FOR CALEB

(1)

Usually they argued in the kitchen ripping their lives apart piece by piece in that one room where food and love are forever entwined? Three places were set at a breakfast table in the corner awaiting the family to gather amidst expensive trappings of granite counter tops, a Viking stove long enough to land a Boeing 787, and a ceramic floor of hand-thrown Mexican tiles Gabbie just had to have. Tall and lean, groomed so not a hair of the severe chignon was out of place, she gulped chardonnay over Botox lips her plastics guy made, the same guy who added cleavage to her chest.

Trey Dawson, her husband, owned a square face, linebacker shoulders, and curly hair that would have made Julius Caesar jealous. He held a longneck beer bottle he used much like a sword to thrust and parry hateful words that spewed over his wife's fake lips, words intended to wound deeply. Gabbie temporarily ran out of bile.

Trey nodded in the direction of the table where a red sippy-cup waited. Winnie the Pooh and Tigger forever danced around it. "Why do you do that?" he drawled.

"What? Oh, it makes me feel better," challenged Gabbie, spitting the words.

He pointed the beer bottle. "Ya'll delusional."

"We set the table at church with the body and blood of Christ. Tell me, Mr. Big Shot, how is this any different?"

"There's that religious voodoo again. Can Jesus bring Caleb back?" he said jutting his chin at her, a habit he learned to intimidate bullies when he grew up and lived with an elderly Aunt Mimi who went to bed when the sun set.

"Caleb would be alive if it wasn't for you!" Gabbie screamed the blood vessels feeding her poisonous brain like multilane mole runs.

"Don't start with me!" Trey warned. "If something's worth doing, by God, you should do it yourself."

Her face went crimson. "Oh, cut the cornpone crap with your long-lost father's hayseed sayings. You're a two-bit, crippled writer of junk thrillers aimed at 8th grade dummies not a damned engineer of backyard gym equipment. If it wasn't for me selling real estate, we'd live over a garage somewhere so you could continue writing meaningless stories nobody reads."

"It was an accident! Okay?" Trey said. "Don't think for a minute I don't regret it. We've walked this ground so many times it's a damn rut. Come on! It never would have happened if you didn't insist on a citified, $11,000 custom swing set when Caleb would have loved a plank swing suspended from one of the oaks in our backyard, but, no-o, that wouldn't look good, too hillbilly. Caleb enjoyed helping me. We had fun." He set the beer on the counter, finished with it and Gabbie. "We won't survive if you don't cut it out," cautioned Trey.

"You killed him," she said through clenched teeth. With dead eyes, Gabbie came slowly to him. She tossed the rest of the wine in his face, added her spittle to it then threw the goblet in the direction of Caleb's plate. Like their marriage, the crystal shattered in a million pieces. Gabbie stomped out sobbing. The Cayenne roared into life. Gears whined in reverse and then the screech of stressed tires running away.

Trey left that night neither knowing nor caring if Gabbie came home.

Traffic in Atlanta at two in the morning was still ridiculous, one of the myriad things Trey would not miss about the city. Numbed by the prospect of the sign-less road ahead, his to choose or shun, Caleb's spirit rode shotgun in the club cab pick-up, the F-150 in which the little guy loved to ride, yet another part of Trey that Gabbie hated.

He called Morty Mandel and rousted his prickly agent out of bed.

"Yes, I'm aware what time it is and, no, I'm not drunk. Look, Morty, I gotta have an advance. Yeah, I know my sales stink, but so are most every writer's in the digital era. No, it's not another woman. The problem is it's the same woman. I left Gabbie tonight. Yeah, thanks, man. I appreciate. You know, this project I'm working on, *Fledgling Warrior*, could make a gangbuster movie with the right director. How about you dangle a few green carrots in front of Giltwood Studios to buy the rights like last time? You'll make some calls tomorrow, you say? Morty, by God, you're not so bad for a kid from Flatbush."

As soon as Trey hit Macon, Georgia to merge onto I-16 headed east, he felt the honied pulse of the old South flash past his headlights. Cypress swamps made mysterious with shifting veils of fog whizzed by, and palmetto palms mixed with saw palmetto grew at the feet of primordial cottonwoods. A sense of freedom though yet swaddled in Caleb's shroud returned as soon as he took Rte. 17 headed for the Sea Islands, the Atlantic Ocean, and the magic of the Low Country he had once called home. At daybreak crossing the Chechesee River and the wide blue water of Port Royal Sound, the new sun gilded the rivers under a tangerine and butter sky.

He was home, a place where he could get a new start.

Trey turned off onto a very secondary road that ran parallel to the Sound. Abandoned long ago, the lumber cut he hunted led to the marsh where he and Mary Beth Love used to have fun. It gladdened his heart that the cut was still there unchanged. The big truck bumped along until the track ended and offered a sweeping vista of spartina grass tempered by the sapphire of the Sound. He shut the truck down, settled his head on a sweatshirt, and closed his eyes. No one knew where he was. No one could hassle him about real or perceived blemishes in his character or the loss of his faith or the fact he was, by God, imperfect.

Before he dozed off, Trey reached down to pull up his jeans pantleg to unlace the titanium prosthesis. He tossed the apparatus on the empty seat and rubbed the stump sighing with pleasure. Like the absence of Caleb, he still felt the whole leg although he left it in pieces on a mountaintop near the Pakistan border.

Trey slept the sleep of the wounded.

(2)

He wakened around two that afternoon and decided to stop by the man most folks in Sea Branch called the Village Voice, Dexter Love III. He owned a gas station and tire business called Don't Tread on Me. Nothing went down in the town of 2,200 that he didn't know about.

"Well what in the world, THE Trey Dawson, best center fielder for the Shuckers I ever did see. Just what in billy hell ya'll doin' home, son?" asked Coach Love, an unlit White Owl Blunt stuck in the corner of his mouth. Genetics gave him a basketball face and a body equally round. At least three days of beard grizzled him.

"I guess ya'll could say I'm in Sea Branch to lick wounds," Trey replied. "I need a small place to rent for a time."

Love had been a coach who cared more about his kids than winning, fortuitous since what was left of Trey's father returned to Sea Branch in a military issue coffin with a flag for a comforter. Dexter Love was Trey's baseball coach through his senior year when Trey earned the honor of All-South Carolina, a five-tool center fielder with a .512 batting average and a rifle for an arm that could nail a cheetah trying to stretch a single.

"Hiding out, are you?" Coach Love prodded.

"Yeah, you might say that."

"Swinging for the fence?"

"Like always, Coach. Singles are for candy asses."

That made Dexter Love chuckle. The cigar migrated from one side of his mouth to the other without noticeable help, gliding as though pulled along by a ghost. His look hardened. "I sure was disappointed you chose to become a Marine," he said, "rather than enter the MLB draft." The Coach cocked his head to one side. "Still trying to impress your Dad are ya?"

"Lots of folks are disappointed in me. Get in line," said Trey, annoyed. "You know, there are a few higher callings than becoming a major league ballplayer."

Love spat in the dust. "Let me make a few calls," he said.

"Thanks. I'm headed to get some grub."

"Mary Beth down to the Dixie would love to see you," Coach said. "Come back when you done, son." Evidently Coach figured his reward to find Trey a rental was Trey's visit to his daughter who happened to be his steady the final two years of school.

Trey took the Glock from beneath the driver's seat and tucked it under his shirt in the waistband. Gabbie despised his armed carry, but Trey found it reassuring. "Contemptable cowboy," she used to call him.

Trey wandered to the Dixie Cafe. An occasional car or a roaring logging truck passed. He questioned what kind of reception he'd get at the better of the two restaurants in town as Trey passed by the True Value Hardware owned by the Tenny family miraculously still in business after a big box outfit opened a super-store three years back in Beaufort, and Donna's Laundromat, its door seemingly always open, then past the Carnegie Public Library, and Harkin's Jewelry, and finally the one-bay fire station. Memories peopled State Street. He recalled the homecoming parades and the time the Sea Branch State Bank was robbed by two gunmen who were never caught.

As soon as he crossed the threshold of the Dixie Diner, it was as if he never left. "Well, lookie here what the cat done drug in," Bob Jones, the State Farm agent said to the waitress behind the counter. Instantly, Mary Beth Love's writhing nakedness under him technicolored Trey's mind. Guilt took over. What was Gabbie doing? Should he care? Should he call?

"How you doin'?" Trey asked of Mary Beth through a weak smile remorseful about dumping her so many years ago. He had his pick of mushroom stools. Trey hunkered down on one in the middle where he sat ogling her breasts, revisiting their glory. They stuffed her pink blouse so completely the buttons were stressed. Trey noted she put on weight since high school and her waist was thicker but the brown Q-Tip look of a bouffant hairdo that looked for all the world like carnival cotton candy was the same.

"You look good, Trey, real good, in fact," Mary Beth said biting her lip fighting back tears. "It's near suppertime but I remember what you like." Her body in an s-curve, she twiddled a strand of brown hair eying him. "Three over easy, hash browns crispy," she said writing on the ticket book, "coffee black, orange juice small size, link sausage, and white bread toast with strawberry jam, not jelly, jam."

While he waited for his food, Mary Beth went on a fishing trip. "Where you at now?" she asked poring coffee.

"Here for now."

"Is that so? I heard you lived in Atlanta."

"Did."

"Ya'll here to write another chapter in your book, ain't you?"

"Yeah, you could say that."

"How did you get started writing. When we was together you didn't write."

"Four years ago, I was wounded and laid up in a military hospital in Wiesbaden, Germany bored out of my gourd so I cobbled a story and got after it."

"I've read every one of your books, some twice they was so good. If you'd like help proofing, is that the right word?"

"Yeah, it is."

"I read a lot after the boys go to bed, Bobbie and Roy Junior. Your writing kept my mind off Rebound Roy after we divorced. How much of what you write is for real, you know, your own experience?"

Never one to wallow in melodrama, he sipped his coffee. "I don't know what will come out of my head. It's like fishing. You have no idea what's on the line until it surfaces."

"Hey, Mary Beth," Bob Jones called from a booth near the entrance. He pointed at his empty coffee mug.

"Excuse me, sweetie," she said to Trey.

The dinger on the shelf between the kitchen and the counter chimed. "Order up," an enormous black man cried out. Throughout the meal, Mary Beth acted like a defense attorney. She asked question after question from where he had been stationed, to did he win any medals, to what the Taliban were like, to why he enlisted years ago. Trey was patient with her. He felt it the least he could do.

Finished with the meal, she tore the check from the ticket book and set it on the counter, leaning over, amused by where Trey's eyes fixed.

"Piece of Maybelline's coconut cream pie?" Mary Beth asked. "On the house. It's mighty good. Ya'll always used to like it back then."

He put the paper napkin next to his plate. "I'll pass," he said, "thanks."

Mary Beth's hands became parentheses to her waist. "You come back, you hear?"

Throwing a ten spot on the counter, Trey dismounted the stool. "I sure will. Nice to see you Mary Beth," he replied in the hope his words sounded less phony than those he heard in his ear.

Trey walked from the Dixie past Grumpy's, the second-best restaurant in town, and the other bank, the Second National Bank, where he bought rolls of pennies, nickels, and dimes so he could look through them eager to add to his coin collection. Cash earned mowing lawns for the summer provided a grubstake.

Trey came to Fish Camp Road which was a residential street canopied by ancient live oaks. Here and there palmetto palms poked the sky. The houses were neat but modest. There was where the Thompson's lived, the George's, the Hardy's. All had been lawn mower customers. He wondered who lived in these houses now. And, just around the corner in the next block, was the roomy bungalow where Aunt Mimi tried to be his mother.

As a squall of melancholy rained on his heart, he paused on the sidewalk.

Coach Love was never one to dance around a fire. "How'd Mary Beth look?" he asked.

"Good, Coach. Find anything?"

"Yeah. Loretta down to Coastal Empire Realtors has a three-room house out in the country. It's an old overseers place from when the Tomotley Plantation was burned by Sherman." A mournful scowl furrowed his forehead as though the tragedy happened just a few hours ago.

Trey thanked Dexter Love and made his way to the realtor's office. A lady he failed to place in Sea Branch told Trey that Loretta Queen was on the road to somewhere and would meet him at the house at five. She gave him the address. "If you leave now," she said, "you'll catch her just right. Good luck, hon," the woman said and winked at Trey.

The small clapboard house's outside was grayed by the weather and the roof was split cedar shake covered in places by emerald moss. It lived next to a tidal creek that let onto Port Royal Sound, its front rich with magenta azaleas, grand live oaks garlanded by Spanish moss, and a magnolia tree ready to bloom. The house belonged just where it was, a feeling Trey felt confident would return to his life too.

A late model Cadillac pulled up next to Trey's club cab F-150. Fancy Loretta Queen stepped out and began to talk two miles to Sunday.

"Why, ya'll must be that famous writer war hero, Mr. Trey Dawson, from right he-ah in backwater Sea Branch. Ya'll do me an honor meeting with me. She ain't much," Loretta said, indicating the house with a sweeping gesture, "but it's cheap, furnished, and clean, and, Mr. Dawson, quiet, yes, that's the word. Could you use some quiet in your life to write all by your lonesome?" She batted nylon eyelashes big enough to cool Pharaoh. "The place has no heat but does have a fireplace, a well in the front yard, and indoor plumbing. Linens are provided and furnishings as well as kitchen stuff. The yard is your responsibility. A mower's in the shed. Four-fifty a month cash, five-fifty by check, and no credit or debit card."

"Yes, ma'am," Trey said.

He took a spin around the place and met Loretta on the porch. "Got a month-to-month contract?" he asked.

"No need. I'd just ask for it in services if'n you was late," she purred, batting those eyelashes again.

Trey dug for his wallet. He counted nine Benjamins. "Three months," he said figuring there were few renters in Sea Branch. She snatched the cash from his hand.

"Come by the office any old time. You can pay the next three months there." She made to leave but came back with a bemused look on her powder and paint face. "You a war hero and all but, tell me something, ya'll ain't afraid of them things that go bump in the night, if you know what I mean, 'cause this house is haunted," she whispered.

"Ma'am, two-legged bearded monsters in live fire fights scare me, not ghosts."

That late afternoon, Trey made a start in erasing his tracks. He drove to Beaufort and returned with a satellite TV system to establish an internet connection. Up and running, he opened a new e-mail account and closed the old one. He also changed his phone number but sent an e-mail to Morty letting him know of the new contacts. Existing Instagram and Twitter accounts remained the same so fans could continue to follow him.

The rest of the week and the next and the next he listened to night sounds rather than complaints from Gabbie.

For six hours a day, he wrote copy for *Fledgling Warrior*. He felt more immersed in his characters than any other narrative he had spun from imaginary threads cultured in his over-active mind. They jumped from his fingers to the page, alive, carrying the storyline on their backs warring, pleading with him for primacy. He was alone only in the sense that not another human shared his space yet Trey was far from lonely. The peace he felt in that Civil War house healed him. He was thankful in the knowledge he never had to squeeze himself to fit into someone else's idea of a life. Yet, he knew himself well enough that what he needed more than peace, more than another lover, more than a companion; he needed an outlet for his anger. If he could, he would have re-upped for another tour. Trey found battle cleansing with its ability to strip bare trivialities that masqueraded the banality of everyday civilian existence. An adventure whose outcome was dangerously ambiguous, the very reason why he signed up for three tours of duty, became a burning ember fanned by disappointment, deep sorrow, and loss. A battlefield born intuitive instinct warned him about the deceptive softness of Low Country air. It was a shapeshifter and tricky liar. Evil; he could feel it and for that reason Trey ran four miles every other day come rain or shine and lifted weights three times a week at a gym on the Old Savannah Highway. He would be ready. Yes. Trouble always found Major Travis Dawson.

A dwarf somersaulted through Penn Smith's closed bedroom door. The imp rose to his feet to strike a defiant pose, his clenched fists at the waist of a court jester's outfit, one leg black, the other white set off by a crimson waistcoat. Everyone in the Smith family knew Gauche as the spirit, *Arupe* – dwarf in Yoruba. He stared at the sleeping African Queen, his charge for life.

"Ignore me again, are you?" he said in Medieval French. The last few years, their relationship turned soured so Gauche planted his forehead on the rug, pointed his rump at Penn, and let loose a thunderous fart. He rolled to his side laughing deep belly laughs that caused the bells sewn to his tri-part jester's hat to tinkle and pointed silk slippers with curled toes topped by bells to quake, too.

"Awaken, my Queen," Gauche said between laughs.

Her eyes fluttered open.

"You foul little man," Penn grumbled, stretching. "Can't you think of something less vile to get my attention?"

"It wouldn't be as much fun," he said getting to his feet. He jingled to the side of Penn's four-poster bed as he pulled at a luxuriant black beard.

"For whom would it not be as much fun?" asked Penn.

"*Ma cher*, it's always about me," he teased spawning a crooked smile that exposed gray, uneven teeth two of which were missing on the upper left side. He often boasted he lost them in a battle with the British to settle an affair of the heart.

Penn raised up to rest her back on the tall headboard. She swiped her cellphone. It was early morning, 3:14 AM. Shiny hair was braided and coiled on the top of her head setting off a strong face with high cheek bones, snappy dark eyes that brimmed with intelligence, and a queenly bearing consistent with ancestral leadership of the Yoruba of Senegambia.

"Look, midget, go away. Go back to France. Hook-up with that unhappy, chubby German guy again, you know, Martin Luther. Go reform some more Catholics."

"By your father's balls," Gauche blustered, "I'm not a midget, I'm an Imp. Midgets can't do this." He withdrew an ivory flute from his tights as if it was a sword, played an antique tune, and danced the Renaissance Pavan around the bedroom. At the end, Gauche executed a perfect backflip followed by a courtly bow.

"Ah, come on, you can do better than that," tormented Penn.

"Once you were such a dear girl, but now you're critical of me every single time I visit. How long have I been faithful to your Muslim Faraji family? Huh?"

"Look, fossil, you've told me how you wooed my ancestor, Rahima, at least fifty times. It was on the island of Goree off West Africa," Penn said in a sing-songy voice mocking him, "where you French collected my people like cords of firewood to stack in slave ships of staggering filth and disease. You bought her at auction on the island, didn't you? Let me ask a question. Did you know Rahima had the eye?"

"But of course. She wore the root doctor to the tribe like it was a golden cloak as you do too. Plus, Rahima's spirit powers were, shall we say, titillating."

Penn shook her head. "And you believed you were in love," she goaded, "so for once in your life you were gallant until the British voided the auction contract. Rahima was sold again in the slave market, this time in Charles Town. Your overgrown instinct to seek revenge bought you a cheap death."

"Ah, but I did not die, did I? Here I stand before you. I was and am yet in love with Rahima," Gauche declared with a heavy sigh. "Where do you think you get your cocoa skin?"

"Am I supposed to thank you for that?"

"You wound my sentimental heart," Gauche said, pouting. A tear trickled into his beard. "How many years have I given foresight to your family? Huh? Well, I'll tell you; it was the year of our Lord, 1562. Now divide by four, take the square root, subtract half and multiply times pi, and I get 456 years, but who's counting." Gauche hooked the red embroidered coat with his thumbs and puffed out his chest evidently proud of himself. "We sailed in a private cabin aboard the *Hind* out of Guadeloupe. The weather in September was dreadful. Reports of hurricanes menaced the Middle Passage. Ah-h, we made love for hours. Your Fahima was glorious. Sweet Penn, the sea rocked us to sleep."

"What a sentimental old gas bag you are," said Penn with a smile, "yet wise enough to play the fool."

"Now you're being an ungrateful brat. You will remember I came to your great-great-grandmother to inform her that she and your family were free by Mr. Lincoln's pen months before news came to the Gullah. And what about your uncle, Lucius Aurelius? He went missing in action in

Vietnam. I came to your grandmother, Collette, to tell her that her nephew lived in a cage like an animal but would survive that stupid war. Be fair to old Gauche," he said, his image flickering.

"Concentrate, Imp," Penn urged, wondering why the ancestors dealt her an ADD Imp. His forehead wrinkled by the effort, Gauche regained clarity.

"Connectivity issues," he said with a sheepish grin. "Only such we had back when was to play hide the salami," he said, making obscene hip gyrations at Penn, one hand behind his neck and the other on his grinding hip.

"Enough of it. Now, tell me, warn me, whatever it is that sent you to intrude on my sleep. I'm due to try a court case in Beaufort in four hours. Look, old Imp, I'm sorry to be cranky but, it's just … just that you make me afraid. The last time you showed was close onto when Gran Collette died of a stroke. So, what news? Is it good or bad?"

"Yes, it is," he said, crossed his short arms and sprung onto the bed to sit Indian fashion in front of her. His hazel eyes were serious. Gauche cleared his throat, pointed a short index finger at the ceiling, and said, "East is East as far as the Orient, but thoroughly abhor-ient, and those from Cathay who play are most fey. Beware, they will slay to have their way." He pointed at Penn, "Hold a tray to survive the fray."

The jester moaned a woeful moan.

"Hey, don't pack your bag," Penn said. "What's up with this childish riddle?"

Gauche paid no heed. He rocked back and forth to become progressively indistinct until he slid off the bed as water would to re-form long enough to complete three neat somersaults out the bedroom door.

After a Ramen noodles supper, he fell asleep watching an improbable documentary about ancient star travelers who came to Earth in prehistoric times to show primitive humans how to live. A timid knock came to the door just loud enough to wake him. He glanced at his watch. It was late.

"Trey," a woman's voice said through the screen door. "Trey, ya'll in there?"

"Yeah," he said rubbing his eyes. "Sounds like you, Mary Beth?" he said shuffling into the kitchen scratching himself.

"Can I come in? The mosquitoes are real bad out here."

"Guess it wouldn't hurt none," he drawled and unlatched the door fighting the urge to tell Mary Beth that all that perfume she doused herself in is like a flashing neon sign advertising supper on the house to every biting insect within a hundred yards.

She stood inside the door, her arms crossed over her ample breasts, fresh lipstick a red slash across her face. "You ain't been to the Dixie since that day, you know, so I just wanted to see how you was a'doin', and all. How you doin'? Can I sit?"

"The place came with two chairs," he said, amused. "Ought to be about right."

"Thank you," said Mary Beth jiggling to the kitchen to commandeer one of the straight-chairs. "You always was kind 'cept when you walked out of my life. Didn't even bother to tell me why. That was a real hard time, real hard. A body don't never like it when you been run to ground. You gets the feeling you're not good enough, you know? Not a day gone by since that I have a thought about you, about us, I mean. It was like a dream when you come in off the street completely out of the blue, I mean, I seen you in my mind do it a hundred times, but it is really, really you," she said her voice softening to a mere whisper.

"Look, I'm sorry how I did what I did," Trey began, "I guess I left because, well I don't know, Mary Beth, I guess it was all about people's lives changing. You know, they head in different directions. I'm not the man I was when I was eighteen," Trey said.

"That why you're separated, at least that's what Daddy said. You changed."

"Yeah, something like that," he answered walling himself off not wanting to have a discussion with her about his dead marriage.

She leaned over to touch his left hand. "I see you still got your wedding band."

"Look, Mary Beth, I'm very much married and, frankly, too angry to begin anything, or, better said I guess, continue where we left off."

"Why? I don't bite, you know," she said, smiling. "I ain't asking for a commitment. It's your leg, ain't it. Poor guy. Well Trey Dawson I could give a fig about your war wound. You are the most bravest man I have ever known. I would be fulfilled to help you with it. I mean you limp a little and all, but it's barely noticeable."

"Don't need help nor sympathy," Trey said a little too frosty.

Mary Beth sighed and got to her feet to stand in front of Trey. She looked him direct in his eyes and pulled a string on the blouse she wore that fell to her waist. "Did you forget how pretty they is?" she cooed, cradling them in each hand thumbing her nipples. "You used to not get enough of them? Remember? This one," she jiggled the left breast and laughed, "why, you named her jello, and this one here, puddin'. So cute."

Trey couldn't help but stare. "I wrote about those puppies in *Hell Hath No Fury* right down to the names. They are immortal, Mary Beth, and I'm still married."

"I could give a care," she said shimmying some to set them in motion.

Trey was having a tough time refusing her implied offer so he could think of nothing better to do than lie a lie so obnoxious she would leave him be but not hurt her feelings.

"Look here, listen to me," Trey stammered still staring, buying time for emergency creativity. "Ah, one of the major reasons I left my wife is that I picked up syphilis in Iraq. You don't need any part of that."

Mary Beth backed away pulling her blouse up. "Oh, Trey, that's awful! You're right, I don't need any part of that. I got two kids to feed and raise. Is Rochester gonna rot off?"

"Naw, not any time soon. I'd appreciate it if you keep this between you and me, okay?"

"Sure, you got it."

"Ah-h, jeez, Mary Beth, please could I see them one more time?"

Mary Beth chuckled. "Once is enough. Do come by to see me, Trey Dawson? Okay? Friends?"

"Yeah, of course."

"At the diner, right, the Dixie where I work. Bye, Trey," she said, tears coming quickly. "I Will always love you." She ran to him and kissed him softly on his lips then Mary Beth went out into the night.

Trey poured himself a healthy Jack Daniels, then another.

In the quiet of an early morning out on the front porch Trey edited a printed copy of the pages he wrote the day before, a craft habit he adopted years ago. The daily effort was recorded on a thumb drive kept separate from the computer. Something compelled him to look up from his work. Out of the rising mist off Silver Creek, a bedraggled stray dog wandered on the property, its ribs an angel's xylophone. The bluetick hound with its outrageous floppy ears trotted to Trey, slowed, then hesitantly, a step at a time, ready to flee, he came up close to the house. The bluetick refused to come on the porch despite coaxing and sat at the bottom of the last step, his bloodshot eyes brown as an old saddle fixed on Trey as if to say, 'it's your move, pal.'

"So, here we are the two of us, both strays," Trey said. The dog cocked his head. "Looks like this is your lucky day. Hold on, partner. I'll be right back." He emerged with a beat-up ceramic mixing bowl of chocolate rice Krispies and another bowl filled with clean water from the well. In seconds the rice Krispies were gone.

They drove to town to buy Cerberus a 50 lb. bag of kibble, a manly chain-link collar, and stopped by the animal hospital for a check-up. The vet said he was probably four or five years old and in good shape, but she advised a full round of shots just to make sure. The strays settled into each other easily. Trey took to calling him Cerberus, the three-headed Hound of Hades.

Most of Trey's days were spent at the laptop pounding away at fresh copy, raw with fat finger typos, and plot inconsistencies. It was an indulgent pleasure to dissolve himself into the words inwardly pleased no interruptions were going to intrude on his concentration. Gone were glitzy cocktail parties and the dozens of boring people without substance with whom Gabbie surrounded herself. Gone was the inane world of golf where every whiny duffer couldn't putt that day or his game off the tee box was terrible just like Tiger Woods. The seclusion and the beauty of the tidal marshes of the Low Country that surrounded him each day gave of itself, helped Trey to force Gabbie to surrender more and more territory in his head. In military terms he understood. He took back territory previously lost to the enemy.

In the middle of the night, not long before dawn, his cellphone rang. "Are you alone?" It was Gabbie. She was drunk.

Groggy, he replied, "How'd you get my number?"

"This house is so empty and cold without Caleb and you," she said, her voice shaking. "It's a daily torture. I see you shaving at the mirror and Caleb playing with the wooden train set Santa brought his last Christmas. He loved that train. Come home, please. I' beg you. Things will be better. I promise to never accuse you again, okay? Please, Trey. I miss you." She cried hard now.

He cleared his throat as he fought a rush of emotion. "If you still feel the same in the morning," Trey said gently, "call me."

All the next day, Trey kept checking his phone to make sure it had a charge and to make sure Gabbie hadn't called and he missed it. The cellphone never rang. It occurred to him she must have hired a private dick. Otherwise, the new number would have been difficult to get. He had nothing to hide.

(5)

Pure and simple, the old place on Silver Creek had gone to seed. Trey turned a blind eye to keeping the weeds at bay. A trumpet vine partnered with Kudzu, the Japanese vegetal import that did to the South what their troops couldn't, the super vine and its ally threatened to eat the chimney.

Dollar weed climbed the porch, its miniature lily pad leaves following the sun. On the yard, a prairie of weeds flourished to grow knee high in the places where the sun could get at them.

One mid-morning, Ticker set to baying. He jumped to his feet and charged out of the bedroom. A rap came to the screen door, tentative, almost an apology. A white-haired black man stood outside in oft-patched overhauls, a tee-shirt underneath, a baseball hat advertising Purina Feeds sweated through, and a gentle flat face marked by enormous brown eyes, a kind face, a generous face marked by sorrows yet smiling.

"Mr. Writer, sir," he said in a deep baritone through the rusted screen. "This here Jonah Grant's house. Yes sir, found he dead right there in the front room. A good man."

Trey and Ticker stepped out on the porch. "Trey Dawson,' he said offering his hand.

"Lucius Aurelius Smith. Live not too far, uh-huh." He pointed toward Silver Creek. "Be a deer path that way to my trailer house. Not to be bothering you none," the old man said in heavily accented English so much so Trey had to concentrate to understand. It was the cadence of his speech that was hard to catch up with that made a sentence difficult to parse. So fast were the words they became soldered together, rising and falling peppered by strange accents and clucks. This was speech like no other he had heard. The Marines schooled him in languages, but this one was unrecognizable.

"You're not bothering me at all," Trey said, intrigued. "Actually, I could use the break."

"What's that? Don't hear real good no more, Mr. Writer."

Trey patiently repeated what he said. "Okay, thank you for that. My head leaves me at times, oh, it do. That Jonah Grant, he crazy worry, walk the woods by night. Now, sir, he carry a thick rain stick to worry those tings seen and those that ain't. Every once't in a while why he'd thump the ground to scare off critters most specially in the spring when bull gators be out roaming round looking for some girl gator to love on. Yes, sir, that right. You needs paint your door blue so's the haints cain't come in. Old Jonah, now, he laugh at me when I tell him of his spirit business but just right now who got the last laugh, uh-huh? I run my mouth, Mr. Writer, but what I was asking was can I help you which the place? Paint the door, mow, trim it up real nice like? Fix things." He paused. "Protect you," he added looking into Trey's cheerless eyes.

That night, mid-evening, showy heat lightning flashed above the Low Country advertising his despair. *Sweet Home Alabama* drifted through the screen door. He cradled his head in his hands waiting for the blackness of his grief to lighten. Overcome with guilt, he broke one of his own rules and sent an e-mail to Gabbie. I MISS YOU he typed and waited an hour then a nodding two hours before he and Cerberus gave up and went to bed.

The next afternoon, a gray van rolled into the dooryard. Trey watched as a man with a face as sharp as a hatchet got out. He held a manila envelope.

"You Travis David Lawson?" the courier asked advancing on Jonah's Place.

"Last time I checked," Trey replied, testy.

Climbing the stairs, the man said, "Ya'll been served, sir. It's a suit claiming, what they say," he glanced at the back of the envelope, 'alienation of affection.' The source is one Gabriella Justine Lawson."

Trey exploded out the door, Cerberus right behind him. He snatched the man by the collar, pulled him off the porch, and down the steps to toss him like a ragdoll on the dusty front yard. Ticker went nuts bugling and snapping at the prostrate man. The courier rolled over trying to dig something out of his right pocket. Instinctively, Trey stepped on his arm to pin it to the ground.

"I'd like nothing better than to break your god damn elbow then stomp it to sand so be a good little girl and lie still." The man did as he was told, Cerberus inches from his jugular slobbering sticky goo on his neck. Trey fished out a vintage Smith and Wesson .32 and promptly fired every round in the cylinder at the feet of the courier, emptied the spent cartridges in his hand, and threw them and the revolver into Silver Creek.

"Listen up, shit-for-brains, ya'll come back, I'll kill you with my bare hands and enjoy every candy ass scream you make."

(6)

Lucius came by to mow and trim bushes as well as to check on Trey. After Lucius finished, Trey asked him to install a front door lock he'd bought in Beaufort and to recontour several old doors so they fit the jamb without sticking, an OCD bubble-up Trey never could control. As he worked, Lucius softly sang or hummed sometimes. Sometimes he's tap out the rhythm on the woodwork. It would be months before Trey met someone who explained it was common in the Gullah community for men working with their hands to sing work songs their ancestors used in the fields chopping cotton, or plowing, or simply rowing a boat, a soulful and haunting holdover from Mother Africa.

Done with his tasks, Lucius went to a classic Toyota pick-up he affectionately called Matilda. Only one headlight survived the years. Lucius dug around the cargo area and emerged with a round red plastic cooler crowned with a once-white top.

He poked his head into the bedroom where Trey concentrated on his laptop. "Mr. Writer, you got time for lemons made? It fresh this morning. Hardly need no sugar they so sweet. Pick the fruits right off God's tree in the Eden of my garden."

Trey cracked his knuckles and stretched. "I guess so," he said and went into the tiny kitchen where he took two plastic iced tea glasses from the drainer. Lemonade poured, they went out onto the porch to sit side-by-side on the upper step surveying the dooryard.

"Place looks nice," Trey commented.

"Thank ya kindly," replied Lucius. "I'm knowing you some and you sure are startin' to warm on me, but, Mr. Writer, I ain't seen no one in a long time who need to know Jesus any more than you."

Trey ignored the implied obligation to talk religion. Instead, he took a sip of lemons made. "I have this thing about doors not closing," he said.

"Is that what you do?" Lucius persisted. "You closing doors?" Trey shrugged. "Mr. Writer, I am deacon in our church. We be happy for you to meet our friend, Jesus. Worship is at 9:00 on Sunday mornings. I be by to pick you up." Lucius held an index finger in the air. "No love hath greater glory than that of our Lord Christ Jesus. Mr. Writer, we been brought together for a reason for there are no coincidences in Jesus."

"Truth be known," Trey started, his head down. "I haven't seen the inside of a church since my son's death."

"Blame Jesus, have you?"

"Some, yes, but mostly myself. It's complicated and –"

"I don't aim to pry, Mr. Writer. Will you come?"

"I'll think about it," Trey said. "I believe your place is on the way to your church."

"It do."

"I'll let you know when ya'll get here."

Sunday morning brought a faultless sky. It promised to be hot. In the church's lot, Lucius parked the wheezing Toyota under a giant live oak for the shade. The vintage pick-up never did have air conditioning. Lucius wore a white long-sleeve shirt, and black trousers, his normal stubbled beard raked from his face. Trey had no idea what to wear so he pulled on khakis and a purple polo shirt. "You clean up pretty good, Mr. Writer," Lucius said on the way to Shadrach outside of Beaufort, South Carolina.

The First Free African Church was a white clapboard structure designed with gothic casement windows whose black shutters became angel wings to each side of the shortened bell tower. The church had a blue metal roof and the number 1862 free-hand painted above and between the front doors, a detail Trey took to be the founding date for the praise house. This was a Gullah term he learned from Lucius on the way. His community, the Gullah people were freed slaves who never left the Low Country after the war. It struck him that 1862 was three years before the war was over, but some would say that the war never really ended for the South.

On each side of the sanctuary were three sets of double-hung sashes of clear glass, eight lights in each casement. The windows must have been at least fifteen feet tall and open at the bottom that morning. Cheerful golden marigolds, harlequin zinnias, and moss rose with their waxy pastel flowers made a good living by the double steps. One door led to the men's entrance, the other to the women's, both painted the same color as the Sunday morning sky. Trey found it ironic the freedmen congregation so long ago decided to segregate their flock by gender but kept his thoughts to himself as Lucius greeted friends, and family, and introduced him all around calling him, 'Mr. Trey Dawson, the famous writer,' which he wasn't but Trey found it ingratiating and kind.

Perhaps forty-five to fifty people came to worship in the white, painted plank interior he found severe in its simplicity. Trey took in the ceiling that was planked too and was surprised to see two operating kerosene lamps. The sanctuary smelled of lemon oil polish, women's perfume, and roses long gone to dust. His was the only white face. The people were cordial but distant as though Trey had skipped the payment of his tithe.

Lucius looked up at Trey. The old black man, a perpetual smile on his face, pointed where they were going. "We sit in the middle. That way, don't have to choose no sides," he said chuckling. He waved at more of his relatives. At exactly 0900 the preacher came from hob-nobbing with his flock to the front of the church. He held a wireless mic. "This is the day our great and mighty Lord has made for us. Let us rejoice and be glad in it," the preacher man said in a big voice run through the gravel.

Lucius whispered to Trey, "He Bowen Potter. Been which us long time."

"Look to the left, look to the right, look to the front, and look to the back," Preacher Potter encouraged, "and greet all your neighbors and friends with a hug, a kiss, a firm handshake, and wish all of them eternal peace with our Lord, Jesus Christ, the only true path to life without end rocked in the bosom of God'a. Can I hear an AMEN," he said and the people said, AMEN. "Am I doin' aw-right," Reverend Potter asked. "Yes, oh Lord, yes," his flock responded.

From a side door, a choir of eight, four men, four women dressed in royal purple robes joined the preacher and when they reached their practiced positions, an upright piano gave out the first few chords to *What a Friend We Have in Jesus*. They sang with great volume, and joy, and clapping hands, and smiles on every face. Trey had never felt a deeper sense of community outside the wartime military. He got caught up in the moment and was on his feet too, clapping and singing. A beam of pure gold sunlight shone on a choir member he had failed to truly see. The woman stared right at him or at least that was the way Trey remembered it. Questions filled her eyes. She stepped closer to separate from the choir and belted out the third verse *a Capello* in an unfamiliar but moving call and response between the woman and her choirmates. She wore tight braids coiled on the top of her head set off by fancy hoops dangling from perfect ears that evidenced a demeanor that bespoke royalty, not haughty, but in control, not arrogant, but humble, and not brassy, but resolute and, rich, and strong.

Lucius must have seen Trey gawking. He leaned to him. "She my niece, Penn."

Trey couldn't take his eyes off her.

Two hours later, the Reverend Potter said, "And so, my children, it is writ large in the sacred blood of our Lord. Love thy neighbor as thyself. Leave nothing undone in the eyes of God. He loves you, he gave his only son so that you may have eternal life. Would you give your only son to affect the lives of millions? Go forth in peace."

That struck Trey deep. Lucius got up but Trey sat where he was as he struggled not to bust apart in front of the Gullah. His chin joined his chest, eyes closed, lost in painful recriminations.

Lucius put a protective hand on Trey's shoulder.

"In a minute," Trey said in a soft voice.

"Would you like me to pray which you?" Lucius asked gently.

Trey still couldn't face Lucius. "See you in the Community Room, okay?"

"Sure ting, Mr. Writer. I be waitin'."

(7)

Gauche somersaulted across Penn Smith's mind the whole service laughing at her consternation. His sassy behavior, although typical, led her to accept the fact that the Imp's riddle meant this man, this Trey Dawson who sat next to Uncle Lucius.

Earlier, Lucius talked with the family to tell them what he learned about the unhappy man to offer facts and impressions instantly spread by Gullah drums just as in the old days. Most everybody heard about Trey long before he set foot inside the church for Gullah's are talkers among their brethren, a function they trusted as they did the Gullah way in slavery. This secrecy preserved their language to the present day for theirs is an oral history, a tradition rich with the nuances of storytelling.

As the choir filed out, Penn took quick peeks at Trey who seemed to be in distress. She yearned to comfort him but thought better of it. Uncle Lucius stood at the end row of the pews waiting for his new friend to gather equilibrium. In a few minutes, Lucius led him to the Community room, a modern multi-purpose hall with a basketball hoop, kitchen, and stage. It was here that coffee and sweet tea were served along with two huge glass plates of homemade sweets. Children let out of Sunday School lined up for the refreshments, some of whom, piled high with goodies, dashed out the hall to play among the live oaks.

"He that man what rents Jonah's old place down by Silver Creek?" Foley Grant, one of her choirmates asked Penn. Foley sang bass in the choir. They were putting robes away in the music room.

"I believe that's so," Penn said. "Lucius has nothing but good to say about the man."

"Best not get close," the older Foley cautioned, turned, and walked away wagging a finger at her.

Taking her time, Penn used the ladies' room to make sure she was put together. Only a blind woman would miss the I-want-you look exuded from Trey Dawson's blue eyes. She knew he'd wait but what was Gauche getting at, and what about the Asians? She settled for the observation that fated destinies brought them together because of an other-worldly nudge from Gauche.

As soon as Penn came into the noisy Community Room, she felt his eyes on her so she struck up a conversation with chatty Mrs. Norton. "Well, I guess you heard Rayshawn, my middle grandson he fell out the tree and broke he arm in three places and then the storm last week, why girl, it blowed a big pine on the sure dead right over the very grave of my dear husband and then, have you ever done this, I went to fix my morning coffee, can't drink but one mug according to the doctor, and, girl child, do you know what I done, why, I added salt not sugar then I had to make another pot and then my car on the way here with Mavis O'Rourke, you know her, well, my car started to act up and you know what, I done run out of the gas so Bob Burke come by, seen me and give me a gallon from a big can he use in he landscape business and then –

Penn reached for both of the woman's hands. "Please excuse me, Mrs. Norton, but I need to say something to our guest before he leaves." Penn excused herself. She had been watching Trey out of the corner of her eye as he worked his way toward her. In the hope she wasn't too obvious, Penn wandered into Trey's path. They met in the middle of the room.

He tapped Penn's shoulder. "Ma'am, that was wonderful, ya'll's solo. Trey Dawson," he said offering his hand.

"Penn Smith. Thanks for the praise. You must be the one I hear about, the guy from Atlanta. You're the news everyone is talking about, I'm here to tell you."

"In person," Trey said feeling nervous. "At risk of being nosy, can I ask you a question?"

"Ask it and we'll see."

Trey chuckled enjoying her feisty response. "How in the world did your uncle Lucius get tagged with the name of an ancient Roman Emperor? I mean, it must have been rough on the playground."

"The short answer is that my grandfather was a teacher and loved Roman history, kind of like a hobby. He studied and studied in an attempt to bring light to the roll of Africans in the Empire, even wrote a book on what he found but, in the end, no one wanted to publish it, I guess because he never went to college. Grampa Ben was certain Cleopatra was black, yet, now that opinion is mainstream."

Lucius joined them. "Hi, you beautiful man," Penn said and kissed her uncle on the cheek.

"You in great voice this morning. Lit our Praise House just like that ray of sunshine what searched you out. I see you meet Mr. Writer."

"Yes, I have." She returned her attention to Trey. "Ya'll worship with us anytime you like," she said. "I have a vestry meeting starting three minutes ago." She pecked Lucius then held her hand out to Trey. "I'm pleased to know you," she said with seriously honeyed words and was off.

On the way to Jonah's Place, they stopped for a burger. Trey ordered a good-dog extra meal for Cerberus. Seated in a booth overlooking Carteret Street, Trey changed the subject from the NFL to something far more important. "So, Lucius, what does your niece do besides sing like an angel?"

"Uh-huh, she a lawyer. Got this fine office a couple blocks from here."

"I'm impressed. Would have never guessed it."

"Em-huh, graduated which honors from up to Columbia where the school, they got them a school to make lawyers. But, first she work as a deputy sheriff, she did. Couple years, uh-huh. We sure proud of her."

"What kind of law does she practice. I ask because I'm shopping for an attorney." Trey's face clouded over. "Gabbie, that's my wife, and I are separated."

"Sure sorry to hear so. That why the Lord he kiss your heart at worship today."

"No … no," Trey said, emotion again threatening to get the better of him. "I'm not sorry about Gabbie. We were married for the wrong reasons. I'm done with it. What kind of law does Penn do?"

"Legal stuff."

"Like real estate?"

"That's right."

"Divorce?"

"Uh-huh, and she did a murder case, too, and got him off. Gullah like to work for Gullah, if you know what I mean."

"Um-m, is she married?"

Lucius smiled and shook his head. "Never been. Say, you hear 'bout the kid from Beaufort, a safety who played at Clemson, well now, he drafted in the second round?"

It was obvious Lucius didn't want to talk anymore about Gullah matters with an outsider, something Trey respected.

Cerberus was thrilled with his special dividend.

(8)

Dark as a mine on a moonless night, Trey sleeping whiskey sleep, Ticker launched off the bed bugling. And then Trey heard what set Cerberus off. It sounded as though someone detonated explosive charges deep in the earth. He patted the bed for Cerberus to join him, rolled over, and went back to sleep, his mind set on determining the source in the new day. The big bluetick awakened him two more times.

The dregs of the coffee pot poured into a stainless-steel travel mug, he and Cerberus were off by 0615 hours. Special Ops trained him to search in grids guided by compass coordinates. He headed toward the ocean first, a search that turned up nothing, no construction sites and no industrial or manufacturing complexes. He passed collections of trailers and modular homes he supposed were family enclaves populated by Gullahs most of their doors or at least the trim or in a couple of instances, the roof, were blue.

He took a road headed northwest then another trending west and saw nothing that could have generated the rumbling. Not far from Jonah's Place, Trey noticed an ocean-going container semi common in the Low Country. It hauled a faded green cube marked with Asian characters. The rig turned onto the same county road Trey traveled, but it came from a gravel road just like the countless number of such he saw that morning that led off into pine woods rich with palmetto palms and saw palmetto covering the under-canopy. No signage appeared to tell the world what went on back there. Trey did a power U-turn spitting gravel and raced after the semi.

"Now we're having fun," Trey said to Cerberus whose head was out the passenger window, his ridiculous ears horizontal like Dumbo's. At the junction of a Beaufort county road and SC-17, the semi turned as though it was headed to I-95 ten miles further south. Trey kept far enough back he wouldn't draw attention to his tail. Soon, the semi merged onto I-95 South and exited at Port Wentworth, Georgia, the fastest route to the international container facility in Savannah.

Two and two was for sure whatever was in that metal box was headed to the Far East.

Trey retraced his journey. He had a little difficulty discovering the discrete gravel path into the woods, but eventually followed it NNW for perhaps a half-mile until it opened on a large industrial plant enclosed by razor wire steel fencing. The installation was no more than four miles from Jonah's Place. Trey saw zip signage here, too, but what he did see was a locked gate manned by two Asian guards dressed in white jumpsuits, shiny black military boots, and a white helmet. An olive drab mesh belt held a commando knife and an automatic pistol. Each of them had an AK-47 slung over a shoulder.

He stopped in front of the gate and got out. The guard on the left, the taller one, unslung his rifle while his comrade put a hand on the checkered grip to his sidearm.

"You not welcome here. Please leave!" the tall guard said in halting English. "No list on day book. No welcome."

"Who can I talk to about all the noise ya'll make?" Trey said.

The guards started rapid-fire talking in what Trey took from his Marine training to be a Mandarin dialect. The shorter one stepped into a glass-walled booth and made a phone call, a tip-off. It told Trey that whoever the owners were, they installed a dedicated phone system to ensure total privacy.

The tall guard barked at Trey. "We bring trouble to you, citizen. Leave now!" Trey's Glock was under the seat but he wouldn't get that far if they opened fire so he one-finger saluted and returned to his truck. Just as he started to drive away another semi identical to the one he tailed burst from the towering industrial structure headed toward the gate creating a grimy rooster tail. It came to a halt. The driver handed the tall guard a piece of paper. He scanned it while the other one kept an eye on Trey then braced to salute the driver.

On the way by the F-150, the Caucasian driver, his window rolled down, hollered, "Don't, Buddy."

Headed to Jonah's Place, his mind on overdrive, Trey's phone rang through the communication package on the dash. The ID read, 'Unknown Caller.' "Accept," Trey said to the screen. "Dawson," he said.

"Hello, lucky neighbor," a man's lightly accented voice said. "You visited my worthy company this morning. You must understand we are suspicious people. I am Li Xie Ling, your friend and neighbor at your service."

"What goes boom in the night?" asked Trey.

"I beg your difference?"

"What goes boom in the night?"

"If you insinuate we make boom, Mr. Lawton, we don't make booms at night or any other time. We mine good American water for our people back home in our blessed country of wealth. Our wells are very deep but no booms. Ten-thousand-year-old water. Very good water. Please, do not trouble your head. Everything is AOK. Goodbye, Mr. Lawton."

Questions ping-ponged in Trey's head. How did this man know his name even though it was clear he changed it to irritate Trey, and how did he know Trey was his neighbor and why the military checkpoint? What were they hiding? Maybe their discretion was the reason the plant carried no signage.

He tried to call Li Ling back but the phone didn't register a source for the call. Trey and Cerberus headed for Beaufort.

(9)

According to a brass plaque affixed to the brick façade, the building on Bay Street began as a pharmacy in the late 1800s. An old-fashioned mechanical doorbell announced his arrival to a high-ceilinged area where the kingdom was ruled by a hefty receptionist. The name tile read, 'Joselyn Smith.' She looked up. "Hello," she said pleasantly. "Why, ya'll that famous writer what moved into Jonah's Place. Saw you at church." The words carried the same rise and fall that characterized Penn's and Lucius' rollercoaster voices. "Fine lookin' dog," Joselyn said and made smoochy noises. Cerberus looked up at Trey as if for permission to allow her to adore him. He trotted to her desk with treats on his mind. "You here to see Penn?" she asked rumpling Cerberus' floppy ears. "Ain't he cute?" she said allowing Cerberus to lick her nose tip.

He took off his Atlanta Falcons hat. "Yes, ma'am," Trey said.

"Well, Mr. Writer, I'll just go and check on Penn."

Trey took in the impressed tin panels that covered the ceiling painted white, flaking in places, and the worn Southern yellow pine floorboards of various widths that complained when walked on. The walls had been taken back to the original red clay brick.

Penn came into the reception area confident, tall, and dressed in a tailored gray suit. He thought her hair looked exactly like Medieval chainmail; beautiful, heavy, shiny, and worth defending.

"Nice to see you again," Penn said.

"Could I ask for a few minutes of your time?" he ventured.

"Of course, this way," she said, her finger a waggling hook. "What's your dog's name?"

"Cerberus," he replied, but Penn already knew all about the stray. She sent him to keep Trey company.

He followed Penn into a bright room lit by a large skylight and populated with modern furnishings of stainless steel and black leather, a glass conference table and desk tops. Photographs covered the brick wall behind her desk chair.

"Please make yourself comfortable. I'll be right back," Penn said.

He scanned the picture wall curious to see the snapshots of her life, the awards, the many diplomas. There Penn was at maybe 10 with a dozen crabs in a wire trap accompanied by an older man, perhaps her grandfather or a younger Uncle Lucius, hard to tell. And there was a photo of an enormous Atlanta Falcons football player who resembled Penn in the face, his shoulders easily 3 feet across. Trey took in images of big family feeds, church doings from christenings to picnics to gatherings of black people helping black people build decks, and docks, and nailing new roofs, and several aged black women on walkers smiling broadly for the camera, some with bandana headbands and ankle-length dresses that reminded him of photos he saw at the Smithsonian in Washington depicting slaves just after the Civil War. One of them was pictured with her arm around a teenage Penn whose skirt held what looked like malnourished potatoes.

Thoroughly lost in a world he could only imagine, Trey was startled when Penn said in Gullah creole, "As you see, we a strong family the Smiths, on-huh. You should know I was the first Smith to go to college. Graduated and went to work with the Beaufort County Police Department. I quit not long into the job. My brothers and sisters killing one another was such a waste so I decided to do what I could to stop the loss of African-American lands to delinquent taxes and heir's property issues. My people, the Gullah, our way of life is disappearing, Mr. Writer. I aim to slow that decline. From 1910 to-date, over 80% of black-owned land has been deeded over to whites, many if not most times without just consideration," she said, her words aflame with passion.

"My trivial matter is a whole lot less important than the destruction of your culture," Trey said. "Could I ask you to go on?"

"For another day," she said, inwardly pleased that the taste of her story tantalized him. "How may I help you?"

He recounted his guard gate episode, the follow-up call from Li Ling, and the ground shakes at night. "Look, could I hire you to dig for me? This whole thing doesn't pass the smell test. I mean, can you look for incorporation papers, site maps of the compound, shareholder's proxies, stuff like that."

"You did say they were Chinese."

"They spoke a dialect of Mandarin."

She handed Trey a brochure. "You're a lucky man. I'll take your case. These are my rates. But, if you don't mind, what about your divorce? Do you need representation?"

Trey laughed lightly. "Can't slip past the rooster called Lucius, can I?" he said. "And, yes, I do need an attorney but it can wait. I'm grateful you're taking me on," he said. "It's so far off your normal casework."

"Mr. Writer, you work plots out for your novels, right?" Trey nodded. "This doesn't pass the smell test for me either and if my instincts are right, it tells me somewhere in this plot might be an embedded loss for my people."

"Well, that said, maybe we can talk *pro bono*?" he toyed.

"Not a chance," Penn laughed. "I saw how many weeks your last book was on the *New York Times* bestseller list. Simple math says you made middle six figures on it."

Trey chuckled and glanced at his watch. "How about we go out to dinner some place nice."

"Maybe," Penn said.

"Too bad. I hear there's this little place where Pat Conroy used to eat."

"The owners are my clients," Penn said with a flash of temper. "I'll have my assistant to call you when I have anything to report, and, by the way, Joselyn, she's my cousin too."

That night Trey slipped off his wedding ring and dropped it in his ditty bag.

(10)

Penn's kitchen was sleek like the complicated woman who cooked in it. A half-empty glass of wine sat on the granite counter of stone mined in Gambia and marketed as African Cream. Three handmade redware three-footed pottery bowls decorated in a black slip referred to as colonolware had come down from slave days. They were aligned like soldiers on the parade ground each holding a different root. She busied herself grinding pieces in a ritual brass mortar and pestle taken from a locked cupboard. The ancient metal pieces contacting one another sounded exactly like Gauche's bells. She replaced the remnants of the roots in the cupboard as she had been taught; one careful piece at a time and locked back up. With scissors, Penn cut a square of hemp tow sack and transferred the mortar and pestle contents onto the hemp that she tied off with moistened cat gut to make a neat bundle. She put it on a polished brass tray. Penn took it to the second story porch off her bedroom. She reached in a pocket of the print dress and pulled out a flash drive filled with Gullah spirituals from their days as someone's belongings. The music that issued from her iPad was earthy, timeless, heavy with syncopated drum rhythms, and a brass rain stick much like Jonah Grant carried. In a trance, her head lolled from side-to-side, Penn lit the bundle. She washed her face and arms and hands in the sacred smoke repeating in a loop, "Trey, Trey, Trey, my way, my way, my way." The bundle now nothing but ashes, Penn spat on an index finger then picked up some of the ash to slash a swipe across her forehead, down each cheek, and another stripe down her nose. She sang;

O, Death

O, Death

O, Death

Won't you spare me over another year?

But what is this that I can't see

With ice cold hands taking hold of thee?

When God is gone and the Devil takes hold

Who will have mercy on your soul?

O, Death

O, Death

O, Death

No wealth, no ruin, no silver, no gold

Nothing satisfies me but your soul

O, Death

Well, I am Death none can excel

I'll open the door to heaven or hell

Oh, Death

O Death

My name is Death and the end is here.

Finished, exhausted, molten silver tears streamed down her cheeks as sirens somewhere across town wept with her. The spirit meeting over, the spell cast, Penn's forward sight sensed that people would die.

A couple of weeks later, Trey and Cerberus went over Morty's edit demands for *Fledgling Warrior*. Gravel crunched outside. Cerberus leapt to his feet and started barking his fool head off. Trey opened the long drawer under the top of a beat-up wood desk he bought at the Church Mouse Thrift Store on Hilton Head Island that he and Lucius lugged into the house. He racked his Glock and took it to the screen door. Penn was just stepping out of a creamy beige Audi-4, a leather document case under her arm. Cerberus nosed through the screen door, sniffed the air his tail a metronome then trotted to her. "I was visiting Lucius," she said fussing over Ticker. "They broke his back in Vietnam, you know. He has the lumbago so I brought dried wild willow branches to ease his pain. Thought I'd combine it with a meeting with you."

"I appreciate your penury, Penn."

"That was punishing," she said laughing. She shaded her eyes. "What's with the pistol?"

"I didn't know who was driving in, is all. Guess I have a case of the yips out here in the wild. Come on up," Trey urged waving her to the porch. "Lucius never told me anything about his troubles," said Trey impressed with the old man's stoicism.

"Yeah, we have lots of Smith's hurt from wars, some outward, some with the broken spirit. We Gullah are taught to never complain because God will take care of you if one stays faithful." She looked off to the marsh. "I'm afraid I bring small news, Mr. Writer."

"Can I offer you a cold beer," Trey said.

"Maybe another time."

They sat at the kitchen table; a 1950s rusted loop leg affair with a used gray top and a pair of mismatched chairs. When Penn was seated, her creation rested his maw on her thigh to gaze up at her with unabashed adoration.

"You were right. The owners and operators are Chinese," Penn said as she stroked Cerberus with long fingers.

"Government or private?"

"From what I could tell, government, but the trail turned faint real fast."

"What's their product?"

"Water," Penn replied.

He pounded the table with his fist. "We knew that from Li Ling but with guards at the gate armed to their teeth? I don't think so."

"Hush, now," soothed Penn. "We think better when we're calm." She patted his forearm like he was a little boy. "There's more. Be patient. I went to Columbia to see if I could run down a list of shareholders but, of course, that was a waste of billable time. Since it's not a public company, under South Carolina law, a list of shareholders doesn't have to be accessible in the public domain. This goes for proxy statements as well."

"And their name is what?"

"Gu Shui Industries. That translates to Ancient Water," Penn said. "I called two major grocery chains to ask if they stocked it and the answer from both was, no. Then I went online. The place has no website."

"That's suspicious in this day and age," Trey said.

"You bet. On the Port of Savannah's website, I found little specific information, but I did discover an intriguing metric. Since Gu Shui opened a little over a year ago, they've shipped, on average, 11 containers a month most of them destined for Hong Kong. That's a boatload of water." Penn said, snickering. "We're even on the puns now, Mr. Writer."

Trey raised his beer to toast her, took a finishing gulp and got up to toss it in the trash. "They had to have passed inspections," he said. "Could you find any regulatory paperwork?"

"I thought about that too. I have a friend working for the SC EPA so I tapped her --"

"Ouch," Trey winced playfully, "Guess that puts me down 2-1."

"Mama Collette always said the words we use are images of our soul."

"I like that. Think I'll use it on the project I'm finishing."

"A five percent royalty is traditional," Penn said, laughing. "Anyway, my friend attached copies of their EPA application as well as the most recent health department report. Trey, they're playing by our rules."

"They had to have passed a field code inspection which I would guess included a schematic of the plant."

"Yes, this same friend is working on that as we speak. And perhaps the most interesting tidbit is on its way. Drum rolls if you please. I called around casting the net for anything more. Gullah country is nosey country. The name Gaylord Russell kept bobbing to the surface. We've danced many a time in court over heir's property he tries to buy for taxes on the courthouse steps."

"That name sounds familiar," Trey said.

"It ought to. He's a retired two-term Governor with Low Country ties going all the way back to the Confederacy. My people never did cotton to him," Penn told Trey. "Three to one."

"You need either a muzzle or a laugh track," Trey said good-naturedly.

"You'll find I'm a great winner. As I live and breathe, Mr. Writer, his family cheated us as freedmen after the war, stole our lands to the tune of thousands of acres and hasn't stopped stealing yet. It so happens that a parcel of 62.265 acres where your friend and neighbor, Li Ling, runs the plant was transferred from Gaylord Russell to Gu Shui Industries of Hong Kong 28 months ago. The price, you might ask. A dollar bill and other just considerations. That was in the Beaufort County transfer of property records. The parcel he bought was taken from the Grant Family consisting of more than 75 individuals who held ownership privileges all the way back to 1863. A firm in Charleston litigated the action. I was co-counsel. Russell won. My people and the Low Country lost."

"Can they do that, I mean, buy property for a dollar?"

"Yup," Penn said. "What do you guess he got from the Chinese; stock, interest deposited in Switzerland, money laundering, smuggling, a vacation home on the beach somewhere nice … what?" Penn finished, riled up.

"Are you sure you don't want a beer?"

"Yeah, I think I would. Thirsty work uncovering the Devil."

"Seems like we have more questions than answers, doesn't it?" he said on the way to the antiquated fridge.

"For sure," Penn was quick to say.

He set the long neck on the table. "I believe I ought to call on the Governor first thing tomorrow morning," Trey said, "ask him if he'd like to give an interview to a hotshot novelist interested in modelling a new character after the Southern gentleman he isn't." They clinked bottles. "What I'd like you to do is discover if Gu Shui has been issued blasting permits and while you're at it see if onsite inspection records exist." Trey touched Penn. "You've done a fabulous job. Thank you."

Cerberus ran after Penn's Audi when she drove away. Trey's heart followed her too.

(11)

That night, Trey searched the Governor's website to find his mobile or home phone. That was a bust but he did find a current e-mail address for an office in Beaufort. Trey typed a quick message asking for the interview.

While he was on the Governor's personal website, he read about the man's political career. It became clear Gaylord Russell was a bully who loved nothing better than to step on poor people. However, Trey did find the material about the family mansion intriguing. It was known as the Russell-Wentworth House and was built in 1763 by the family's slaves. They fired bricks on St. Helena Island across Port Royal Sound. They moved them by sailing ship to the worksite. African slaves brought to the Low Country through Charleston for their rice growing expertise also learned how to be carpenters, masons, and painters particularly Senegambians. Wealthy families kept fine homes in the cities but not on their cotton, rice, or indigo plantations. Plantations houses in the rural Low Country were normally more lavish hunting camps than mansions. Standing fresh water incubated mosquitoes by the trillions. The area was rife with malaria or the ague as it was known in the 18th Century. White owners and their families stayed away and lived in palatial city homes. Because Africans are genetically afflicted with sickle cells in their blood, they were mostly immune to the disease.

In the self-aggrandizing online article, Trey also learned something he was going to use. The handle the Governor preferred, New South Man of the People, was a lie. His great-grandfather was a wealthy carpetbagger from New York who made a fortune selling gunpowder to the Union Army. He and his family arrived just after Appomattox to speculate on real estate, one of the thousands of such Northern vulture entrepreneurs who swooped down on the region to buy land and housing on the cheap.

In the morning, an e-mail arrived on Trey's laptop. He was invited for an afternoon meet at the mansion.

The Governor himself answered the door. The man had albino white hair rippling along his pink pate combed back to expose a high and broad forehead unblemished by worry lines. The man was decidedly pink. The only thing calloused about him was his soul. Trey shadowed him into an impressive library with bookshelves lined by tome after tome accessible by a wooden ladder on a railed track. An enormous Oriental, palace-sized rug big enough to be Ali-Babba's NASCAR ride was prevented from flying away by an equally enormous desk piled high with stacks of newspapers, files, and books.

"Please do have a seat," the Governor said. He walked around the desk and plumped down on a tufted leather office chair with an incredibly tall back. He studied Trey for a few beats before he said, "I enjoyed your last book. Helen and I took in the movie too. So, what does a famous writer and decorated war hero hope to glean from me. And, by the way, I am flattered you called."

"Mind if I record our conversation?" Trey said holding a pocket-sized recording device into the air for the Governor's inspection. It was theater but the Governor didn't have to know.

"Go right ahead," said the Governor looking very pleased with himself.

"I read about your family," Trey opened, "your education, career track, and such. I'd like to maybe cut to a more macro window if I may. South Carolina from its very beginning was a commercial dynamo trading foodstuffs and raw materials to the world produced by Africans in bondage. How do you see the State in the next half-century and how are you positioning your personal wealth in this new multinational and technological age?"

He knit chubby fingers to rest on top of a prodigious belly. "The New South, sir, has developed into the direct opposite of where we were in 1860. The Union had most of the manufacturing capacity before and during the war. As such they out-technologized the Old South and used that advantage to win the war by attrition. We, on the other hand were forced to negotiate with Europe for war materiel then try to outrun the Union's naval blockade. The solution remained incomplete. Today, the New South is a destination for over-taxed unionized companies domiciled north of the Mason-Dixon Line and for that, we not only compete for Northern manufacturing, we beat them head-to-head at every turn. You asked, me, sir, where I have my family's capital? Why, it's in companies like Gulfstream, Boeing, Volvo, Michelin, and BMW; all of whom have made sizeable investments on the future of my State. We started with the sale of agriculture and raw materials to global markets three centuries ago and we have very profitably come full circle."

"Yes, sir," Trey said. "If I'm not mistaken, those you listed are all American or EU companies. What about the Chinese?"

The Governor pushed back from the fancy desk and stood.

"They are a discrete people, Mr. Dawson," he said, an edge to it. "Let's leave it at that, shall we?"

"I found a dead limb on your family tree."

"You what?" the governor said.

"A dead limb."

The Governor shook his head, baffled.

"Your great grandfather and grandmother didn't live here at the start of the Civil War. They lived in New York and came south after it was over. It was they who bought this house after the war bankrupted the Wentworth's."

"And just what in hell is your point, sir?"

"Carpetbaggers, your immediate family –"

"I assure you, my pedigree is pure, sir," the Governor said growing pinker.

"I understand a Chinese company is doing, quite literally, a booming business right near my house. Do you know the company, Gu Shui Industries?"

"This isn't about my family at all. Is it?" the Governor huffed coming closer to Trey.

"You couldn't be more wrong. It's all about family, Governor. What did they compensate you in return for the land you stole from the Grant family? You get 10%, 20%?"

"Get the hell out of my house," the older man fumed, pointing the way with a finger shaking with rage. "You don't want to be my enemy. Trust me on that one."

"Aw-w, this was getting to be such fun," Trey wisecracked.

He drove to Penn's office sifting impressions on the way. Reading between the lines, if for no other reason than the Governor's fast anger when the subject of the Chinese came up, it was certainly the Governor had some kind of financial interest in the Chinese plant. But exactly what?

At the end of an impossibly busy workday, Penn called out to Joselyn, "Girl, you get you wide body in here this minute if you know what's good for you." Within seconds, Joselyn pranced into Penn's office carrying a fake attitude. The way she walked with extra arm swing and hip joggle gave it away.

"What you want which me, girl, yo'self?" Joselyn asked and flounced onto an easy chair.

"I've had it with this Reardon case," Penn said. "That is the single most stubborn bunch of people I ever saw. I brought them another more than fair settlement and the fools didn't sign this one either." She threw her arms up in exasperation and left her desk to join her cousin.

"Em-huh, you been slaving over it for six months, that right?" Joselyn said.

"But, especially here lately. Such a slog."

Her cousin chuckled. "That 'cause you got you head full of him."

Penn sighed and leaned back in the chair. "Why is it we Gullah can't get enough of bad boys? Ever think about that?"

"'Cause we think we can tame them, that what. But there be a bigger problem than that," Joselyn said, her brow furrowed.

"Don't start with me," Penn cautioned, her hand kneading her temples.

"He ain't Gullah," Joselyn said.

"So what?"

"Tradition that's so what. Look up on that wall behind you in pictures of our lives. Do you see a chalky face in any of 'em? No, you do not." Joselyn wagged an index finger for emphasis. "Now, I ain't got nothin' against Mr. Writer in particular. He cute but them blue eyes they carry trouble. And, girl, he married. My advice to you is play but don't pay."

In all the years she had known Joselyn, Penn never discussed the powers that rested in a Gullah spirit world that coincided with Senegambian ancestors who believed in a three-part death cycle; the body, the soul, and the spirit, a structure not too different than the Trinity of the Christian religion which they embraced as passionately as they did the old ways. When a Gullah dies, the body is buried in the earth in the natural cycle of life common to man. The soul lifts out of the body to "cross the waters" to heaven but the spirit remains on earth. That was the realm in which Penn's powers were exercised most dramatically. Instead of the truth about her root doctor training, Penn acted as simply the healer, the shaman for the Gullah community using ancient homeopathic remedies whose applications stretched far into the African past well beyond recorded history birthed on the continent where man first walked upright. That didn't mean Penn didn't thirst to tell all to her closest friend, especially about the spell she placed on Trey. In the deep past, stolen from their homeland, her people survived slavery then wove a cocoon around their community to embrace old,

old African ways, developed their own language, and cuisine; all accomplished in the mysterious Low Country living daily in a secrecy born of caution when dealing with white people.

"Well," Penn said, hesitating after Joselyn's guilt-infused salvo. "I'm working on that divorce thing."

"Em-huh," Joselyn scoffed. "You sinning, that which you do."

Penn rose. "Oh, stop with the moralistic palaver."

Joselyn snickered again. "You use them big words when you steamed. Girl, you know I right. You cain't hide in them words, you understand, don't you?"

Trey told Penn all about his visit to Gaylord Russell.

"We have to get in that plant," she said after he gave her the basics. "Snoop around to see what they're really up to. You know, at first, I thought you were some reactionary Loonie Tunes obsessed with conspiracy theories running the world, but the bigger the hole I dug on our pal the Governor, that stink you talked about got to me, too."

"Agreed," he said. "Tell me something, please. Why do folks call me, Mr. Writer?"

"Is Gullah ting. Kindly like when you white folks freed the serfs. Like slaves back then, they had only first names, no last names so you work in a gristmill, you become Trey Miller or if you Daddy build houses like our Lord Jesus did, you be Trey Carpenter. We Gullah the same so your identity is a writer. Mister, it be added out of respect. We could have known you as Mr. Soldier too."

"You researched me?"

"Of course, we did just as we do with all of my clients," she said slipping out of Gullah.

He studied Penn for a few beats. "Do you have any government regulators you can contact?"

"You probably don't remember but I already told you I do, a college roommate, Michelle Langley the Pious. She was the one who PDF'd a few papers she found and ones I shared with you."

"What's with the Pious?"

"Well, her fanaticism working for the EPA is most like her religion. I'm here to tell you she's righteous about keeping the environment clean and loves nothing better than to bust the chops of evil corporate polluters. She's a mid-level admin in Columbia. I think I can incite her to riot, pretty easy to do actually."

Trey paced the floor thinking out loud. "With your friend's help, maybe dressed in fake uniforms. Yeah, that's it, we could pass for watchdogs, walk around, see the sights, look at some files. But you gotta promise to let me do the James Bond thing," Trey said all serious.

"Chivalry not only died a long time ago, it never existed between a very white man and a gorgeous, vital Gullah woman like me." Penn fluffed her braided hair then shook it. Something stirred in Trey's belly, something visceral, something primordial born of desire.

Penn was satisfied she had Trey's heart but did he have hers? She thought not and reflected on the fact she had never even gone out with a white guy and never once had she fallen for one. He would stay as close as she would allow just like Gauche suggested. Under the Imp's counsel since she was fifteen, Penn knew better than to cross him.

"You need a disguise," she said. "They have your mug."

"How about I grow a full beard and let my hair grow out?"

"Better than nothing," she said. "Look I need to go upstate anyway to research some real estate documents for a case I represent. I'll look in on Shell."

"Just like that, she'll drop everything for you?" Trey said, incredulous.

"This woman, she is sick with the love I don't give back, but she hopes with a sore heart."

(12)

Michelle Langley was all arms, legs, and hands, her hair an uncombed and equally unruly brown mop edged in silver that threatened to take over one day. She was plain, plainly dressed and plainly into the natural look of no makeup or jewelry or bright colors. Her intense blue eyes were lasered on Penn. They embraced at the door.

As she had always done starting freshman year much to Penn's discomfiture, Shell gave her a quick kiss on the lips then grabbed Penn's elbows to take her all in, beaming with pleasure. "Lord God almighty but ya'll a sight for tired eyes. Whoever said one should paint the sun yellow was wrong. The sun is cocoa and she stands before me and dat is the ting. Come on, have a seat." She indicated wooden chairs in front of her cluttered desk piled high with the substance of bureaucracy. Shell chuckled before she said, "I have to tell you that after your call yesterday, what with all the mystery surrounding this Gu Shui Industries, I was energized. Shit, I was here until after ten last night, girl, and it's your fault."

Penn crossed her legs. "Guilty as charged, your honor. So, what did you find?"

Shell reached across the space between the chairs to place her hand on Penn's resting on her lap. "Well, it might be better to describe it as what the hell was and what is no more."

"I don't get it."

"The incorporation papers are intact, nothing untoward, all the appropriate spaces filled with figures and measurements and people's names I can't pronounce. But I couldn't find a single scrap of information about shareholders."

"I had the same experience," Penn said.

"However, internal memos imply they are current on their water sample reports."

"So, they really do produce water."

"Yes, indeed. And here's another feature that may or may not be important. Let me bring this up on the laptop." She opened the computer, typed then turned the screen so Penn could see the satellite reconnaissance page Shell previously selected. "I called a friend of mine in the state geological department and asked her about the aquifer they're drawing from. She worked on it some late yesterday and came crashing into my office with a weird look pasted on her puss, like she'd seen a ghost or something." The EPA specialist got up to put a hand on each of Penn's shoulders and pointed to the image of the plant. "They built right smack dab on an underground river coursing through a tectonic anomaly."

"Okay, stop with the technical stuff," Penn said. "Keep it simple for a simple woman."

"You are everything but simple, my African Queen. This river bisects a dome of minerals that actually was trying to become a volcano but it never made it to the surface, kind'a like a volcanus *interruptus*. This means there are magma pipes deep underground like you get in diamond mines where high pressure and equally high heat can create exotic stuff. There's one in southern Illinois, for example, called Hick's Dome, that created the world's largest supply of fluorspar critical to the steel industry and for the manufacture of fluoride for the world's teeth."

Shell reached to her desktop and took a file off it to hand to Penn. "Here, this is for you. Inside is a copy of blueprints submitted prior to issuance of a building permit." Penn opened the file to withdraw an architectural rendering of the plant. "Every damn thing you see on this schematic is consistent with bottling and water extraction from deep wells such as automated bottling lines, stainless steel holding tanks, wellheads, you get the picture."

"What about the filtered residue?"

Shell looked surprised. "What residue?"

"From the filtration process."

"Oh, that's over here." She pointed at it with a spidery finger. "Any traces of bad stuff would show in the water sample reports."

"Yeah, unless they're cheating."

"I'm not worried about that so much as I'm concerned with a large room in the northeast part of the plant that is labelled simply, 'storage.'"

"Well, they'd need to have a place to store inventory prior to shipment, right?"

"Sure, but this room is three stories high and 10,000 square feet."

Penn couldn't help herself. "That's a boatload of water," she said.

"Damn straight," Shell agreed. "And one more thing; all other papers in this file besides the ones you see have been on-loan some three years ago to a Robert Habersham, an employee of State Licensing. No such person ever existed and no one knows where the hell the paperwork is today."

"How convenient," Penn said. "I do believe you have a mole."

"No shit, Sherlock."

"Listen, we need to be hugely careful. Do you know of any political operatives in either of these departments?" Penn asked thinking Gaylord Russell might have paid informants to lurk in the shadows.

"No, in fact, hell no," Shell said, indignant.

"Can you raid Gu Shui?"

"Yes, but it'll take time to clear it with my superiors."

"Go for it girlfriend," Penn urged.

(13)

On-staff attorneys moved the gears to open the gates of Gu Shui Industries but it took three weeks for them to open, plus, Shell was hesitant to allow Trey to go with them. Penn was no problem because Shell could reason that a *pro bono* attorney was a good idea, particularly one with a law enforcement background. In the end, Shell convinced a superior to approve Trey but not before he signed a four-page hold-harmless document that indemnified the state for anything short of nuclear holocaust. His official job description was 'bodyguard.'

In the municipal parking lot near Penn's office, a chilly introduction made, Penn and Trey staged Shell's late model Tahoe. It was clear to Trey that Penn's friend disliked him immediately.

On the road, Shell drew boundaries. "I want you guys as extra eyes. Nothing more. We're bending the rules as it is. Any commotion could spell trouble for me." She caught Trey's attention in the rearview mirror making it clear the barbed words were for him.

"Do they know we're coming?" Trey said from the backseat.

"Of course. It's the law," responded Shell, but it sounded like, 'of course, stupid.'

Penn spoke up. "I'm interested in the quality of the water, the mystery room, and where they discard filtered residue."

"Spot on," Shell agreed again looking in the rearview mirror for dissent.

Twenty minutes later, they turned off the county blacktop. As before, two guards were on duty, their faces chiseled marble. Shell lowered her window, "Officer Michelle Langley, South Carolina EPA," she said offering her credentials. The guard gave it sneering attention, consulted a clipboard, grunted then gave it back.

"Get out of the car," he said. "All stand by side."

"This is bullshit," Shell fumed.

"You want in, Michelle Langley, you do as I say."

"Jackass," Shell blurted but opened the door and got out.

The other guard carried a handheld portable device. He held it in front of Shell's face, depressed a button, and flooded her with a curious purple light. Apparently satisfied with the information that appeared on the video screen, he mumbled into the device then moved on to Penn. Trey's face was the last to be illuminated.

"You," the guard said very officious, "you no go." The other guard unslung his AK-47. He glared at Trey waving the barrel at him. "Put hands behind head," he said, and when Trey didn't respond he jabbed Trey in the belly with the muzzle. "Do it, now, Trey Lawson." Trey spat at the guard's feet and did what he was told. The frisk turned up the Glock and his cellphone. "I keep both," the guard said triumphantly field-stripping the 9mm rounds from the insertable clip. The bullets fell in a pile on the sandy ground. "You, Lawson, stay outside, I keep you too." He turned to Penn and Shell. "You enter."

I'm disappointed in you," Penn whispered. "We discussed bringing a weapon and thought better of it."

"I don't trust these lying bastards," he whispered back.

"Nor do I, but now we have just two pairs of eyes, not three and all because of your temper. We'll leave the car," she said, displeased.

Issuing from the front entrance to the plant, a multi-seat ATV sped toward them with a driver and one passenger in the back seat. The guards closed the gate and escorted Penn and Shell inside the perimeter, their way blocked by the taller of the two who held his rifle aslant across his chest.

"Looks like Humpty-Dumpty called Uber," snarked Shell.

Penn studied the passenger. He was a beer barrel of an Asian man dressed in a fine tailored black suit, black leather shoes perhaps Italian designer, a black fedora, and white shirt capped off by a dreary tie. She estimated his age at maybe fifty to fifty-five and assumed the guy was the head honcho. Like his guards, he showed zero emotion as though someone wound his porcelain self at breakfast, patted him on the behind, and sent him on his way. The ATV came to a halt and the man got out. He was surprisingly agile for his size and advanced toward them hands behind his back with purpose in his step.

"If you please, ladies, remain where you are," the man said in clipped Etonian English. "I must greet my neighbor and friend." He bowed then walked slightly hunched with his hands grasped at the small of his back through the gate where Trey took in the diplomatic ballet.

"Li Ling, I presume," Trey said.

"Why did you try to sneak into my business with such blatant artifice?" the plant manager said. "Furthermore, you are naïve to think our facial profiling capability would be compromised with a childish attempt to grow a beard."

"Well, I just wanted to meet my neighbor and great friend." Trey goaded.

Li Ling's eyes closed slightly. "If you had called in honesty, I would have personally taken you on a tour, but now, since you lied, I must treat you like a child by withdrawing your privilege."

"Nice technology."

"What do you mean, Lawson?"

"Dawson," Trey said, "that's Dawson, not Lawson and that's the third time you did that. Now who's showing disrespect?"

Li Ling drew himself up. "You shall remember this is land owned by my people of China. You stand on our private property at MY option."

Trey ignored the nationalistic bravado. "Never seen a portable facial recognition scanner," he said. "A new toy for you ChiComs? What's the range?"

"Why, if you must know, it reaches all the way to Beijing but you already presumed that specification."

"You use my Special Ops image, did you?" Trey said trying to get under the man's skin. "No, never mind, look, let's chuck this cock and bull. You're an employee of the Prople's Republic of China, likely up to no good, and I aim to find out just what that is."

"Ah, you remind me of that fine actor, Bruce Willis, in *Death Wish* movies. And, oh, by the way, the titanium that makes your left leg probably came from our mines in the Gobi Desert of Mongolia where I managed the richest deposits on the planet. See how nice we can be."

"Yeah, and that mortar round you assholes made that took my leg was being nice and then the high quality steel tube that killed Caleb."

(14)

Penn and Shell were driven to the plant. Steam rose from pipes on the roof. The humming of air conditioning and internal electric industrial processing made the place sound exactly like a huge beehive. This was the first industrial site Penn had ever visited that lacked a parking lot. The absence helped her draw the conclusion that the employees who ran the operation were prisoners inside the fence and likely to be 100% Chinese nationals.

The portly Chinese plant manager led the way down a gloomy hall, his gait like an ice skater, the palm of his hands pointed behind him, the arms swinging in rhythm to his steps, back and forth, back and forth. Walls were devoid of display cabinets showing off their production or history. No employee of the month picture was on display and not one single announcement board. For whatever reason, the Chinese also chose not to light the florescent ceiling panels.

Li Ling opened a door just like all the rest. It let onto a monkish office. Not a single picture hung on the corrugated steel wall, or on the credenza, or his orderly but modest desk. The only picture was a framed image of the current Chinese President. Unlike Shell's wreck back in Columbia piled high and deep, one single folder was squared on a green felt blotter. It was bright red, embossed in gold lettering. Penn read upside down: Gu Shui Industries – Global Material Solutions for Global Issues.

Penn and Shell shucked out of their backpacks and set them on the polished concrete floor. Li Ling pushed the folder toward Shell and with his knuckles resting on the desk said, "Inside are truthful answers to the list of questions for which your office has asked. You were especially concerned about quality control of the water. Inside this folder you find thrice-daily measurements for the last six months that follow EPA protocol. By the way, on that wish list you demanded a record of our shareholders. I cannot nor will I divulge a single name," he said.

"But, that's –"Shell sputtered before he cut her off with a slicing gesture of his hand.

"Our attorneys are clear we are in no gray area."

"What about filtrated residue?" Penn said. "We insist you show us your disposal site."

"I assure you it is safe."

"Not sufficient," said Shell, prickly.

"Tests for the filtered waste are also within the reports. We take extra steps for you. We sterilize some of it and the rest we incinerate at high temperature. Now, if you will follow me, I take you to a private room where you are able to evaluate our world-class operation. A girl is provided for immediate assistance."

"We asked for an open tour," Shell said not twitching a muscle.

"That is not going to happen," said Li Ling firmly. "It is beyond your purview. Need I explain that your charge is to ensure the safety of the water we produce and to certify that we are not polluting your precious swamps. That can be accomplished by reading the completed forms your department so kindly sends quarterly, of course, with the esteemed counsel provided by Mademoiselle Smith. Unlike my own progressive nation, your country has gone too far in regulations. We encourage business to grow. We do not try to strangle them with useless make-work." He held the door open. "Shall we?" he said.

They proceeded along a corridor of closed, windowless doors and turned a corner to walk about half the other corridor. Not a sound could be heard save their shoes on the concrete. No ringing phones came from within nor human chatter, or music.

They came to an unmarked door. Inside, a small woman in her twenties leapt to attention to stand rigidly, her arms at her sides, eyes straight ahead and blank. She wore a white shirt and a black unadorned skirt to mid-calf. Penn took note of surveillance cameras mounted in each corner.

"You have all you need," Li Ling said, "desks, chairs, nice cool air, quiet, no need to worry about lunch. We bring it to you. If you must use the restroom, Miss Chen is here to accompany you. Am I clear?" Li Ling didn't wait for an answer before he was gone, locking them in from the outside.

"This is outrageous," raged Shell.

Miss Chen didn't blink. Instead, she glanced up at a camera and said something in Chinese. She extended her hands toward Penn and Shell. "I shall have your phones, now" she said in a crisp voice.

"In a pig's butt," Shell objected.

Miss Chen addressed the camera again and when she was done she said, "I have asked my people to jam both phones. As such, no messages will be forwarded or received or recoverable. You may keep your precious phones most of which were made by Chinese citizens."

Thinking about the greater good, a concept her father, Denmark, was fond of, Penn shelved a stand for freedom of communication. It was useless to fight this skirmish. Other more impactful ones would follow. She rummaged her backpack for the laptop.

"Do not bother with your computers," Miss Chen said. "We have good Chinese machines for you loaded with our excellent software."

"Yeah," Penn said disgustedly. "Stolen encryption from good American companies."

"No matter," said Miss Chen, her indifference maddening. "You take notes on our technology. You take and make copies of what you need, okay? No internet."

"No internet? What's the deal with that horseshit?" Shell exploded. "How do you suppose I'm going to link with my department?"

"Not our problem. Please, do get to work," Miss Chen scolded. "You want bottle of our water? Very good."

The better part of an hour went by finding little. "It's too Goldie Locks, if you ask me," she said to Penn, "and, yes, I understand they can hear me but I don't give a rat's ass. Hey, puppet girl," she said to Miss Chen, "I need to take a leak."

"Leak?" Miss Chen said turning slowly to Shell like an owl sighting dinner.

"You know, urinate, pee, make one of your yellow rivers that Mao used to swim in, or, how about drain the lizard."

Most humans would have smiled but Miss Chen couldn't. Instead, she said something to the camera, rose from her seat, and left the room with Shell in her wake. The door was locked from the outside.

Penn conceded Li Ling won this first game on home turf. Somehow, she and Trey had to find a way into the complex. But, Trey didn't look Asian in the least nor did Penn so it would be madcap to act like they were employees. If caught, she would be disbarred and left flapping in the media winds as they picked her bones. Her dreams of making a difference for the greater Gullah culture would end or at the very least be pruned to insignificance. Trey, on the other hand, would likely see a jump in sales. She pictured a headline – NY Times Bestseller Trey Dawson Tries Espionage Gambit for Real.

Her mind strayed to Trey. She felt trapped by the prospect of tying up with him to where his future was her future, but that was exactly what a four-hundred-year-old Imp told her to do. So far as she knew, if Trey became her lover that would be one of the only such interracial affairs in Smith family history. And, what would her parents say? Would she be banished by her extended family for diluting Senegambian blood? She had recently completed one of the online DNA kits, so she was keenly aware of who coursed through her veins. The information was shared with her parents and siblings. Penn learned she was 80% Senegambian, 6% Gola, 4% Gold Coast, and the rest Northern European from Gauche's French Huguenot legacy plus a few animalistic rapes by owners. If other Smith's who no longer lived in the Low Country were tested, Penn suspected their DNA would be less African-centric owing to the high value Low Country Gullah place on the most important unit to her people, the family. The relative isolation of the Gullah over the centuries distilled the former slaves into a concentrated culture suspicious of outsiders. Trey Dawson, no matter his accomplishments, was one of those.

A key turned the tumblers in the examination room admitting Shell in full meltdown. "Look, Pee Wee," she said to Miss Chen, "at the top of our list is a complete walking tour of this facility, not this bullshit of a jail cell filled with your snotty technology, which by the way, sucks a big one."

Miss Chen didn't blink. She relocked the door and assumed her seat as Shell continued to blister her. Shell pointed a very sharp finger at the camera. "I'll talk with Ling Ling and right now," she said. "Do you hear me in there? I can make things real goddamn uncomfortable for you guys. Maybe shut the plant through court order. Isn't that within your understanding of statute, Barrister?"

"Indeed so," replied Penn enjoying the bluff.

Calmly, Miss Chen rose and spoke to the camera then sat back down, her black eyes giving away nothing.

"That's it?" Penn said. The woman made no answer.

"I'm making an official request that if not heeded will give you a one-way ticket back to whatever hole you slithered from," she said, looking down on her jailer.

The door lock clicked. In strode two guards clad like the outside ones except for no rifle. "Come with me!" one of them demanded. "Leave equipment and backpack."

"No way, Jose," Shell said.

A guard whipped out a baton and moved very quickly behind Penn sticking it like a sword in the small of her back.

"Move," he said with menace. "Colonel wait for you."

"So, the Jolly Yellow Giant is military," Penn said to Shell.

15

Furious they confiscated his pistol and phone, Trey started the Tahoe. Big truck tires kicked up a torrent of gravel as he spun out. It pinged the guard box and sent the guards for cover within. Trey zoomed away down the narrow track.

He quickly found what he looked for, a path like the one he and Mary Beth used years ago. He pulled in, initiated the four-wheel drive, and bumped toward the north perimeter of the plant but deadfalls left over from the track of hurricane Matthew blocked the way. He got out, looked around then started off on foot. Trey hadn't gone far until a heavily accented, tinny voice came from above. "Lawson, leave immediately, I repeat, get out immediately." Just then, a large drone at least six feet in diameter, zipped above the pine tree canopy. It whirred to a stop over his head.

"Return to the main gate. NOW," the machine demanded.

Two, gun ports pointed at him. It was no use to try to evade or overpower the machine. He vowed the day would come when he would be equipped to do battle with the aerial robot.

"I might not be the brightest bulb in the pack but I'm here to tell you," he said to the drone figuring it was capable of two-way communication, "Mama didn't raise no stupid kids,".

"Leave!" the drone ordered again.

"Okee-docee, ace," Trey said and did just that.

Li Ling was as still as the grave, feet wide, and manicured hands locked on a wide waist. Stormy weather played on his face. "Your threats are unnecessary," he said. "We want what you want; clean water. You must follow me."

The colonel led them to an internal entrance where a keypad was mounted on the wall. He placed his hand on the screen, a red light blinked, and the door opened directly into a noisy bottling line in full swing. Half a dozen uniformed personnel checked each plastic bottle that clattered down a stainless-steel line at the end of which was a packaging automaton that stacked filled, red labelled bottles in twelve packs, wrapped them in clear plastic to be stacked on a wooden pallet that disappeared through a large hole curtained by black rubber veils.

"We fill 20,000 bottles a day," said the sullen Colonel.

"What's that over there?" asked Shell indicating a large stainless-steel tank next to equally large pipes equipped with wheels on their top, one painted red, the other blue.

"They are water pumps that refill the tower."

Shell headed for them. She touched the top of each one. "Interesting," she said. "One is cold and the other, the red one, is really hot."

"At the depths we go to find prehistoric river, we approach the interior of our planet that is a core of molten rock. The fresh water we pump is over 90 Celsius, near the boiling point. We must refrigerate it before bottling. If we do not, the plastic melts."

"What does this do?" Penn said, touching a refrigerator-sized metal box.

"Well, that's a specially designed reverse osmosis filtration system filled with the best technology available. We are proud of it."

"How much sediment do you generate in a normal bottling run?" Penn said.

"That figure is in the paperwork you reviewed."

"Oh, yeah, he's right," said Shell, embarrassed she missed it.

"We have video and audio record of you viewing the page. I refer you to the work we have already done and not bother us in our important mission having to do and do again and do again." Li Ling shook his head and walked off toward yet another guarded entrance.

They walked into a bustling warehouse and loading dock outside of which were a baker's dozen intermodal cubes uniformly stenciled 'China Shipping.' Preternatural cranes like massive metal spiders ran on an aerial track designed to secure a cube with iron claws and pile it on a waiting tractor trailer. The place swarmed with Asian men backlighted by the bright outside appearing as animated silhouettes while scarlet fork lifts scurried between pallet stacks and an empty cube.

"From what port do you do most of your shipping?" Shell asked.

"Again, Michelle Langley, if you did your homework you would know that 89.6% sails to various harbors in mainland China from the Port of Savannah. The balance ships from Charleston. Roger Forsyth, the Port of Savannah's director has become very good friend unlike your sidekick, Lawson. Now," he said, "I have a surprise for you. If I recall, you are paranoid about how we dispose of particulate waste. Our brilliant engineers have turned an industrial problem to a cultural joy. I play Pied Piper. Right this way."

They exited into dazzling sunshine. It took a bit before their eyes could focus properly. They stood in a formal garden that contained a myriad of flowers, rose bushes of every color filled with blossoms, manicured boxwoods, and a gurgling water feature that ran over black glaciated rocks. Here and there cast-iron benches invited one to relax where Koi were colorful clouds in the pools.

"My friends, I have plants from China living well from the new earth, ancient water moistening their feet. I visit this oasis many times to cleanse my mind. It is much like my garden in

Quandong Province my wife and I tend. One more stop and you may leave," Li Ling said abruptly

pivoting away.

Back inside, they were led to three over-sized portals. Two guards flanked it. The Colonel

said something to the guard on the right who let them in. They were on a viewing platform high

above the floor. No people rushed about. Two large, domed structures at least three stories tall

dominated the area. Bots fashioned from fork-lift chassis roamed the aisles some cleaning the floors,

some lifting filled palates, some checking the many, many gauges.

"We are fully automated in this pasteurization section where all impurities are removed and

the water is sterilized. These are our ovens. They are the latest state-of-the-art technology only the

People's Republic of China has to give its citizens."

The space held aisle after aisle of three-story metal shelving. Plastic bottles were everywhere,

some filled but most empty. Several mountains of wooden pallets were neatly ordered near a long

conveyor belt that snaked out presumably to the bottling area.

"Do the pallets go to the loading platform?" Shell asked.

"Where else?" said Li Ling sarcastically. "Have you seen enough?"

Ever the humanist, Penn asked, "Where do your workers live?"

"Onsite. Full dormitories, cafeteria 24 hours the day, a dedicated physician, and stores to buy

necessities. We are good to our workers, I assure you. Because I am done with this, you are done with

this. I escort you to the entrance where your backpacks may be retrieved."

Li Ling bowed and said, "Should you have questions, you have my contact information. It has

been loaded on your phones in the Notes app."

16

As the ATV taxi approached the gate, Penn was dismayed to see Trey arguing with one of the guards. The other guard stood with a pistol draw but at his side. Trey's arms flailed the sky. He stood toe-to-toe, nose-to-nose. "You lousy, conniving son-of-a-whore, give me back my Glock," he yelled above the whine of the approaching 2-cycle engine.

"You no have gun," the guard said. "You Americans have too much guns. Very dangerous."

"Give it to me now, or I'll crack your head like a walnut."

"Trey, look out, the other guy is at your back," shouted Penn.

So angered by the theft was Trey that he forgot a cardinal rule of combat, 'never give them your back.' He heard the arming of the pistol in the advancing guard's hand then the cold steel of the muzzle jammed in his neck. Trey simmered down, put his hands in the air to say enough and backed away to the SUV sending off a charged stream of vulgarities.

"Well, that was stupid," scolded Shell as they stood beside the SUV.

"Listen, the sons-a-bitches stole a $1,000 dollar pistol I've owned for years, plus my phone, and you don't think I have a right to be pissed?"

"Now it's my turn to be pissed." She pointed at the coating of South Carolina dirt all over the side panels, doors, and wheel wells of her tricked-out Tahoe. "You pig," she said to Trey. "Where in hell did you go to slime my ride this bad?"

"Well, I got kind of bored so I found an old road that might take me to the perimeter of the plant. It didn't. Come closer you guys." He waved them together. Shell looked dubious but did it anyway. He whispered, "Your phones are compromised. Do not say anything negative on the way back. You'll need to replace them as soon as you can."

"Bullshit on the cloak and dagger, Mister Man," Shell blustered.

"You wouldn't have lasted five minutes under my command," he said and got in the vehicle.

A few minutes on the road, Shell said, "I believe they're on the up and up. I'm going to file a complementary inspection report."

Penn caught Trey's attention. Out of Shell's line of vision, she shook her head in silent disagreement.

The rest of the way to Beaufort was spent in discussions of what Penn and Shell had seen, Shell advocating for Li Ling, Penn playing Switzerland. He kept silent about the encounter with the drone, an omission he was sure the ChiComs would notice.

They pulled to the curb in front of Penn's office. It was well past closing time. Shell hugged Penn, gave Trey one last disapproving glare, and took off for Columbia.

"Come on in," Penn said handing Trey her phone and opening the office. "I need to use the facilities while you defang, okay."

He bared his teeth at her and growled.

"I hate to eat alone," Penn said when she returned. She gave him a come on along arm swoop. They left Penn's phone on Joselyn's desktop. Once outside where she could talk freely, Penn said, "What say we walk a couple of blocks to the G-Spot, get a cheeseburger and a couple of beers, reminisce about old times?"

"Oh, come on. You're pulling my leg," Trey said. "The G-Spot for real?"

"Hey cowboy, get your head out the gutter. G for grilling, get it, and okay to the grub."

"Hey, Pete," Penn said to the black barkeep of indeterminant age as they made their way to the back of the small establishment.

"Hey you own beautiful self. When you gonna marry me?" he played in Gullah.

"Oh, maybe first ting tomorrow, or maybe not," Penn said. She led Trey to a faded red naugahyde booth next to an old-fashioned jukebox.

"Went to high school with Pete," she said by way of explanation.

The compact bar and grille's walls were covered by colorful Gullah paintings offered for sale serenaded by down and dirty delta blues from ceiling speakers. A couple of customers were hunkered down on stools at the old oak bar their arms fences that guarded their drink. It struck him that not a single patron turned their head or gave them a murderous stare. Instead, heads nodded them back to their table. The culture had changed while Trey was away at war.

Within seconds, a blousy middle-aged woman breezed to their table with once clear plastic glasses of ice water and utensils wrapped in a paper napkin. "Long time no see," she commented to Penn, crossed her arms over enormous mounds of breasts, cocked a hip, and said, "And where did this handsome probably delicious man come from. You ain't from around here, sticky buns, 'cause I know where all the talent is in Beaufort."

"Buttercup, this is Trey Dawson, my client from Atlanta."

"Great name," said Trey with a smile.

"You that fancy pants writer people gossip about."

"Yes, ma'am, in the flesh. How about a couple of Buds and two cheeseburgers with American cheese." He looked at Penn to see how he was doing.

"And fries," she added. "Doing good, Mr. Writer."

Buttercup sashayed back to the kitchen in the hope that Trey noticed the giddy-up in her tailgate.

His salt and pepper beard in both hands, Trey leaned toward Penn. "So, what do you think? Keep or shave?"

"Keep. It makes you look like an Old Testament prophet."

"You can call me Moses if you like. He and I are like this." Trey crossed his middle and index fingers to illustrate. "Come closer," he whispered. "They have drones," he said.

Penn gave him a disbelieving look. "I'm sorry.? They have what?"

"Drones."

"What for?"

"For preventing people like me anywhere near their campus. One stopped right over my head, told me to leave, even knew who I was, calling me Lawson. Guess who that might be?" He omitted the gunport observation for fear it would terrify her.

"I'm for dropping this whole thing," Penn said. The beers arrived. They clinked longnecks. "I mean, this keeps escalating. I'm an officer of the court, ya know. I've no business in this business. Look, Trey, we should tell the police about our suspicions. Give it over to the authorities."

"No," he said emphatically. "I'll go on without you if you're uncomfortable. If we hand it to the FBI they'll tie it up with Justice and State Departments. I double guarantee it would take forever to get anything done. The last thing they want is for an international incident to blow up between the countries. However, if we, I mean, if I uncover what they're up to and have incontrovertible evidence, it's one private citizen doing his nation a favor, not the government. Besides, the Chinese have become increasingly militant especially in the South China Sea where they have taken islands that belong to Vietnam and others, constructed airstrips and ports on them. Plus, they dishonored international waters laws to the point where the ChiCom navy has placed live rounds across the bows of US Navy warships. No, State wouldn't want anything to do with this small stuff possibly inviting China to rattle their aggressive sabers for a sympathetic press. Add in a trade war with the US just for fun and we've got one hell of a mess."

"Yes, yes, I get it," Penn said. "But what are there, maybe fifty Chinese in that compound. How in the world are you going to penetrate their defenses? Drop out of the sky like Iron Man. Come on, confess. You're his brother, right?"

"I haven't figured it out yet," Trey said unamused, "but what I have figured out is that I want Li Ling's ball sac hanging on the wall in the living room of my next house."

Penn sat back in her banquette. "You scare me some," she said.

"I'll tell you straight," said Trey, agitated. He fastened her eyes to his. "I write because if I don't, I'll go mad. The offal I've seen, the carnage of kids blown to pieces by suicide bombers, those images don't go away, Penn, never," He said and looked away from her. "It's time you heard the truth about your client. Let's begin with the fact I'm estranged from my wife, Gabbie, who blames me for the death of our three-year-old son." Trey sighed and ran a hand under his nose. Penn could see he was struggling much like what happened at church. She covered his folded hands with one of hers, and kept quiet so Trey could lance poison. "Um-m, yeah, well, see," he sniffed, "Gabbie believed it was time Caleb had a backyard swing set so she shopped it and when I saw it would cost over $11,000, I threw a hissy fit. I called the company to cancel delivery. Over the next month of weekends, he and I built a swing set and loved every minute of it. We used a heavy iron pole painted Commie Red as the top rail to which three seats were attached. Gabbie was furious with me but what was new with that? She spent her days and nights with her head shoved up my colon anyway." Trey inhaled deeply to steady his emotions. "Caleb and I were swinging together, you know, trying it out, Caleb on one saddle seat, me on the other. I was teaching him how to pump so he could touch the stars. The bar broke in half. A jagged end went right through that little boy's tender heart. He died in my arms, his precious blood on my hands."

Penn was openly weeping. "I am so sorry, Trey," she sniffled.

"Guess where that rotten iron came from?"

"China," she answered quickly.

"Yeah, dumped in the country illegally. Those bastards owe me, Penn, beautiful Penn. This isn't for me. It's for Caleb."

Wrapped in their own thoughts, they were quiet until the burgers arrived in the hands of the ever-efficient Buttercup. The two made small talk, intimate talk until Trey pushed his empty burger basket away. "If you'd excuse me, gotta see a man about a horse."

"Lordey, I haven't heard that one since my brother, Caesar, moved to Greenville. While you're gone, I'll run back to the office to use the landline. I need to check on something."

As she came to her office, Penn noticed that both of their vehicles listed hard to port and when she got to them, she found out why. Their tires were slashed.

"God A-Mighty," Penn said looking around her, freaked. She hastily opened the office, took her phone off Joselyn's desk, and hustled back to the G-Spot constantly looking over her shoulder.

"Where's the ghost?" Trey said upon seeing her.

"They slashed our tires."

"Sissy thing to do, the bastards. Can I borrow your phone?" She handed it over. He asked the woman in it for the number of Don't Tread on Me, dialed it, and got Coach just finishing supper.

"Hey, have a huge favor to ask. My truck and a friend's sedan need two tires each. Looks like we got on the wrong side of someone's shit list. They slashed our tires. What's that? No ... no, not going to call the cops. We can handle it." He gave Coach the make and model of their vehicles and where they were parked.

"I don't believe I got no tires in stock for that fancy Audi," Coach Clem told him, "but your truck should be a cake walk. See all ya'll in half an hour."

In the offices of the Bureau of National Treasures just off Tiananmen Square situated deep underground an unreadable face looked back at Li Ling on a securitized satellite link the program for which was plagiarized line for line from Skype.

The bespectacled and balding Red Army General, fittingly handicapped by gigantic Alfred E. Newman ears as though advertising his profession, was saying, "We have reviewed the digital recreation of your meeting with the Americans and find no fault in your actions. You are to be complimented for bringing the vulgar and aberrant regulator, Langely, to our side."

"I am thankful, sir," said Li Ling, his head bowed. "However, sir, this Trey Dawson is a concern. Your able department suggests he has issues with us whether they are real or imagined. Should we arrange a convenient accident?"

"Too early," the General replied. "Yet, I think, oh, how they say in United States? Ah-h yes, we must make Colonel Dawson as nervous as a cat in a room full of rocking chairs. Place GPS sensors on his truck and her sedan. They go nowhere without our knowledge. If the situation arises that you can scare him with mis-aimed live fire from our drone squadron, do not hesitate. That is all, Colonel."

(14)

Not far from the G-Spot, former Governor Gaylord Russell and a man by the name of Roscoe Tanner enjoyed a couple of Tennessee sour mash highballs. Now retired, the State Police captain acted as the Governor's trusted bodyguard for the last decade. They sat in white wicker chairs on a veranda that overlooked the marsh and the Beaufort River. An overhead fan stirred air fragrant with jasmine that bloomed in Helen's extensive backyard gardens. The two reminisced about the good old days in Columbia until the subject of the present bullied its way into what had been a pleasant conversation.

"Who'd you hire to do the tire slashes?" the Governor asked.

"Do you recall that black junkie we paid to lie under oath in the racial scuffle over property the Chinese eventually bought?"

"Why, sure I do," the Governor said. "I also recall that Penn Smith, that darkie lawyer, she gave him a hard time on the stand, sure enough. Did everything but call her black brother a liar, which of, course he was."

"Yes, sir, I give that boy a chance to get even," said the trooper, "and you know how them Gullah like to use a knife to settle grievances."

"How much did you pay him?"

"Fifty bucks."

The Governor slapped his knee he laughed so hard. "Hell, Roscoe, those damn tires will cost four times that. Ya'll have any more fun and games you'd like to discuss?"

The Trooper sipped the honey-colored whiskey and set the tumbler down on a nearby tabletop collecting himself. He folded meaty hands together church steeple fashion, a tic he developed as a cop. It meant somebody was going to play hell.

Dressed in grimy overhauls, Coach came into the G-Spot like he owned the place to make sure to say howdies to nearly all the patrons. He worked the room to stop here and there to pass out his business card like a politician in November until he got to their booth.

"You Penn Smith that lawyer," he said staring at her.

"Nice to meet you, Coach," said Penn.

He turned to Trey. "Y'all fixed up but, ma'am, we ain't got your size. Had my son to order them special. Should be in tomorrow. You want I should trailer your car to my locked lot for the night? No charge, ma'am."

"That's awfully kind," Penn said. "My Audi's so old the tires are more valuable than the car."

"Yes, ma'am," Coach said. "I live to serve. See you tomorrow, slugger." He made to leave then pivoted to face his former all-star. "You know, the Braves are having an open tryout next month in Atlanta. What say we go?"

Trey lifted his pant leg to his knee then hiked the prosthesis onto the table. "Probably not this time, Coach, but thanks."

Coach considered the appliance for a couple of beats, "Sorry, Trey. I heard tumors about what happened to you, but the reality of it done took be a'back." He sucked at his gums. One could tell he turned over what to say next. "Ya'll ought to reconsider. You know, that one-armed pitcher for the Yankees, that Jim Abbott pitched hisself a no-hitter, yes sir, made history and the big bucks."

"I'm working on another kind of wealth," said Trey winking at Penn.

Penn and Trey walked hand-in-hand to his truck feeling invincible. He held the door open for her but instead of helping Penn in, he threw his arms around her. They kissed tender and slow until Trey pulled away. "Been wanting to do that for weeks," he said. "I feel like a schoolboy around you, lady. Come home with me to Jonah's Place. Be my love."

She put her long arms around his neck and pulled him close so she could kiss him proper. "Yes, yes, yes," she whispered, each one a kiss.

Cerberus on the braided throw rug on the floor at the foot of the bed in which Penn and Trey slept as spoons.

In the morning, wearing one of Trey's long-sleeve dress shirts she found in a dresser drawer, Penn brewed coffee before he awakened. Waiting for the coffee maker, she took a seat, the same one she used during their first interview that seemed a geologic age ago. The coffee done, she and Cerberus went out on the front porch to enjoy the day-clean, Gullah for sunrise. Penn never tired of the red sun birthed from the marsh, a place her people looked at as both a place of life and a place of death.

Trey pushed through the screen door. He kissed Penn. "Mornin' sunshine," he said and sat next to her on the porch swing.

"Glad it's Saturday," she said. "The only thing I need do is help clean the praise house in the afternoon. We got plenty time," Penn said in fast Gullah.

Trey shook his head, bewildered. "Who are you, lady? I caught maybe half of what you said."

"What I said translates to; I don't have to do anything until mid-afternoon."

"I mean, I heard plenty of folks talk the way you do but, I mean, is it Gullah?

"Yes, it is. The old way of speaking comes from West Africa, in particular, Senegambia. I'm mostly Senegambian but also a tiny bit of Northern European."

"I thought maybe that was the case."

"Long story," she said, taking his hand. "I'll let you in on a secret. Africans are rich with oral histories since we lacked an alphabet. In 1565, it has come down through time that my ancestor,

Fahima Faraji, a Muslim, was bought by a French dwarf named Gauche. He fell in love with her but he was unaware until later that Fahima did the magic."

"You're pulling my good leg."

"No, Trey. Look into my eyes, please. I do the magic and it do," she said in Gullah. "Gauche, he come at troubled times."

"Like one of your haints or something?"

"Yes and no. More an image, a presence."

"Did he come to you before all this?"

Penn nodded. "I tell you this because you are in mortal danger. People are going to die."

"I've accepted that since the beginning. War, if you've smelled of it, you feel it when it's near, you embrace it like a brother. That's the smell I mentioned at the git-go."

Penn put a fist to her nose, her chin on her chest. "Let's stop with this. It disheartens me," she said. "You should hear that the slavers, whether they were Portuguesa, or French, or British, they bought Senegambians because we were known to them as intelligent people, tall, ebony skinned, with kindly eyes and shapely noses like mine. Fahima Faraji worked as a domestic in the house of Jean Ribault, a French naval officer and the leader of a Huguenot group who landed above what would become Charleston on the Ashley River in the mid-16th Century. Fahima became his right arm while he dealt with Natives, other African slaves, the Brits, and Spanish as well. War in Senegambia was a perpetual reality. She had plenty of experience plus Fahima knew the language of slavery, some say Creole, most say Gullah. We worked in the houses of wealthy merchants until the middle of the 18th Century when they sent us to work in the Low Country on plantations, namely one called Frogmore on St. Helena Island where my parents and family still live." Penn reached over to kiss Trey. "Is there more coffee?"

"Plenty," Trey said getting up from the swing. "How do you take it?"

"Black, of course."

He was back quickly. Penn had stretched her long legs out on the swing so Trey took an aluminum, webbed lawn chair.

"By the middle of the 1700s," Penn continued, "cotton became more and more important as did rice and indigo. Wealthy white planter families from Charleston, Beaufort, and Savannah bought thousands of acres of land and built plantations worked by African slaves. By this time, we developed our own sort of sub-culture based on the Christian religion but seasoned with African ways and spirit use. We became isolated. It allowed us to maintain the purity of our traditions. When your nation split from England, Tory planters either sold their land cheaply to the Patriots or they abandoned them taking their slaves to Caribbean plantations where my people led brutal lives in the cane fields, far worse than growing Sea Island cotton where the task system was used."

"I don't follow," Trey said hanging on every word.

"Well, each morning at day-clean, the driver would assign a task for each field man or woman. It might be to hoe 10 rows of cotton, or to haul and spread 6 wagon loads of manure. Once the task was completed, the driver happy, the rest of the day belonged to the slave."

"Isolated as they were, what in the world did they do?"

"Well, many had buck patches which were small garden plots on land not under plantation cultivation where they could raise vegetables they would have eaten in Senegambia."

"Where did they get the seeds?"

"Women sewed them into the hems of their skirts before the passage."

"Clever."

"Survival," corrected Penn. "Sweet potatoes, peanuts, millet, benne seeds, okra, and field peas such as black-eyed, pink-eye, and crowder thrived in the sandy soils of the Sea Islands. Hot, dry summer conditions were very similar to our homelands. On their own time, my ancestors were allowed to raise fowl, fish for shrimp and oysters, and snare small game. Any surplus not dried or salt-cured to hold for winter was sold at market or to the big house. That's important to what happened after the Civil War, but I get ahead of myself. Because our diet was so varied and plentiful, because we were encouraged to create family units, and because we converted to Christianity, Colonial Low Country Gullah had a longer life expectancy than their contemporaries inhabiting Latin America. Our owners thrived. More slaves came onto the land. In fact, whites were outnumbered in the rural counties of South Carolina by as much as 3-1. A field worker man could pay for himself in 4-5 years. Here's something else you might not know. Have you ever heard of indentured servants?"

"No," Trey replied.

"Well, they were white folks from England who dreamed of a new life in the Colonies but couldn't afford the passage so they sold themselves to their New World masters. Typically, the indenture lasted 10-15 years then they were freed usually to pursue trade work after manumission. White indentured servants were sold in the Charleston slave markets just like we were."

"No way," Trey scoffed.

"I'm here to tell ya," Penn said smiling at his incredulity.

"Well, with Gullahs outnumbering whites by such a margin, why didn't they rise up?"

"Oh, but we did. There was the Stono Rebellion in 1739 in South Carolina led by a literate slave named Cato. He organized 60 men to rebel. They headed south for freedom and land promised them by the Spanish in Florida. Mounted militia cut them down long before they got there. Those who survived were executed but some were sold to new owners in the West Indies. Another revolt was Igbo Landing in 1803. A group of Igbo slaves mutinied their ship on the way to a plantation on St. Simons Island in Georgia. The Igbo were known for their independent flare and not well suited to slavery. They killed their white captors. The ship grounded on a marsh and the men either died in the marsh or were retaken by bounty hunters. But the most intimidating rebellion was led by Denmark Vesey, a free, literate carpenter who lived in Charleston in 1822. As the story goes, he won a lottery and bought his freedom with the money. He founded the second largest African Methodist Episcopal Church in America but was accused of organizing thousands of Charleston and country Gullah to an armed rebellion. The plot was discovered and Denmark was hanged as were dozens of black folks but not one single white man was injured. My father's name is Denmark in honor of this man."

"What happened to ya'll after the Civil War?"

"Honestly, Trey, we were scared. We prayed for freedom and the chance for an education for centuries but we were like the dog that chased the cart and didn't know what to do when he caught it. The Union came to the Low Country in November, 1861, to take Hilton Head Island and Port Royal Sound, the deepest port on the Eastern Seaboard. Ten thousand slaves were liberated. The planters fled for fear of reprisals or the risk of being thrown in prison. We didn't know what to do so we mostly stayed on the plantation to farm it for ourselves until authority came but it really never did. Gauche, he warned our people. My ancestor, Odah Faraji, was the spirit doctor on Frogmore

Plantation. She possessed great powers. The people demanded Odah and her family live in the

plantation house. It would be over a year before we saw any Union Army officials. We were told we

could stay where we were as long as we sold what we grew to them for fair market prices regulated

by the Freedmen's Bureau in Washington. We were also told we could buy land abandoned by

planters because General Sherman had given Field Order 15 to the Gullah making it legal for us to

own land. All those dollars and cents we got from our buck patches and fishing and hunting was dug

from the ground. The 603 acres my folks own today as heir's property was the result. They were

shrewd people. War in Senegambia coursed through our veins. We understood it would end and when

it did, the planters would come back and buy our labor on land returned to them. Tradition goes that

Odah asked Gauche where Buckra Smith, that was Gullah talk for master, might have kept his gold or

jewelry. Gauche, he came through for the Faraji. After the war, Frogmore House was bought by two

women who were Northern Abolitionist missionaries from Philadelphia. They were of the Quaker

faith. One of them, Laura Towne, founded what became the first black education center in the

country. They named it the Penn Center in honor of William Penn."

"So, that's where you got your name?"

"Yes, sir," she said. "The first classes were in the Frogmore big house until a proper

schoolhouse could be built. Odah Faraji Smith was one of the eager students. Before this time,

plantation owners considered a literate slave was a dead slave. We lived a quiet life for another

century to include lots of wars Gullah men fought for white America, but it was the Civil Rights era

that delivered the most change. Just as Carpetbaggers flooded in from the North after the Civil War

intent to buy distressed property during Reconstruction, with the Civil Rights movement came real

estate developers determined to run us off the land we have been husbanding for 300 years just so rich white folk can enjoy what we have enjoyed over the centuries. In a way, today's not much different than the years right after the Civil War."

"I'm shocked to hear you say that," Trey said.

"Don't be. The way we see it is that the government has become Buckra. We fight to hold our families together, in the meantime, and I do mean, mean time, they offer cash incentives for fathers to stay out the family. I get it, I can hear you thinking. You believe welfare is a good thing. Couple the disintegration of the Gullah family with developers who continue to deprecate Gullah land, and you have the decline of my people. I am the first of the Faraji-Smith's to graduate college. I hold a desire to help those of us trapped in the system so I became a Beaufort County police officer." Penn looked out over the beauty of the land and sighed. "It was sad, Trey. Tragic, really. I can't tell you how dejected I was to see young black men, some just teenagers, shoot one another in a never-ending parade of blood and broken hearts because Buckra let us down again. I quit the force to go to law school and the rest is history."

Trey got up to kiss Penn. "You are such a sensational woman," he said.

"Now you. Who is Trey Dawson?"

"Not much to tell, really," he began retaking his webbed aluminum lawn chair. "My father, Robert, was drafted and never came home from Vietnam. I have no memory of ever meeting him. His pictures all over the house freaked me out. It was as though he was staring at me with eyes full of expectation. Mom was Thelma. She raised my big brother, Ned, and me by herself. Oh, there were a scattering of family around Sea Branch but we weren't close. It was me and Ned, and friends to ride bikes with and play baseball and basketball, school, and the Catholic Church. Mom was devout as well as deeply religious about Ned's and my grades in the belief that academics were the only way we were going to be able to get up and out of town to do something special with our lives. Mom demanded excellence and she got it. She ran a community daycare facility. I don't believe she ever went out on a date. Mom made my father into a household god. He became her personal martyr, her fulcrum to leverage good behavior from perfect boys made in the image of their perfect father. She would whip out blistering statements like, 'Your father would be disappointed in you,' or, the one I hated the most, 'Father wept.' I was never quite sure if he meant Robert or God." Trey paused for a moment to gather himself, sighing and rubbing his nose with an open hand. He started pacing the porch. "One Wednesday night," he went on, "pouring buckets as it can do in the Carolinas, Mom followed her routine. She drove to church in the rain. Wednesday night mass was her one escape from me and Ned. The last thing she said was, "Boys, after I visit our Redeemer, and you guys have your homework done, we can go to McDonalds when I get back. I love you both." She was killed by a semi that ran a red light out in front of St. Stephen's. I was ten, Ned twelve. He and I were divided. I went to Aunt Mimi's house in Sea Branch, and Ned, he was shipped to Phoenix to an aunt on my father's side. I missed my big brother and Mom terrible but tried hard not to show it. An inward rage provided the material to grow a world-class chip on my shoulder. Even the slightest of slights, I came out with fists blazing. I didn't much care if I got my ass kicked, in fact, in a perverse sort of way, it felt good to get clocked. I know how weird that might sound but that's the honesty of it. So ... so, I fought myself through fighting with others until it came time for college. I wasn't big enough to play Division One football, but I did play a pretty good center field. That got me a scholarship to play baseball at Duke. In Raleigh/Durham, I signed up for ROTC for the extra money and graduated with a degree in English. I deferred my military obligation. Duke found me a starter teaching job in a high school in Savannah. Oh God, how I hated it. The kids took up space day after day. They were corpses. The world's best writer's words skipped off their thick skulls like pebbles thrown at a granite boulder. Deeply disappointed in myself for the monumentally shitty life decision, I enlisted. The military thing led to Special Ops. I really don't like to talk about it much, but fighting is the only part of life I completely understand." He shrugged. "That's about it."

"Are you and Ned close?" asked Penn.

"Naw, haven't seen him in years. Don't even know if he's alive."

"What about your wife? You haven't talked much about her."

Trey snorted in disgust. "Well, she filled a physical and social need but there is no 'we' in Gabbie. When Caleb was born, the little guy became the only family I had. Life was good again. Although I missed my brothers in Special Ops, it was alright ... alright to be back from the war ... I guess. They kept saying at the VA, 'You're lucky to outlive the loss of the leg. You could have died.' And you know what, it was like getting my clock cleaned in school, I deserved to die, not my brothers. And now I have Caleb's blood on my soul, too, my only family left." He sighed. His lips compressed and trembled as he stared off into space shaking his head. He looked at Penn, his torture apparent. "Now, I have you for family and that's better than alright, I mean, don't I, don't I have you?" he asked.

Penn came to sit on his lap. She stroked his hair, comforting him. "I'll teach you what family is all about, my brave Colonel," she murmured.

(17)

Cerberus sleept on the porch floor, his muzzle on his big paws, and Penn gone to the bathroom, the advance warning system that he was, Cerberus all of a sudden jumped to his feet baying long, soulful calls. He bolted down the steps and continued to bay until a late model white, uber-expensive

Mercedes SUV decked out in shiny new Georgia plates with a pair of peaches modelled on it that looked for all the world like a pair of testicles zipped into the dooryard.

Out jumped trouble.

"When is enough, enough?" Gabbie asked advancing on the steps. "Truce, Trey. Okay? Come home. Come live with me again. I can't stand it anymore. I belong in your arms. You forced me to hire a private firm to track you down. How humiliating! But you enjoy squatting on me, don't you, dear laddie?" She took in Jonah's Place, her disapproval obvious. "This looks like a negro shanty," Gabbie said.

"It was and by the way, never say that to me again."

"What's that, lover?"

Gabbie stopped at the bottom of the steep stairs staring up at Trey.

"I mean that ignorant damned, 'laddie.'"

"Scout's honor," she played holding up her right hand.

"They would never have allowed you in the Girl Scouts. Maybe Witches United but not the Scouts."

"Trey, darling, why are you so unpleasant with me? Please, please come home. I love you so much." She dabbed at her eyes with a tissue that appeared out of nowhere. "Maybe that new doc we hired, you know, that Pakistani fertility specialist, maybe he can finally do me some good. The new drug he prescribed is supposed to work wonders. I read about it in *People Magazine*."

Thick arms folded over his chest as Trey stood mute at the top of the stairs. The screen door sighed behind him.

"The cleaning lady, right?" Gabbie said flustered and then she recognized the shirt Penn wore, Egyptian cotton of Italian design in a blue and white stripe, size 18 ½. She bought the pricey shirt to wear on an upcoming book tour.

Gabbie looked like she was going to pass out.

"You should have called," he said.

"I don't have your number. You changed it, again, damn you to hell."

"There's nothing to talk about. Go back to Atlanta."

"It taste like chocolate, does it?"

"Actually," Trey replied, "Penn tastes more like caramel."

"You sonofabitch!" Gabbie screamed. She reached down to grab a handful of chat and threw it at them. "You'll hear from my attorney," she seethed. She couldn't get out of the dooryard fast enough.

His phone rang. Trey ignored it in the belief it was Gabbie. "You okay?" he asked Penn. She nodded as she comforted Cerberus who she prevented from running after the Mercedes. "Bit of a wildcat, your wife. We should go after her harder, get this divorce thing done."

"Agreed," he said.

Trey swiped his phone. "Yeah," he said impatiently. "I know who you are, Governor. You'd like to come by my place? Talk with you about what? I'm not in the mood to play guessing games. When? Two minutes, you say?" Trey shook his head in disgust. "Come along." It was obvious the Governor had been waiting outside on the highway and equally obvious he'd probably seen Gabbie burning rubber out the drive onto the hardroad.

"The Gov is stopping by for a chat," he said to Penn.

"How terribly nice of him. Shall we dress for the occasion?"

Trey laughed. Ticker was howling again. "Gullah are not fond of Gaylord Russell," Penn said. "About that we'll talk."

A silver Bentley pulled in next to the truck. An old black man in livery opened the back door. Tugging the seersucker vest over a belly gone cannonball, Gaylord Russell put on a costly Panama hat. There was no way Penn and Trey would know he bought the handmade extravagance during a recent Windjammer cruise to Havana. Like Gabbie, he stopped at the bottom of the stairs taking the couple in. "Well, ain't we having fun, now. Might I sit with you a spell?"

"Not until you tell me the name of the geniuses who manage your retirement portfolio," Trey said deadpan.

"Nice ride, Gov," added Penn, piling on.

Trey waved him up and stepped aside. The Governor had difficulty with the climb and wheezed by the time he stepped on the last riser.

"Whew! Don't we have covenants mandating elevators?" the Governor puffed. "By the way, what in God's name did you say to that wild woman in the Mercedes?"

"That, Governor, is soon to be my ex-wife."

"Ah-h. Now, that makes perfect sense. Clear up another something for me. Dawson, this here is Grant land. What are you doing on it?"

"That would be called renting," Trey replied.

"Real snot, ain't ya? Didn't care for ya'll none after you duped me into that sham interview and what in hell were you up to trying to impersonate an officer of this State to a foreign national?"

"Why, Governor, I'm honored to be Penn's bodyguard."

Gaylord Russell lost his toothy grin as though a switch was thrown. "This ain't no penny thriller where the studly British guy wins the maiden and takes down the bad guy in an hour and thirty-six minutes. By the way, I really enjoyed *Hell Hath No Fury*. Me and the Misses, that would be my Helen, streamed it but I stray just as you have, Mr. Dawson. Let's not play, shall we? Southern neighborliness goes just so far. I am prepared to have my attorneys contact Miss Smith about slapping a suit on your arrogant ass, or, maybe take more direct and less mannerly action, but, Mr. Dawson, I prefer not to do that. Am I understood?" He set to leave.

"Whoa, Governor," said Penn. "If I heard you right, you just threatened my client with bodily harm. Last time I checked the penal code, that's a misdemeanor."

The Governor snickered wickedly. "I'm the law around here," he sneered. "And by the way, why don't you make ten times what you make now and come work for me heading up the legal division to my real estate assets division? Ma'am, the Bible recommends making friends out of enemies."

"Some things do not have value because they are priceless," Penn said. "Gullah haven't been for sale since 1865, sir. Greed hath no season, Governor."

"Indeed. Life liberty and the pursuit of happiness is what I'm all about. I wish you a good day," he said tipping his Panama hat.

They watched the Bentley drive off. "There's that smell again," Trey said.

"Getting stronger, too," concurred Penn.

He took her by the elbows. "Look, I have to fly to NY tomorrow to meet with some people about various publishing problems plus have a long chat with Morty Mandel, my editor and agent. We're at cross purposes with my latest manuscript. I'll be back Saturday afternoon into Charleston. Why don't you drive up and we can meet at some outrageously expensive hotel and try to find someplace we could get a decent meal and a good bottle of wine?"

"Sure," Penn said, "but it will have to be on the clock. Since I met you all I've done is clean up your messes." She flashed perfect white teeth at Trey. "My payment will be to take Cerberus with me and board him down to home Saturday so we can party. I could use the break."

That afternoon they went to a gun store to replace the Glock, buy another one for Penn, and several boxes of ammunition. They also drove to their telecom carrier's store to pick out new cellphones making sure to ask the young woman who worked with them to change their numbers. Penn's infected phone was crushed under his heal and dropped in a recycle bin.

(18)

Running north to Charleston early Sunday morning, few cars were on the road except for older black folk all prettied up headed to see Jesus. Trey rounded a corner near Cuckold's Landing where a derelict outbuilding decayed. Of a sudden, a thumb-sized hole blossomed in the passenger side of the windshield creating stress cracks in the tempered glass. The round exited through the passenger door window and then another bullet did the same thing. Trey jerked the truck to the side of the road, reached underneath the seat for the new Glock and snaked across the console getting out by the passenger door careful to keep the truck between him and the shooter. They were the same diameter as an AR-15 .223 Remington. He'd seen thousands of holes just like it in Iraq and Afghanistan.

A container carrier whizzed by identical to the one he saw leaving the water plant. The invisible driver blared the horn as the big tractor swerved to sever the sideview mirror bracket and in so doing scraped the entire side.

He sprinted into the woods darting tree to tree to work his way back to the abandoned shed. Directly across the road from it, Trey braced behind a large pine tree trunk and spat three rounds from the Glock, two into a window and one through the rotten door that rested at a slant. No return fire came from within. Trey didn't bother to clear it. The guy was gone. It was an intimidation move. All casings would have been picked up. The question hung in the tense air; was it the Chinese or was it a goon from the Governor's stable, or were they tag-teaming?

The sound of high-speed fans descending from an elevated altitude got his attention. The drone flew past just above the high tops of the loblolly pines and came back to hover far enough away that shooting at it with a pistol would be folly. The drone's move suggested they were equipped with infrared scanning technology. It was half again as big as the one outside Gu Shui that chased him out of the woods. Four red lights blinked at the corners of the contraption. Was it armed like the newest generation of military drones? When he heard the whoosh, Trey knew exactly what headed at him. A miniaturized rocket propelled grenade exploded ten feet in front of the tree spraying sand and bits of tortured vegetation all over him. His mad up, Trey emptied the clip at the drone. Unharmed, it buzzed off to the south-southeast toward the Atlantic.

The live fire was an escalation he could not turn his back on. Far from chasing him away, the increase in threat level only heightened his determination. His instinct was to run at gunfire. The drone attack convinced him the AR-15 ambush came from the black heart of Gaylord Russell.

Doing 80 to Charleston, he called Penn. "Hey, I just got bushwhacked then a drone tried to tattoo me with an RPG. Please, Penn, don't go back to your condo tonight except maybe to get some things and Cerberus. Stay with your family. Please don't argue with me. The next shots might not be a warning."

The Smith Family's two-story white clapboard house rested on an up-rise by the Coosaw River for 150 years on land originally owned by a planter out of Charleston named, John Morton so locals started calling the area, Morton's Bluff. Time renamed the settlement Smith's Bluff for the Gullah family that owned it. This had grown over the last hundred and sixty years to a collection of fifteen homes, some 12-wide trailers, some modular that arrived in two pieces and were nailed together. Similar to the wishes of the family in 1862 for Root Doctor Odah to live in the abandoned Buckra's house, Smith freedmen raised the house for their spiritualist. The next structure to be raised was on down the road, the First Free African Church, the one Trey attended as Lucius Aurelius' guest.

Supper dishes in the drainer, Cerberus fed, Momma Emeline and Denmark Smith sat with their youngest daughter on the back porch on inviting, wooden rocking chairs, eight in a row. They sipped sweet tea appreciating the breeze off the water and watched the Coosaw digest the sun. A white egret rose out of the spartina grass flying low out over the water on the way to roost in a willow grove up the Coosaw, the bird intending to join its kin for the night, just as Penn had done. Yet, as peaceful as it was, unanswered questions sizzled like static electricity between them.

"Momma, the shrimp were awesome," said Penn, "better than any this season. Pedro, he caught them in the net up the river?"

"Yes, chile. He not well, my Pedro. Got the arthritis in he knees from that football, em-huh, but he keep a-going."

"And your gravy on the grits," Penn said, "Momma, it was heaven."

"Now we talk," her father said. He gave Penn a stern look and cleared his throat. Denmark Smith was never a man who had difficulty telling you what was on his mind. "None of us Smith folk like you with a white man," he said. "I got this to say, em-huh. Listen to me, now." He stopped rocking and waited a beat for effect. "Blue Jays is Blue Jays and Robins is Robins," her father said.

"That's right," Momma Emeline added She smoothed her skirt and resettled the sweetgrass basket she plaited on her lap. "I see babies in you eyes, but now I got this to say too; you may believe this is the New South and us folk, we can do what it is we want with whoever we want. It ain't true out her in the Low Country. Maybe the city, I give that. They's lots of crackers leftover in these piney woods."

"But, but —" Penn sputtered before her mother interrupted her with a stop sign hand.

"You break tradition," her mother said, sternly. "We got some white blood running in these veins 'cause uppity slave owners force theyselves on our ancestor women but that was tragedy away from our God-given free will."

They went quiet for a bit chewing on what just happened.

Penn broke the tense silence. "First-off, nobody's marrying nobody. We met a few weeks ago. Second, he's a decorated Navy Seal. That speaks for itself."

"But, what about that leg, now?" Denmark said. "He white and he ain't whole. You deserve a whole man."

Penn got up and went to the porch railing. She crossed her arms like she did in court at a critical time in the proceedings. "You raised me by two codes," she said slipping back into English, "Gullah tradition and God's laws. I have tried to honor my family by following both sets. Let me ask you; do you think your views on Trey are prejudiced? You don't even know the man yet you don't want me to see him. I mean, did he do something that would make you disrespect him?" She was having a tough time holding her temper. Cerberus sensed it and came to sit at her feet looking up at her asking if everything was good. Penn patted his head waiting for a response from her parents.

"It ain't that we exactly prejudiced," her father said, measured.

"So, you're not PRE-judging him, on-huh?"

"Sis, now lookie here, we go about day to day guided by the same traditions we have for long time," her mother said.

"Oh, so he's not accomplished enough for your daughter?" Penn huffed. "Well, he has a degree from Duke, is a New York Times best-selling novelist, and a military hero to boot. The man has three Purple Hearts, a Bronze Star for valor, as well as a Presidential Commendation." Penn's hands flew around her she was so worked up. "Plus, he's going after a shady Chinese outfit all by himself because he doesn't want the police or military in for fear they'll cave to political pressures. It's for Caleb."

"Who?" her mother asked.

"A three-year old little boy, his son, who was killed on his swing set in their backyard when a defective piece of Chinese steel broke and killed him. Trey built it so he feels responsible, poor man." Penn wiped at her eyes.

Her parents rocked in their chairs as though nothing of particular import was going about.

Denmark stopped rocking, "Think it'll rain?" he said with a smile, the question one asked in the house since remembrance in a farmer family's never-ending quest for the perfect growing conditions for his crops, much as the Smith's were doing because they loved Penn and wanted nothing more than a satisfying, good, and Godly life.

The three burst out in laughter.

The air cleared, Denmark said, "We don't cotton to what he's doing with that Chinese outfit either. What little you tell at supper make us afraid for you. That what we have police for. Let them take the risk. They paid for it."

"This is personal with Trey. First, it's his innocent son then it's too many of his buddies killed by weapons designed and assembled in China for sale to any two-bit tyrant with a pocket full of oil money."

"It's like Nam that way," Penn's father, a Vietnam vet, said.

"They steal our military secrets with impunity," Penn continued. "Trey says all of their most modern fighter jets look exactly like ours. He feels certain the Chinese will continue to steal our country blind to the tune of $100s of billion a year in trade deficits. Things you and I wouldn't even notice, Trey notices like the guards at the gate of the plant. Their helmets were exactly like Chinese foot-soldiers wear as was the jumpsuit. The commando knife, the AK-47s were also military issue. And just what in the world are they so secretive about? The numbskulls are supposed to be drilling for water."

(17)

Trey missed the flight to La Guardia and had to take one that went wheels-up four hours later. That meant no dinner on Morty. It was a very long two days in the city. The noise, and bustle, and too many brassy people snaked under his skin. The Low Country called out to Trey. He was anxious to get back to Penn.

The trip did afford sufficient downtime to scope his finances and catch up on e-mails, reader's Tweets, and texts. He discovered Gabbie cleaned out not only their joint bank accounts but also their brokerage accounts which, according to Morty, she had every right to do but that a leveling of assets in court would occur later on. For now, Trey was screwed. The only means he had to live on was what was left of the $30,000 he'd hidden in another bank behind Gabbie's back and the $10,000 check Morty cut him the night he left Atlanta. Now he understood where the money came from to buy the fancy German SUV.

He was religious about keeping Penn in the loop. On one call, he said, "It's fine if your family is hesitant about us. That will repair in time. Do you think they would object if you and Cerberus moved back in with them until we know the end of this story? That, or you can move in with me."

"Whew. You a race car driver too? I really don't have an answer for any of it."

"Listen, this is really important. You told me Gauche's riddle about staying close to the tray. Right? Best do what he says."

The New York meetings went well enough, however Trey had difficulty concentrating to the point Morty asked him if he was okay. The fact of the matter was he couldn't wait to see Penn. He accepted a compulsive need to protect her from whatever nest of ground hornets he had kicked open. He was as responsible for her life as he was Caleb's. Looking out the window of the hotel, watching yellow cabs paint Fifth Avenue with white and red streaks of light and the cacophony of incensed cabbies honking their displeasure, the lonely angst he carried since Thelma died forced Trey to accept that he simply couldn't live with himself if anything happened to Penn because of his animus toward the Chinese, a hatred that transcended rationality. This was his duty, this was his call to war.

He landed seven-ish early evening in Charleston. First thing on the ground, Trey searched for local gun shops online to see which ones were still open. He found one on the Old Savannah Highway where he bought two pairs of night-vision binoculars and a couple of Kevlar vests.

He called Penn. "Hey, lady. I'm in the truck on the way south. I picked up some presents for us for tomorrow night."

"Two bottles of Moet and Chandon?" she teased.

"Yeah, something like that."

"I'll catch up with you in the A.M," she said. "We have a birthday party at the house. Gruncle Smith is 94."

"What's with the Gruncle?"

"You know, grumpy uncle? I pray you live long enough to become one.

Jonah's Place was too quiet what with both Penn and Ticker gone to Smith's Bluff. He turned in early and rose with the sun to work on his growing arsenal until Lucius showed to work on the yard but really, Lucius came to take Trey's temperature. It took him less than thirty minutes to mow and trim. Over a glass of lemons made, Trey was curious.

"What do you hear about Penn's parents? They all had a pow-wow when I was gone. She hinted they weren't too pleased."

"Evy-body talk 'bout you two. You welcome with us. But they is one ting."

"And it is?"

"You got to come to church, worship the Lord God. Gullah say, 'No Jesus in de heart, no heart a'tall."

"I see," Trey said but he realized that was a stretch, well, no, it was a lie. He changed the subject because he could think of no words for Lucius about Jesus. "Ah-h, could I borrow Matilda tonight?" Lucius looked at him with raised eyebrows. "I get it that's from left field," Trey said, "but, I mean … although … I have to tell you, your attachment to her frankly intimidates me. If anything happens to the old girl, I'll buy you a new one."

"Ain't no soul like an old soul," Lucius said.

Trey dangled his keyring in front of Lucius. "Trade?"

He walked with Penn to the Roasterie Coffee Shoppe around the corner from her office under strict orders from Joselyn to bring her back a latte. On a personalized new leash, Cerberus trotted by their side looking forward to a cool drink of water from the stainless steel dog bowl by the front door.

"I've been thinking," he said, seemingly forever on point. "Somehow, we have to put eyes on the plant. That's our nearest objective. They know our vehicles, right? But they won't recognize Matilda."

"Who?"

"You know, the vintage truck your Uncle Lucius drives."

"Okay," she said, very tentative, "but, what about those drones?"

"Simple. I go bird hunting tonight. I bought a 12-gauge shotgun. We knock a couple of them out of the sky, maybe they'll back off and tell us what they're up to."

Penn shook her head. "Do you really think for a minute they'd blow their cover and admit to wrong-doing?"

"You don't have to go."

Penn stopped to face Trey. "I go where you go," she said, "period, the end. I get it. All the same, that Li Ling makes my liver quiver. There's an evilness about that man. He gives me the creeps and, for the record, if we go where I think you're headed out into the piney woods tonight, I hate no-shoulders. They give me the creeps, too."

"Snakes?" Trey guessed with a smile.

"Yup."

"We need Wellingtons." Penn looked at him funny. "You know, tall rubber boots."

"I knew that," she said then added, "Gotta put a nickel in it. I have to earn a living. The deadbeat man of letters who's stacking untold billable hours hasn't paid a dime yet."

"Oh, but the residuals can be very interesting," Trey said. "Come to supper?"

"Momma Emiline's cooking or yours, on-huh? Let's see."

He took her hand turning it over in his. "This could get hairy," he said.

"Yes, sir, Colonel sir," Penn smarted off, saluting.

Matilda had a 3-speed stick shift on the floor capped off by an eight-ball knob so old the number was nearly rubbed off. She was a 1990 Toyota pick-up assembled so long ago it was made on Japanese soil in Toyota City outside of Nagoya. It must have been a bright blue right off the factory floor the hue of the Pacific Ocean a few miles away but it faded in the unrelenting Low Country sun to a steel gray, a shade that resembled a Johnny Reb officer's uniform.

Penn decided to bring Cerberus, but even with his face in the wind the whole trip from Smith's Bluff he whined and came to Penn demanding attention which was very much unlike him. Cerberus was worried. His humans were acting a lot weird, especially at Jonah's Place when Penn wrapped her head with a colorful scarf and withdrew from a pink tote several plastic bags and a small Smith Farms burlap sack tied off with catgut.

"What are you doing?" Trey said not knowing whether to be fearful or make fun of her.

"I'm headed to the creek. Please keep Cerberus inside. Be back so you don't notice."

Penn left by the back door. Trey and Cerberus watched as she made her way to the creek bank. She sat on the ground with the bags of herbs and roots taking a pinch of this and a tad of that until a small mound rose from a colonolware plate of rustic finish, unglazed, and dusty red. It had come down from slave days when they were allowed to make their own fired clay objects. Penn lit the dry materials, blew on them to kindle the herbs, got it to smoke then sang low and melancholy as she cleansed with the smoke. Done, she dug a shallow hole into which she poured remnant ashes and covered them over with dirt.

Penn came back into the house. "When the time is right," said Trey, "I'd like to learn about what you just did."

"Only in the broadest terms," Penn reacted. "I would risk the loss of my powers if I disclosed our secrets. Nothing personal. My father doesn't know what Momma Emiline and I do, either."

"I guess a dressed-up hog is still a hog," Trey said, feeling perhaps too keenly the thoroughness with which Gullah fence their territory. "I think it best you to drop me off a mile or so away from Gu Shui and pick me up at a time specific."

"No, and double no," she said incensed. "I've had live fire on me before and I've suited up on several drug busts like we're about to do, so don't you be playing the biggity ... honey," Penn said.

"Okay, okay, soldier," he said holding his hands up in mock surrender. He went to the sink, got the book of matches he put there earlier, struck one, and toasted black the bottom of a wine cork. A shallow bowl of salad oil was brought to the table.

"Come, sit here," he said.

"Something a little ironic about a white man applying blackface to an African," joked Penn.

"You haven't been out in the sun enough, sister," Trey replied, laughing and smudged her cheek.

"By the way, women are better in a tactical mission than men ever hoped to be. I have eyes sharper than an eagle's and a nose better than the bluetick's to pick scents out of the air you couldn't even begin to smell, after all you're just a man. Besides, my Dahomey neighbors in West Africa had their own version of Amazons. They were called the Ahosi. They fought alongside the men of the tribe. Many of them were involved in the slave trade taking captives in raids on other villages then selling prisoners to slavers."

"Uh-huh," Trey grunted, not much interested in her lesson on international feminism, concentrating on the work at hand. "Have you been trained in night vison?" he asked.

"Yes, sir."

"And how about Kevlar vests?".

"Yes, Colonel, sir," Penn said with a flicker of impatience.

As they suited up, Trey went over the plan. "The booms in the night start right about now," he told her. "We go in to reconnoiter. I don't expect manned resistance; besides, we'll be on Federal land in the ACE Basin. However, the drones are another matter. By the way, I made a fake abandoned vehicle sticker for Matilda of the type you see on the interstate just in case someone gets curious about her parked like a derelict. "You have your Glock?"

"Yes, dear," Penn said.

"You told me you made marksman at the Police Academy."

"Yup and I prefer the AR-15, if you don't mind. This a 20 clip?" she asked. Trey nodded.

"Ammo is in your Kevlar pockets," Trey added with a grin. "Done. Let's roll."

Cerberus wanted to come but Trey locked him inside. He was vocal with his disapproval.

On the short drive, Penn softly sang the Gullah spiritual, *God is my Rock in the Weary Road Ahead.* Trey felt peaceful Penn by her side. Caleb was with him, too. He glanced at the Breitling Chronometer, a gift from Aunt Mimi he wore since OCS graduation.

It was 2310.

Perfect!

Matilda parked and stickered, Trey put gloved hands on Penn's shoulders. "Stay behind me at all times," he said, "and no talking. Use hand gestures. Weapon safeties off, goggles on."

She slipped on the headgear. It dangled around her neck. Trey could see she was having a hard time finding the activation switch.

He came close to initiate the appliance and when he was done, Trey said into her ear, "I love you with all my heart," kissed the top of her head then proceeded down the road equipped with a big grin on his face. A familiar adrenalin rush flowed inside him as it had so many times in the desert of Iraq and the mountains of Afghanistan.

They stuck to the side of the road. A vehicle was coming. Its lights flickered off the pine trees. They scampered to the edge of the woods hiding behind tall Joe Pye weeds. The pick-up passed without incident. In the misty fog, Trey saw no red lights to indicate the truck stopped or slowed to check out Matilda.

They walked side-by-side for another couple of minutes until the bright yard lights of the ChiCom plant reflected off wisps of fog, the Spanish Moss eerie like the beard of a witch. He touched her arm jabbing the night air in the direction of the woods.

Water was a foot-deep. All around them insects filled the air with invitations to make more bugs. The rank mud caused their boots to create a sucking sound any audio system could pick up. Nervous, of a sudden, Trey halted them so he could listen. Looking the other way to concentrate on a flash of movement on the left side of her peripheral vision she feared might be a snake, Penn ran into his back and fell on her side in the slop. She came up mad but silent.

He waved them on until Penn tapped his shoulder. She pulled him behind a loblolly jabbing an index finger at the night sky then at the direction from which the perceived noise was coming. Trey could hear it now. The whirring buzz grew nearer and nearer. Penn reached for Trey's hand. The night vision goggles allowed them to see a ghostly drone fly past headed in the direction of the plant.

They stayed on the move until they left the swampy section and reached higher ground. Trey directed her to a deadfall where they sat back-to-back. The quiet of the deep moonless night was broken by geological thunder coming from the earth. The rumble sounded just like an earthquake he experienced as a kid. Trey gave Penn a thumbs-up and signaled they should move on.

They got to within a hundred feet of the fence to lie on their bellies, a strategy discussed in the kitchen. The reason they stopped was straightforward. Penn explained to Trey that the plant was built right on the edge of a Federally owned wilderness area called the Ashipoo, Combahee, and Edisto Rivers Basin or ACE Basin, 350,000 acres of Federally protected wetlands, marshes, and softwood forests. If discovered by the Chi-Coms and captured, they would not be trespassing on private land, a fine, lawyerly distinction but, then again, the ChiComs could choose to just shoot them and feed their bodies to the alligators.

Twenty minutes later another drone flew over to land on the rooftop of the mysterious 'storage' room. An out-going flight rose from that same rooftop. This one vanished into the night headed south moving far slower than the incoming units. To Trey, that meant it carried cargo. Was it vectoring to a land location, or, because the Atlantic was only a couple of miles southeast, could the drone land on a seagoing asset that served as both unloading/loading zone and/or a remote flight center? If he could only bring one down, the GPS system could be decoded. That would give Trey answers to his questions.

He tapped Penn and motioned they were to leave. They hadn't gone but three hundred yards when Penn heard another incoming drone, this one from the east not the north as the others. Alarmed, he signaled to Penn to take cover.

The drone kept on coming.

Trey shouldered the shotgun. Penn slugged him on his arm shaking her head furiously. 'No,' she mouthed. He took a couple of steps away from her and shouldered the shotgun again. BAM, the 12-gauge exploded. Fire leapt out of the barrel, then BAM, BAM, BAM. The drone fell out of the sky but on the way down it got hung up in the canopy except for a quarter of the frame that crashed on the forest floor.

"Damn it all to hell," Trey cursed running to the fallen frame section. "If I didn't have bad luck, I'd have no luck at all. We gotta get the hell out of here," he said, picking up the wreckage. "All hell's about to break loose."

(19)

Chinese operatives in the Gu Shui control room were either on the phone or stared into their computer screens typing furiously as multiple wall-mounted claxons blared. The room became the very definition of bedlam. Systems alerted them to a problem with drone DX-4-KL as it headed back to the droneport from making a drop.

Li Ling was awakened and briefed before he addressed his people.

Mere minutes later, feedback violated the PA. "Attention; a National emergency exists," the Colonel said. "We are in lockdown mode. This is not a test, I repeat, we are in lockdown mode level 8. An outgoing drone is down. The recovery team will assemble immediately and report to Gate 2 where you will be issued further instruction by Lt. Colonel Shen. We have not determined the exact coordinates of the crash. Satellite information has been requested. Let me be clear, I demand that every piece, every scrap of that machine be recovered or dire penalties will disgrace your family and your Republic. All regained material are to be added together to make certain the exact weight of the drone matches the deadweight of its type. That is all."

Li Ling handed the mic to a subordinate. "Ring up the droneport," he ordered. Seconds later, a subordinate spoke into the receiver. "Standby for the Commandant," the young sergeant said and handed Li Ling the satellite phone. "Scramble Dragon Fighters three through six," he barked. "They are fully armed and fueled, are they not?"

"Yes sir," came the fast response, "only ... not exactly, sir, four and five have laser issues."

"What do you mean? Be specific, soldier," the colonel barked.

"Neither drone is airworthy. We worked on them all day, sir."

"Fix the bloody things!" Li Ling demanded.

Palmettoes scraped their faces as they ran through the muck hoping against hope they could reach Matilda in time to save themselves. Granted, the old truck wasn't a NASCAR prototype, but, if they had to run, certainly they stood a better chance of success in Matilda than on foot. Trey learned on duty that most drones topped out at 50 mph. He hoped Matilda could do lots better than that.

"We need to shed these vests," he said between panting breaths. "I put a tarp in the back and some concrete blocks there before we left."

Ears on stalks for drone activity, Penn and Trey made the road and ran around the bend. The truck was in sight.

Long guns were dumped on the beat-up bed, as were their vests, and night-vision gear. Trey pulled the canvas tarp over it and quickly weighted the corners with the blocks.

He dug in his pocket for the keys. "Here," he said. "You drive and, Penn, pull up the hoodie to your sweatshirt, pull it over your forehead so your eyes can barely see."

Matilda started right up. Penn executed a perfect spin-out, a trick she learned as a 10-year-old on the family's tractor. Trey slid off the bench seat and balled up on the passenger side floor making himself as small as he could.

"What are you doing?" asked Penn, alarmed.

"Hiding my face, of course," he replied. "Your disguise and hoodie will throw them off. And, Penn, none of your lead foot, okay. If we race off at high speed, they'll suspect we're up to no good so keep it under the speed limit, okay? Now, we go silent again."

The old pick-up clattered north.

Startling Trey, Penn shrieked. Two feet away, a fighter drone with an incredibly bright spotlight, its superstructure bristling with gun barrels and what looked like hand grenade-size bomblets, hovered right outside the windshield. Instinctively, she shielded her face with a hand. Penn braked hard and stopped in the middle of the road blinded by the strobe. It was as though the thing was alive looking like a huge, hostile bug. She could clearly see its oculus scan from side to side, up and down. Trey reached to pat her leg.

"Steady," he whispered.

The machine whirred straight up to inspect the bed flooding it with light. As fast as it arrived, the drone made an equally sudden exit lifting up into the sky.

Both of them realized that if they had driven the F-150, they'd be human hamburger.

"I don't know who's shaking more, Matilda or me," quipped Penn back underway.

Trey stayed where he was until they got to Jonah's Place.

Getting out of the truck, she noticed something was not right with the house. "The front door is open," she said. "You locked it, right?"

"Yeah, I did," Trey replied, "and I don't hear Cerberus."

Trey quickly took the shotgun from the truck bed and dug in his Kevlar vest pockets for more shells to replenish the magazine. They climbed the steps warily. Still no Cerberus. The blue door's knob and lock was blown in. Blood spatter flecked the doormat and the wood flooring. Remembering attack protocol, Trey pushed the door wide open with the shotgun barrel and stood to the side as did Penn. He nodded and they burst into the living room and kitchen.

"Clear," Penn said.

"The bathroom," Trey said. She checked behind the shower curtain, and the back of the door as well as the linen closet.

"Clear," Penn sang out.

Weapons still at the ready, Trey waved her with him to the back porch.

Cerberus spun slowly. They hanged him from a rafter shot two times, once in the back, once to his beautiful jowly face. Blood dripped from his wounds onto the floorboards, his broken body yet warm to the touch.

Cerberus was buried on the bank of Silver Creek in a tattered bed sheet near where Penn made burnt offerings. A piece of yella-wood found in the outbuilding shed became a makeshift marker until something better could be found. Penn collected a Mason jar of dirt from Ticker's grave. She told Trey it was 'gooler dust,' and not to ask questions.

"I made a terrible mistake," she said. "I prayed to God for our safety but I forgot our pal."

Whoever broke in tossed Jonah's Place. The house was wrecked, pots and pans thrown here and there, cushions off the sofa, the mattress in the bedroom on end and every drawer inverted then sent airborne to all points on the compass. He opened the refrigerator in the need of a cold beer. The bastards stole the 12-pack he'd just bought.

His laptop was missing.

The discipline of saving work daily on an independent thumb drive paid off. Trey found it on the floor intact. *Fledgling Warrior* was safe.

But were they?

That night Trey and Penn slept in her condo, Glocks on the nightstand, safeties off and armed.

(20)

The Governor's Beaufort office was closed. It was early morning. None of his staff arrived for another hour. He nursed a third cup of coffee expressly contravening his cardiologist's admonition to drink only one a day and to lay off the half-and-half. He was on the speaker phone.

"Whoa, now, slow down," the Governor said. "When ya'll get all riled up, half your words are Chinese and I cain't understand."

"I was saying," Li Ling replied, the words both careful and acerbic, "One of our drones was shot down in the ACE last night."

The Governor hunched to the edge of his desk chair. "Do what, now?" he said.

"Are you deaf? I said, we had a drone shot down last night. Well, 80% of one. The other part must have been collected by the shooter. Satellite contact was lost at 0016. I dispatched teams to collect what was left. We found steel shot imbedded in the skin."

"Shotgun," the Governor said, sure of his deduction. "It may have been rascal hunters having fun," he offered lamely with a chuckle.

"Rascal?"

"Yeah, raccoon, a popular sport for the good ole boys who made up my electorate. Listen, I told you a year ago the drone thing wouldn't work. Too easy to bring down, you ask me, too fragile, and unuseable in bad weather."

"There you go again questioning Chinese strategy. Our civilization is 5,000 years old. How old is the United States?" The Governor was silent. "Do I make my point?" challenged Li Ling. The Governor shook his head glad they were not FaceTiming. He chose to ignore the gratuitous condescension. If his affront registered, Li Ling paid no attention. "Have you ever heard of a man by the name of, Lucius Smith?" he asked.

"Yes, I have."

"We spotted a truck, a rust bucket actually, driving away from near our compound. Facial photos were inconclusive. My people accessed a link to the State's database for the tag where the name was given to us by one of your associates."

"That guy, Lucius, is part of Penn Smith's family," the Governor said. "He didn't shoot your machine down."

"How do you know that?" asked Li Ling. "Our data shows he's a Vietnam War veteran, spent years as a guest in our Hanoi Hilton, and killed many Chinese. There is your, how do you say, burnt belly motive."

"Li, Li, Li; I got ears and eyes in the back of my head. I sent two of my men on a mission of their own last night. They paddled sea kayaks up Silver Creek to hide in the marsh watching what went on at Dawson's house. Guess what? Who should drive up with the dog but Penn Smith and guess what she drove?"

"The Toyota," answered Li Ling.

"Bright man. They left armed to the teeth about 2300. One of the weapons Dawson carried was a 12-guage."

"They destroyed Chinese people's property!" Li Ling said, clearly hacked off.

"Hold on, don't get your bowels in an uproar, Colonel. While they were gone, we tossed the place, but found nothing. My men had to kill their mutt to get in. One of them was bitten pretty bad."

The Governor weighed the efficacy of mentioning Trey's laptop but decided he'd keep that as an ace in the hole.

"Well, that is a beginning, my friend," Li Ling said, simmered down. "Tell me something. Do you think Dawson can be bought?"

"Li, old buddy, my Momma used to say that wise men change their minds but fools never do. Trey Dawson is a bonafide fool. What do you say I should find a bottle of 25-year-old Tennessee sippin' whiskey and see if we can make it disappear?"

"Just as that foolish someone must disappear."

"Be cautious, my friend. Our opportunity will come and soon. Until then, the next time I see Dawson how about I offer him $10 million of your money to cease and desist?"

They were grumpy with one another the next morning after they buried Cerberus, too much stress, too little sleep.

"This might be a touchy subject," Trey said, brushing his teeth fully cognizant of the egg shells strewn on the floor between them, "but, why don't you call the Beaufort cops to give you extra protection, make up a story like you have a crazy client who scares you?"

"You do scare me."

"I surrender," he said, "but, I won't hear of you driving to work without me glued to your bumper. Period, the end."

"This is not the military and I'm not amused," Penn came back as she slipped into a pair of jeans. "You can't boss me."

"Okay, how about we flip a coin," offered Trey. "I'll take heads. Best two out of three."

"Alright," she said.

The flip spun into the air to land on the cup of his hand. Heads it was. The second was also heads. What he kept from Penn was that the American silver quarter had an eagle on both sides, a souvenir of a poker game in Helmond Province during a terrible sandstorm three weeks before his left leg was pulverized.

Penn made it just fine to her office. She waved as he pulled away.

Intending to head back to Jonah's place to put it back together, he changed his mind and turned toward Savannah to call on a brother-in-arms. Cal Hubbard stayed active duty rather than retire as Trey did, but then, Hub was younger and whole. He switched branches and now worked as the Executive Officer of the Coast Guard air Station on the Savannah River charged with the important job of safekeeping the port. Trey figured it would be smart to just show rather than make an appointment in the belief it's always more difficult to blow someone off in person.

From the website, Trey discovered the Air Station operated various models of helicopters that patrolled the coast, the interior, rivers, and estuaries from North Florida to Charleston. The small airfield in north Savannah looked like the rest of its brethren with steel fencing and an armed guard gate not unlike Gu Shui only the guard was far friendlier.

"Afternoon, sir," the Seaman said. "Sir, what is your business?"

"I'd like to see Mother Hubbard," Trey replied.

"I'm sorry, sir?"

"His Marine handle, Seaman."

"Oh, yes sir," the kid said, smiling.

"I was his CO when we were up ISIS and the Taliban's tailpipes."

"Very well, sir. I'll give his office a call."

Trey watched as the Seaman's head bobbed up and down on the phone, all smiles, and came out of the guard post. "His assistant, sir, said Major Hubbard would be delighted to see Shoeless Joe. You may pass."

Hub met him in the foyer. They embraced with the obligatory hard back slaps.

"Man, this desk job made you into a chunky monkey," Trey said.

Hub patted his Buddha belly. "Yeah, sitting at a desk will do it every time plus a wife who loves to cook."

"Twins?" teased Trey.

"Tough, guy. Some things don't never change," Hub said with a bit of an attitude. "This way. I have maybe fifteen to give you before I have to break for a meeting off-base."

Trey followed him into a dinky office flooded with sunshine whose walls were a sea of family pics and war images.

"You visiting?" Hub asked.

"Naw. Live back in the old hometown. Kind of weird."

"Heard about your son, man. Some shit. Sorry."

Trey looked at his boots. "Yeah. Listen, I'm thinking about starting a commercial drone business in the Low Country for real estate, agriculture, personal surveillance, well, actually a whole lot of applications. One question I've been asked and couldn't answer is bedeviling me. I bet you have the solution."

"I'm game."

"You have military radar and satellite capabilities here at the station."

"Sure."

"Can you guys track drones?"

"Nope. Just between you and me and the fence post, that's a serious issue we are only now beginning to tackle. We used the big ones with turbo engines in theatre, right?" Trey nodded. "They saved our skins a couple of times."

"But, I'm not after that info," Trey said. "Let's say I have a need for lift of maybe twenty-five pounds. It's eight feet across. That bird still won't show?"

"Might," Hub told him, his head cocked to one side as though he was suddenly suspicious of Trey's purpose. "I'll play the devil's advocate. Here's a serious issue for you. What would prevent this make-believe commercial bird from coating the superstructure with stealth materials rendering it invisible?"

"Frightening thought," Trey said. "Does the Port do a lot of business with China?"

"Of course. They are our number one customer. There's hardly a day we don't have one or more Chinese container ships unloading." Hub leaned his elbows on the desk. "Mighty snoopy questions for a civilian. What's up?"

Trey shifted in his seat and crossed his good leg. "Been doing research on the internet," he said, "The ChiComs make the most advanced small drones in the world. I, shall we say, have an aversion to the yellow bastards, no, I'll be less PC; I hate their stinking guts."

"Okay, then," Hub said laughing. "Refreshing to hear."

"Um-m, if I gave you a sample of a substance for identification, how long would it take to obtain a chemical analysis?"

"An emergency, I take it?" Hub said, interested.

"Of course."

"At worst 48 hours. We have a dedicated lab in Oak Ridge, Tennessee up by Knoxville."

"I saw you glance at the clock, so I'll be quick. Do we have helo assets near, like Apaches or Cobras?"

Hub frowned on that one. "The answer is, of course, in spades. The South Carolina Air National Guard hangers are a stone's throw from here. Then we have Ft. Stewart in Georgia maybe ten minutes out, then the Marine Air station in Beaufort that happens to have the most advanced fighter wing in the world let alone the Marine base at Parris Island. That enough firepower, Colonel? We are locked and loaded in the Low Country. Gotta go. You and Gabbie come to supper some night," he said standing. "Linda and I would love to see you. And, if you're looking for investors in that potential business start-up, let me know." He handed a card to Trey. "I really need to make some dough, got kids going into college, plus, we have a special needs child, Katherine, who has cerebral palsy. Linda and me, we have a hard time keeping up with her bills."

"I didn't know that, Hub."

"Yeah, she's one of those 'Oh Shit' kids that come along later in life."

"Now it's time for me to say, sorry." Trey reached for his buddy's hand. "Thanks for the invite," he said. "I'll call but the lady's name is Penn, Penn Smith. And, Hub, don't forget to look into radar echoes of low-flying drones between 0100 and sun-up. Call me if you find anything."

While he jawed with Trey, Hub came up with an idea nothing short of brilliant. As soon as Trey left, Hub fired up his personal cellphone.

(21)

The sun was low on the horizon as Trey and Penn drifted the Beaufort River in one of Penn's client's skiffs. Maneuvering with a trolling motor mounted on the prow, they threw soft baits into the edges of spartina grass attached to a rattle bobber fishing for a sea trout dinner.

"So, in Special Ops, you learn to factor risk for the potential gain," Trey was saying. "The greater the goal, the higher the risk. The ChiComs are airmailing a product. This we can agree on."

"Yes, but what? We're still at the same sticky question," Penn said casting the spinning rod expertly.

"We have to figure how to get in the backdoor."

"What about Gaylord Russell?" Penn said. "He must have files."

"Have you seen his Beaufort office?" asked Trey.

"It's the old South Carolina State Bank building on Carteret Street."

"That's not a bank. It's a fortress."

"All the same, I understand they give tours. What say we head there tomorrow? Snoop around."

Just then his dayglow red and chartreuse needle bobber darted below the surface. "Fish on," he said setting the circle hook.

The two-story gray granite bank building had all the charm of a mausoleum. Because it was added to the National Register a dozen years ago as well as the stroking of the Governor's world class ego, daily tours were open to the public. Trey dressed carefully, keeping a baseball hat on inside while they toured. Penn let her hair down and hid behind heart-shaped sunglasses. They came and went separately concentrating on the bank's layout to look specifically for utility closets and public restrooms.

"This was only one of three banks in South Carolina not to close," the elderly docent said, "during the first financial panic to hit the relatively new nation of America in 1837. Andrew Jackson was President. He was at war with a man named Nicholas Biddle, the President of a bank that effectively was the Federal Reserve system of the day. This was the Second Bank of America in Philadelphia. Biddle learned that Jackson held a grudge until the other man was ruined in a scorched earth policy presaging William Tecumseh Sherman."

"Yes, indeed, all ya'll," an unctuous man's voice said from off to the side, coming closer. It was Gaylord Russell. "The story is writ that Old Hickory --,"

Penn caught Trey's eye and wagged her head in the direction of a hallway leading off to the left. They took care to keep a distance from one another if footage was ever run from the array of security cameras. They came to bathrooms and vanished inside. The windy Governor could be heard through the thick walls. It took a good five minutes for him to stop. The guests gave him a polite round of applause.

They finished the tour to learn that the bank escaped arson in 1864 because Sherman had a cousin with an equity interest as did the black hero, Robert Smalls, a Congressman during Reconstruction. The place closed in the Great Depression year of 1932 only to be resuscitated by conservative Gullah coffee can capital. The sturdy structure's granite exterior was quarried in Barre, Vermont, and shipped from Boston, the lacy iron grille-work from New Orleans, and the marble floors from Tennessee.

Done with the tour, they went separate ways. Prearranged, Trey and Penn met at a tourist trap on Bay Street. They walked the street with its abundance of 18th Century buildings and soft vistas of the old harbor, stopped at an ice cream place, and took the cones to a picnic table by the water.

"Here's what we're going to do," Trey said brimming with confidence. "In a couple of days, we tour the bank again. Half the way through the tour near that hallway we found there's a utility closet. I checked it out on the way back. It's unlocked. You create a diversion, a fainting spell, or a swoon from a change in medication, or how about a Grand Mal seizure if you really want to do it up right? I'll hide in the closet, come out when it's dark and photograph any and everything of interest I find in the files."

Penn dabbed a napkin at a drip of salted mocha ice cream in the corner of Trey's mouth. "Don't you dare go back in the closet, you hear?" she said.

Trey snorted. "As a witness to the artistic way you lick that cone, not a chance."

They laughed together. "I like the plan," she said, "I really do but how does the good guy get away?"

"I checked out the window in the men's room. No wires. I already unlocked it."

"Aren't you clever," Penn said.

Trey bought a throw-away cellphone loaded with eight gigabits of memory and a decent built-in camera. He used it to call the Governor's office manager.

"Ms. Dornan," he said. "This is Jack Meehoff from Low Country Cleaning Services. How you today, ma'am? Mighty fine, mighty fine. Listen, I won't ask for much of ya'll's time for I know you're busy what with the Governor and all, but, Ms. Dornan, are you happy with your commercial cleaners? Un-huh, I see. Well, might I ask you this? How often do they clean and on what nights? You say, Monday, Wednesday, and Friday? Might I also ask how much they charge? Oh, me, that's dirt cheap. I'm afraid we cain't compete. Thank you for your time, ma'am."

The call could never be traced.

The next day was Thursday. They arrived at different times. With cash, they bought tickets for the final daily tour that started at a prompt 1600 hours, an hour and ten minutes before the sun set. Penn stayed all the way in the back of the group of nine tourists while Trey remained up front. Human nature being what it is, they thought it wise for Trey to be in the lead of the group and Penn the very last. Her fake seizure would cause people to concentrate on her rather than Trey so he could slip away unnoticed.

He wore baggy Lee jeans, Wal-Mart suede leather boots, and a checked shirt that featured fake mother-of-pearl snap buttons plus a baseball cap that read; Amateur Gynecologist; his touch, not Penn's. She wore her grandmother Collette's oversized tropical-flora print dress matched to a scarf of the same pattern wrapped around her head Mother Africa style. Collette had been a large woman so Penn stuffed the inside with pillows plus padded her bra with tissues.

The plan executed flawlessly.

Trey sat in darkness for three hours entertaining himself with online trivia games and Sudoku. Time inched. His ears played with him. Once, he thought he heard someone in the building, a sound possibly coming from the Governor's office which was a huge former bank vault in the middle of the old building. But that was impossible until he did hear someone talking.

Trey's heart raced. He slipped on thin kid gloves and got up to open the door very carefully, one small degree by one small degree. Just wide enough, he pulled his Glock out, and vectored the sound source. Down the short hall, light issued from the bank vault where an Asian man worked at a computer screen. Trey plastered his back to the wall concentrating hard to prevent the rubber soles of the new boots to screech out his presence. He came to the office's threshold. The man still didn't know he was there. Trey cleared his throat. The look on the Asian's face was worth the price of admission.

"We no need clean tonight," the man said jumping to his feet in panic.

"Well, then ya'll kin call the cops if you like," responded Trey in a deep Southern drawl. "I ain't goin' nowhere. Got a job to do same as you, looks like." Trey advanced on the man, the Glock hidden at his side.

"What you do?" the man said alarmed, backpedaling.

"You I do, if you don't tell me who you work for."

"The Governor. I work for him."

"Bullshit, Little Eva," Trey said. He took the telephone receiver off the hook and tossed it on the desktop. "Heah, call him."

"It too late. He sleep. Lose job."

"You lying piece of shit." Trey showed the pistol and kept coming. The man ended his retreat against the Governor's credenza. Freaked, he looked left then right for an escape route. To Trey's surprise, the man assumed the martial arts position, bowed his head then advanced on Trey. He reasoned that a body in the Governor's private digs was out of the question. Trey raised the Glock to eye level, both hands on the checkered grip, and fired over the guy's head, the explosion magnified many-fold by the domed vault. The man kept coming. He fired another warning but the Asian was fearless and just a few feet away. He leapt at Trey, a foot catching him on the left cheek, the other slammed into his mid-section. Trey went down. The Asian pinned the wrist of the hand that held the pistol by stepping on it then kicked viciously at Trey's groin missing badly all the while emitting whiny exhalations from the effort.

Training took over. Regaining his wind, Trey seized the ankle of the foot that abused his wrist and gave it a great twist. The man went down. Trey pounced on him. He smashed the Glock into the side of the Asian's head. It felled him like someone pulled the plug of one of those Santa Claus blow-up yard displays.

Trey's head screamed at him as did his belly and wrist but he'd been here before. Pain was the byproduct of a warrior's success. The Asian's belt became handcuffs, his shirt, a gag. Trey reopened the computer, the chair seat still warm from his captive. Rather than use the time to transfer files,

Trey decided to take the laptop with him, borrowing a page from whomever it was that tossed Jonah's Place. He also opened file cabinets all in a rank off to the left. The Asian started to moan so Trey encouraged him to go back to sleep. One file labelled, 'Gu Shui,' gave up document after document of good stuff, their images stored in the disposable cellphone.

He looked at his Breitling. It was 2020 hours. Penn was to meet him in the alley behind the bank at 2030 sharp. He shut down the computer that had Chinese characters on its lid, tidied, and closed file cabinets, straightened the desk and made his way to the men's room but turned back. It struck him that it would be a good idea to uncuff the Asian. He should be allowed to escape so Li Ling could suffer Trey's victory. This guy would have plenty to sing about to his handler. Plus, Trey was curious why Li Ling might spy on the person Trey and Penn took to be his partner. Would the Chinese plant manager think Trey was on the Governor's payroll, or would he continue to think that the white man pestering him was none other than Trey Dawson, Colonel, US Marine Corps, Retired?

Another option came to mind. Take the guy hostage and interrogate him in Penn's condo. He quickly discarded that notion because Trey wanted to send an in-your-face message to the rotund one, plus, if his vendetta blew up in his face, Trey would be charged with kidnapping, not a pleasant prospect.

Trey relieved himself and with the computer under an arm got halfway through the window, stopped, and jumped back onto the floor. He crossed the rotunda, opened the front door, went out, and around to the alley where Penn waited.

"Hi," Trey said as he climbed in the passenger side.

One hand leapt to her throat, the other to her forehead. "Sweet Jesus Lord. You enough to scare me white!"

Stoked following the burglary, Trey told her everything about his encounter with the spy.

Comfortable in her home office, it took a while for her to figure out how to instruct the machine to dump the Chinese characters in favor of English. The keys were not a problem. They displayed both languages. She opened the disposable phone to transfer document images Trey captured. He went in the bathroom to swallow a couple of Advil and wash the blood off his cheek while Penn printed fifty plus pages and more were still in the queue. She handed them out like a blackjack dealer in Vegas.

Trey nuzzled her. "Did I ever tell you fighting makes me horny?"

"You are a piece of work," Penn said. "Just when aren't you horny? Come on. Let's get to work."

"You're no fun," he said.

The story of Gu Shui Industries unfolded gradually. For starters, Gaylord Russell leased the land underneath the plant site for a cool $250,000 a year. For the arrangement, he was given a 15% equity interest capitalized at a handsome number; $14.3 million. The incorporation charter described the plant as "a futuristic mining entity that produces world class premium drinking water from three deep wells averaging 551 feet each that tap an inexhaustible river of fresh water trapped just above the bedrock placed there when the Illinoian glacier melted into history 15,000 years ago."

Penn learned that the Governor received a 5.2% cash dividend from the ChiCom government. This payment was deposited monthly in the Royal Trinity Bank in the Cayman Islands to a cloaked account, the holder of which was the fictitious Spectrum Investments, LLC. The address of the fancy sounding bank was in the British Territory's capital city of George Town. A quick bit of grade-school math suggested the Governor was given annual walking around money by the ChiComs to the tune of

$735,000 none of which, nor any of the balance sheet or income, was shared with the Internal Revenue Service. He, along with his wife, Helen, also owned a fancy condo on the crystalline waters of the Caribbean. Penn opened a real estate website for help developing a best-guess street value of the property and came up with another nice round figure; $3.6 million. Of course, Penn hadn't had the time to research titles to the property, but she told Trey she bet good money it transferred from a Chinese owner or sham corporation. Nevertheless. a copy of a net worth statement dated a year and a half ago gave the Governor a bottom line at $127 million, not bad for a humble country politician whose ancestors were carpetbaggers.

Penn just knew she would find damning information on local land transactions, but it didn't come to light until the bleary-eyed hours of a new day while Trey slept on the couch. The find was an original copy of the heir's property deed for the 62 plus acres the Governor slicked from the Grant family. Penn discovered the Governor and the ChiComs hired a local n'er-do-well to pose as a long-lost Grant relative who needed money and wanted to sell, no, had to sell his interest. This, of course, forced the other family members out of their property. The pathos of it was that the land Gaylord Russell crooked was originally purchased soon after the fall of Port Royal Sound to the Union in November of 1861. It became part of the Port Royal Experiment which was an arrangement that followed Field Order 15 to the letter that licensed freedmen to buy and own the same property on which they had worked for generations, sometimes for as little as covering back taxes. The experiment worked until Lincoln was shot in April, 1865. His successor, Andrew Johnson, a slaveholder planter from Tennessee, rescinded Sherman's order and returned the plantations to the white planters under the condition they pledge fealty to the United States of America and paid back taxes.

Penn now had a clear mission.

Lt. Lu Zhao walked slowly at the point of an AK-47. The young officer with a wife and baby child back in Wuhan, a city in eastern China larger than New York dreamed of becoming an Army officer. He qualified to attend the Chinese version of West Point, the Republic of China Military Academy in Kaohsiung. A bright man, Zhao graduated in the top five percent of his class. And now, six soldiers previously under his command dressed in Red Army uniforms accompanied him through Li Ling's formal garden. The path passed a large bronze temple sculpture to dead-end at a grassy space where two grave markers jutted from the earth like large tongues. A fresh hole yawned open in the black earth next to them.

Resembling an effigy rather than a living being, Li Ling, statuesque, stood at attention at the foot of the shallow grave in his dress uniform.

The soldier whose rifle muzzle indented Lu Zhao's back said, "Prisoner, kneel." He pointed at the head of the hole. Lu Zhao, the left side of his face colorful from the confrontation with Trey and the eye swollen closed, did as he was ordered. Slowly, hands behind his back, Li Ling came around behind Zhao, unbuttoned the flap of his holster, gripped his pistol, put it against the side of Lu Zhoa's damaged head, and pulled the trigger. Brain tissue and bits of savaged skull spattered three of the soldiers. They acted as though it was an everyday occurrence. From the momentum of the 9 mm slug, the body toppled into the hole in such a way that only two soldiers had to get in with the body to pull it completely within its confines. The corpse began to flop, legs and arms flailing the South Carolina air as though rejecting death, fighting it for superiority, the torso convulsing wildly. Li Ling fired at Lt. Zhao's heart three times slowly, a programmed, emotionless robot's actions. Lt. Zhao still, the two soldiers jumped from the grave to stand at rigid attention, their white-gloved hands blades saluting their Commandant.

Li Ling returned to his original station. "We are here today," he said, "out of respect for the useful life of Lieutenant Lu Zhao, a man who had the misfortune to fail his people, fail his fellow officers, and fail the President of the Republic of China. Therefore, his body we bury in enemy territory and commit the remains for an eternity to the silence of disgraced death." He saluted the corpse. At an order by the detail officer, the soldiers unslung their rifles, and awaited direction. Li Ling picked up a handful of dirt and tossed it on the officer's body and barked, "Shoulder arms ... Fire," he said three times.

Li Ling folded his hands behind his back and sauntered the peaceful paths of the garden taking mental notes as to what he would task his landscapers with that day. He approached a large wire cage, 5 X10 and 5 feet high. On the bottom outside it was equipped with another much smaller pen secured to the larger one. This one had a trap door. Rock and earth terraces were built of flat stones arranged in such a way they afforded shady living for its inhabitants.

Li Ling shook the small cage. Mice inside went nuts. He lifted the trap door but all of them withdrew to a far corner where they made a nervous, white fur ball. No matter, Li Ling took a bamboo backscratcher knit into the metal walls, withdrew it, and used it to separate two mice, their pink eyes glinting in the sunlight. He pushed them into the main cage and closed the trap door.

Out slithered one and out slithered the other, a five-foot Copperhead, a six-foot Diamondback Rattlesnake, thick and muscular. Li Ling smiled to see them, his old friends. He agitated the cage with long fingernails drawing them across the top. As if on cue, the poisonous snakes coiled. Li Ling banged the cage with the flat of his hand and was delighted both snakes struck at the noise only to re-coil ready to strike again their fangs dripping milky venom that looked a great deal like semen, the Colonel's favorite part of the deadly ballet. Li Ling enjoyed the macabre pathos of the doomed mice as they scurried from one corner of the cage to the other. He snickered at the futility of it. The rattler was the first to strike.

"Well done," Li Ling said in Mandarin, fascinated, clapping his hands in delight, repositioning his genitals and holding his kneading hand over them.

The mouse lay crosswise in the rattler's mouth. The giant snake shifted the little corpse to go down its cottony throat head first appearing as a lump at the top of the big body just behind a triangular head as big as a salad plate. The Copperhead's kill was nearly identical to the rattler's except for a display that defined the species' aggressiveness. The thick brown snake allowed the wounded mouse to escape briefly before it darted its head faster than the human eye can follow and gulped the tasty treat.

The Chinese Colonel let go his erection and clapped like a little boy electrified by the dance of death.

(23)

Trey and Penn drove to McDonalds to buy a couple of breakfast sandwiches and coffee then drove to their favorite waterside park. Mist rolled in off the harbor to deliver the fresh smells of a fresh day.

"I have a story to tell you about the Governor's house out on the Point and how it fits into my family's past," Penn said as they ate. "We've lived here so long it seems everyone has commonality. Folks call the house the Palace because it has eight bedrooms. Everyone knows my *Arupe*, Gauche lives in the cellar."

"This is the pet ghost you talked about," Trey said.

"Yeah," replied Penn. "He's often seen walking the Palace grounds. The original owner's daughter told stories of serving tea to him on the back porch. Her parents ended the fun because her language grew too coarse for a young woman of means. They rightly blamed Gauche. The Union Army and Navy used the house as a hospital. Its carriage barn and smoke house became morgues. Union soldiers who died there walk the halls. I was drawn to these stories as a child. They gave me endless imaginings of a spirit world opened to me by my Grandmere, Collette Felicité Le Févre Smith.

"Who?"

"Grandmother in French."

"So, you speak English, Gullah, a little French, and a little Yoruba?"

"Yes, sir, but let me finish the story, okay? For the first couple of hundred years of slavery we were owned by the Ribault family. My ancestors learned their language as a replacement for our West African mother tongue some of which yet sticks to our words. In the old country, Grandmere probably would have been a shaman. During my growing, many sick people came to our house and pleaded with her to cast off spells or to buy herbal medicines she learned to make in her childhood.

They were quiet with one another as they sat watching Beaufort wake enjoying gulls crying out to their kin while rolls of fog disappeared in the yellow light of a new and dangerous day.

Trey fired up the truck and drove them to the Palace. They climbed the steep brick stairway and rang the doorbell three times.

Gaylord Russell wore a battered chenille bathrobe, slippers, and a surprised look. Puffy dark circles underscored his eyes. Trey quickly shoved a booted foot across the threshold that stymied the

Governor when he tried to slam the windowless door.

"Get off my porch or I'll call the police," he warned.

"No, you won't," Penn said firmly. "Not after all the dirt we dug on you the FBI and the Treasury Department would be thrilled to see."

"You're bluffing," he said.

"No, sir, we are not," Trey told him.

"It's time you came to Jesus, Governor," Penn said.

"Maybe, just maybe, it will save your sorry, thieving life," added Trey.

"Are you threatening me?"

"We aren't the people you should fear," Trey said.

One of the Governor's neighbors, an antique lady, shuffled past the fine grillwork fence with a yappy little dog straining at a jeweled leash. She waved. "Good morning, Gaylord," she said all chipper.

The Governor cleansed the fury from his face and waved back. "Top of the mornin' to ya'll, Millie. God bless you."

"You wouldn't want your neighbors to see such riff-raff as us on the front porch of their beloved Governor, now, would you?" Trey said. "You can bet Millie's going to set her landline on fire as soon as she gets back to her mansion."

It was Penn's turn. She switched to a sassy Gullah. "You got no news?" she asked.

The Governor stepped out of the way and let them in. Trey watched him closely. The Governor did something stupid. He threw a haymaker which Trey deftly blocked seizing his wrist, ducked under the arm, and twisted it behind his back. Trey shoved him in the direction of his study.

"You need us more than we need you," Trey said. "Your ass has a bounty on it whether you want to admit it or not. Not only that, but your precious gentile, plantation owner charade is in serious jeopardy."

In the study, Trey pushed the Governor away.

The older man looked dazed. He considered offering the $10 million bribe discussed with Li Ling but decided Trey's blood was up and to wait for a better, more rational time.

A mousey woman appeared carrying a pistol and a cellphone which she held in the air. "Lord, should I call 911?"

"No, dear. It's alright." She left without uttering another word.

"Lord?" Penn said, full of scorn.

"That's right. If you don't like it, Miss Smith, get the hell out."

"Sing!" Trey said disliking his tone.

The Governor inhaled, the air whistling in his nose. He let it out slowly. "I've suspected for months now that the Chinese are doing more than just filling water bottles," he said. "The last time I visited I was denied access to various zones some of whose entrances were guarded by armed men as well as newly installed state of the art facial and thumbprint recognition lock systems."

"What happened to the drone we shot down?" Trey said.

"Drone? What are you talking about?"

Penn went into lawyer mode. "Are you saying you know nothing about weaponized drones coming and going from Gu Shui? That's not credible, sir."

"Look, all I know is that the Chinese are squeezing me to sell my position in their company."

"And?" Penn said.

"Well, I can say with certainty there's tons of payola with regulators bought off to look the other way."

"But, of course, you know nothing about that too," Penn said sarcastically.

"Look, I'm sincere when I tell you I made what I thought was a good, no, a great investment for my family and it wasn't until it became like that old-time newscaster Paul Harvey used to say, 'stay tuned for the rest of the story' that I became wary of my business partners. Every time I turned around I had to help them bury another investigation, or lean on this agency, or that one in Columbia, or intimidate snoopers like you two."

"Really?" Penn said. "How in God's green earth could you not have an inkling that things weren't on the up and up, sir?"

"I suppose so but I was helpless to extricate myself from their financial quicksand."

"Level with us," Trey said, "did your team shoot out my windshield and tear up the left side of my truck just for shits and giggles?"

His lips in a thin line, the Governor shook his head. "Intimidation. Now it's time for you to level with me. Why are you risking your lives confronting the Chinese?"

The answer came quickly. "Revenge," Trey said.

"For me, it's getting even for all the hurt people like you've done to the Gullah. For evil people like you, greed has no season."

"Did one of your goons kill our dog?" Trey asked.

"We are not dog killers, sir."

"That is a lie!" Trey raged.

He rose up becoming a very real physical threat for the older Governor. His hands in iron fists at his side, Trey slowly walked around the big desk never taking his eyes off Gaylord Russell to stand behind the Governor's desk chair where he hunkered over the back, freezing its mobility. Only Penn could see it, but the Governor's eyes were wide with fear. Trey smashed a palm into the leather backside of the chair. The Governor's head snapped forward then whiplashed back.

"What are the Chicoms hiding?" shouted Trey, choking down a seething rage, that adolescent chip on his shoulder rubbed raw given new life.

The Governor swallowed hard. "I have no clue," he said. "But ... but, nothing radioactive. I saw no evidence of that. They are secretive, passive aggressive souls," he continued. "One always feels like you are told only so much. They smile at you and knife your back and expect you to enjoy the experience. I invited Li Ling over for dinner one night, got him in his cups, and he let loose a little. I might add that the land I lease to them has a unique geological structure under it," he said veering off course.

Trey spun Gaylord Russell in the chair so that he stopped right in front of Trey giving the Governor no choice but to look up at him. "Cut the crap," grumbled Trey. "We know all about it. Get back to your dinner party."

"Well, okay," the Governor replied, flummoxed. "Um-m, halfway into the supper, Li Ling admitted that chemical interactions in the wells frees up unusual minerals. At that, the bastard laughed his ass off. I'll never forget it. 'We have it, and you don't,' he said, real patronizing like a rich kid on the playground who charges for rides on his go-cart. 'Beijing very happy with me. How ironic that we draw it out right under your noses,' the guy says. I asked him what in hell he meant and he only laughed at me again and held up his glass for more Jack Daniels Sinatra Select at $130 a bottle."

"This is worse than I feared," Trey said to Penn coming her way, his imagination racing.

"Dear God," the Governor said, swiveling back around. He put his head in his hands. "What have I done?"

"What minerals?" pushed Trey. "You said not radioactive, but you can't be sure, can you?"

He offered the weakest of reasons for his perfidy. "They are enigmatic people," he said.

"Think, damn it!" bellowed Trey.

The Governor threw his hands in the air. "I do NOT know."

"You're worthless," said Trey, "and so is this conversation with the deaf, dumb, and blind kid. By the way, we might go drone hunting tonight to shoot down one of their mules. Maybe you could deliver the carcass to Li Ling, tell him his neighbors thought it was his birthday. Want to come?"

"No," the thoroughly defeated Governor said and slumped back in his chair looking out the window at the tranquility of Helen's flower garden. "We have grandchildren coming over for a cookout," he said.

"Do they call you, Lord, too?" badgered Trey.

Penn was impressed by Trey's focused tenacity in the pursuit of exposing the Chinese. He never wavered in his conviction that Gu Shui was evil. He forged ever-forward smoldering night and day with a fierce and unrelenting intensity. Devoid of impulsive missteps, his approach was methodical, thorough, and straight ahead. He exhausted Penn.

Trey rolled out the details of the night's mission. They were to position themselves in what would be a likely path from the plant to the Port of Savannah in the belief the drones they encountered would be loaded at the plant with whatever they were smuggling.

Penn drove so Trey could fiddle with the GPS function on his phone. The goal was to find yet another turn-in to disappear into the woods and wait for something to fly over, shoot it down, and hope this one doesn't get caught in the pine branches.

"There," Trey said pointing at an opening.

Penn wheeled into the overgrown path and shut the truck down.

"GPS coordinates say we're 10.23 clicks SSE from the plant," he said.

"Not far enough for my liking," Penn said.

Gear was checked one last time. They waded into the swamp. Occasionally, a vehicle drove by out on the hard road, but that was it. Hiking once to the east and once to the west they heard not a single drone. After three futile hours, they hung it up.

"Must not be flying tonight," Trey said unloading gear on the truck bed.

Penn cocked her head to one side concentrating on the night. "Sh-h," she cautioned.

It moved SW to S then away from them to the East but in a few minutes came right at them. "Start the truck. The damn thing is searching for unfriendlies," Trey said calmly, then it dawned on him this was a recon drone/hunter not a cargo drone, or maybe they acted the same? "Don't get in the truck," he said closing the door the diesel still turning over. "Stay by my side."

He shouldered the 12-gauge.

The drone came closer and closer, stopped above them then fired laser pulses that cut through the pine tree tops sending branches crashing to the ground. Those pulses that got through the vegetation singed the paint from the truck's already damaged quarter side panels but couldn't get to Penn or Trey. The laser stopped for a moment. Trey sprang up, shouldered the shotgun, and blasted four quick rounds. The drone reacted by rising very fast out of the effective range of the shotgun and exited north at high speed.

"Damn," cursed Trey. "I'll bet it's coming around behind us. Its gotta be running out of juice." They re-positioned and waited.

A drone whose advance they failed to hear, zipped close, quite high, and let loose two rockets. The vegetation triggered their impact sensors causing both devices to detonate in the trees. The air filled with whistling flechettes that became anti-personnel razor blades. The upper canopy was virtually stripped clean of leaves, their tops shredded. If they had been in the open, Penn and Trey would have suffered the mythic death by a thousand cuts.

The drone fired its lasers. This time they reached the truck without dilution. More and more of the laser beams sizzled the truck. Acrid smells of burnt paint assailed their noses. Realizing he had to get lucky, or they would die, Trey popped up and shot six quick rounds from the 12-shot box magazine. The drone wobbled, rocked side-to-side, and fell from the sky 50 feet away.

They ran to the fallen machine. "Come on, baby, let this one be a carrier," Trey said, lifting the wreckage from the swamp. "Light sonofabitch," he observed. "Christmas will have to wait. No cargo, damnit all to hell!"

Trey tossed the dead drone in the bed of the truck, fastened the hard cover, and sped off.

"Let's have a heart-to-heart with the Governor, want to?" he said invigorated by their success. "He's holding something back."

"My take, too," said Penn.

Trey was elated. He played steering wheel drums to the beat of the song on the radio. "We got one of the sons of bitches!" he said.

The speedometer touched 100 on the straight highway running between a corridor of tall pines, twice the speed drones could fly.

"It's the middle of the night. Who's banging on my door?" the Governor demanded.

"The comedy team of Penn and Trey," Trey answered.

"What in Hell?" the Governor exclaimed when he saw what Trey was holding. "Come in! Jesus, Mary, and Joseph. Here, take it to the basement. I have a workshop down there."

The entrance was a truncated door cut beneath the main staircase leading to a basement half the size of the big house, dank even on a hot summer night with a sand floor and walls of round ballast stones abandoned on the beach by hundreds of years of merchant sailing ships heading home loaded with New World cargoes.

Penn wondered if Gauche was home. If he was, there could be no doubt he was entertained by what happened in his house.

"Set it on the workbench," the Governor said. He pushed several unfinished birdhouses off to the side. "Big SOB," the Governor remarked.

"Yeah," said Trey, "About the size we used to see coming over the border from Pakistan into Afghanistan only they were solely for recon. I didn't think the Chi-Coms had the technology to weaponize with such sophistication." He inspected the craft. "Here's lithium batteries weather-proofed in this metal case and the fans on the corners. This here looks to be a telemetry bundle, infrared sensors, laser package, and a set of four hooks that I'd guess are for carrying payloads. Those rechargeable lithium batteries could give it enough range to get from the plant to the ocean, easy. If the machine needs recharging, all the operators have to do is pop in a couple of fresh batteries and recharge the depleted ones. I guess we were far enough off the flight path for the pack mules to fly over that we could only attract their guard dog, or, maybe they were flying them at higher altitudes now to blunt our effectiveness."

Penn looked puzzled. "Who's flying this thing?"

"My grandson has one," said the Governor. "He sits in a chair on the back lawn and flies his toy all over the marsh. Live video can be viewed from an onboard camera whose resolution is remarkable."

"Actually," Trey said, "I'd bet even money someone in Beijing is flying it with the help of a dedicated geosynchronous satellite." He tapped the telemetry nacelle. "This thing operates at the speed of light. Instructions are virtually real-time anywhere in the world. I've been retired active duty now for three years and I'm here to tell you we didn't have lasers on our hand launchable drones yet because the power packs drained too fast even if operated during the day while creating real-time bonus electricity from photovoltaic cells. It helped but it was still not feasible."

"We should give it to Parris Island," the Governor said.

"Not yet. Cardinal rule, never give up what you've won."

"Looks like I better call in the Posse," the Governor said.

"Who's that?" Penn asked.

"Law and order, stand for the flag lovers like me. These men are former State Troopers under my command when I was in Columbia."

"Can you trust they'll keep their mouths shut?" Penn said, skeptically. "From my interactions with Troopers, they're usually real chatty."

"Miss Smith, the Posse will do whatever I tell them to do."

A couple of days after they brought down the empty drone, Trey was keen to have another go at it. This was why Penn found herself sitting in the prow of a Coast Guard launch with Mother Hubbard at the tiller driving up the Savannah River dwarfed on either side by enormous trans-global container ships. A half dozen of the behemoths from around the world were docked along a row of cranes the spitting image of the AT-AT machines in the Star War movies. It took two hours cloistered in Hub's office to convince him to go along with boarding a Chinese ship without official involvement.

"I kid you not, Hub, I've been hearing drones." Trey told him. "They fly over the rental house mostly in the wee hours before sun-up, you know, high passes with no navigational lighting. You gotta believe me. Listen, I heard a rumor another drone company is already operating in the Low Country. If that's true, the feasibility of opening a new one would be ignorant. That competitor might just be Chinese."

Hub rolled his eyes in disbelief. "No way," he said.

"Yes, way," added Penn. "I've heard them too. We think they might make regular drone deliveries. Since the world knows Chinese prefer to do business with their home boys, we thought it would make sense to check out Chinese national ships as the destination for whatever it is they deliver. The fact they're performing them at night implies they're doing something they shouldn't be."

"Interesting," Hub said but his arms were still crossed in a defiant bit of body language.

"You owe me one from that ambush in Kandahar Province," Trey said, scrabbling for Hub's consent and not proud of playing the guilt card. "The one where you were caught in a crossfire. Remember? Tell you what let's do, I'm offering you a ten percent stake of the start-up gratis depending on what we find tonight. It's that important to me."

Hub leaned back in his chair. "Make yourselves at home," he said getting up and heading for the door. "I'll use another office to make calls."

Out on the Savannah River, lightning flickered to the north accompanied by a few distant growls.

"Which one did you say is the Chinese-flagged ship?" Trey asked from the stern of the launch.

"The red one dead ahead," Hub replied. "The *Edge of Heaven* out of Hong Kong."

Hub turned to Trey. "Man, I'm real uneasy about this. I get it that I trusted you with my life. By all rights, both of us should be dead several times over, but I got to tell you I don't like what we're up to. It could earn me a court martial. I'm not that far from hanging up the spurs. They get me, my family has zip for an already inadequate pension."

"Naw, piece of cake. Besides, we'll take care of you."

Hub snickered. "Yeah, right," he said under his breath.

At the waterline, they tied off to a floating wooden dock to which an elevator was accessible that facilitated the five-story climb to the main deck. Hub pushed the red intercom button.

"Major Calvin Hubbard of the United States Coast Guard. I am preapproved and have two inspectors and myself ready to board."

Controlled from somewhere inside the vast *Edge of Heaven,* the elevator opened. As they climbed higher and higher, vistas of the busy port dazzled them. The place worked at capacity 24/7. Small craft and tugs moved slowly along the wide river covered with a sheen of hammered silver light while cranes on multi-story tracks picked up cube after cube to deposit them in either holding areas or trucked immediately to nearby distribution centers. Tungsten vapor lights made it near-daylight making Trey's job that much easier. Hub and Penn were to pretend to check random cubes to ensure they held what the manifest claimed was inside while Trey hunted the top deck for a potential landing and re-launch area.

The Chinese official who met them was armed with only snarly arrogance. Mother Hubbard did the talking. Formalities over, the ChiCom bowed and disappeared through a dogged door.

"Set your phones to airplane mode," Trey said. "Don't call me. I'm shutting mine down completely. Let's make it an hour and a half until contact."

Penn and Hub patrolled the tall canyons of 20-foot iron boxes stacked four tall stuffed with TV's, clothes, bicycles, shoes, furniture and any number of imports destined for big box retailers and internet sites alike. Trey circled the outside rows in the thought that a landing space would, by physical necessity, have to give the pilots enough elbow room in which to land safely. He moved deliberately along row by row until he came to an area in the stern right next to dozens of lifeboats dangling from rusting davits. Another ovoid, dogged door offered access to the interior of the ship. In front of it was a perfect, painted circle perhaps six feet in diameter crosshatched to show the center. He climbed up into one of the lifeboats to wait under the plastic sheeting cover.

At 2349 hours the hatch door squealed open. Trey peered over the gunwale of the lifeboat. Two armed Asian men emerged. They wore the same uniform as the workers at Gu Shui Industries except for white gloves, or at least they were originally white. The palms were a dirty brown now. Both of them on cellphones, they looked up and pointed at the sky jabbering away. Surgical facemasks covered their nose and mouth. The mate to the drone they killed that rested next to Gerald Russell's unfinished birdhouses eased into the floodlights. This drone had saddlebags dangling on opposite sides of the round machines. It landed right in the center of the circle and shut down.

The Asians checked the saddle bags first, unzipped them to inspect their content then started chattering and gesticulating. One of them was beaming. One of them looked unhappy. This one reached into his jumpsuit to get his wallet, peeled off some paper money, and slapped hands. They got back to tending the machine. Trey watched in fascination as one of them pulled the two onboard lithium batteries to seat them on a portable recharger where a half dozen other batteries were digesting new juice. They ran a diagnostic scan of the machine. They chittered away oblivious, chuckling again at something one of them said. They slapped hands again.

Trey came up shooting four fast rounds that found torso and head targets. The men dropped. Trey dismounted the lifeboat and dragged first one of the dead men to toss him overboard then the next one but before this one splashed, Trey stripped off one of the man's gloves and put it in his pocket. He noticed a water hose coiled on the wall. It was used to sluice deck plating of any traces of blood. Trey opened one of the waterproof saddlebags and found heavy, sealed sacks. He guessed the weight at five pounds each.

Trey dogged the sea door, stomped on the inert airship to take it out of commission, and stuffed the sacks in a cargo pocket of his pants. He stooped to pick up the trashed drone and chucked it overboard.

The gold was so heavy Trey had to shove both hands in his pockets to keep his pants from falling to his knees.

He called Hub. "I give up," Trey said.

"What's going on with that?" Hub responded. "Why the hell are you quitting so soon?"

"We've been here over an hour, "Trey replied. "I've crawled all over this tub, nothing. Tell the Chi-Coms we're done. Meet me at the elevator," he said and disconnected.

At the elevator, Hub was confrontational. "What the hell? You hung-up on me, man," he said, steamed as they waited for a ride to the launch. "I didn't stick my neck out so you could quit way too damn early. Out in the field, wasn't it you who said to be patient, to allow the problem to come to you on your terms? You've changed, Colonel ... sir," Hub finished caustically. "Take me where you just came from."

"Alright dude, you got me," Trey said holding his arms up, a sheepish grin on his face. "I didn't go hunting at all. Instead, I hit the wall. So, I climbed into a lifeboat, and took a nap. I'm out of gas. You know, a man slows down as he gets older particularly with all the wear and tear on this high mileage chassis of mine."

"Not the same man I knew in Iraq," Hub mumbled, disgusted.

Penn recognized Trey's gambit. Trey never ran out of gas. She was certain he found something otherwise he would still be hunting.

"Sorry for the wild goose chase," Trey told his old teammate as the launch got underway. "So much for Ant Man Returns to South Carolina, huh?" Trey pulled the glove from his pocket and gave it to Hub. "I didn't totally strikeout. This was in an area big enough for drones to land. Could you find out what all that brown stuff is?"

"You're shitting me, right?" Hub said. "This is all I get, a dirty, lousy work glove?"

"Do it, Major," Trey said.

(24)

Early in his dealings, Gaylord Russell learned that Chinese businessmen prefer to conference at night. He called the plant to invite Li Ling for a heavy dose of that 25-year-old Tennessee whiskey he'd mentioned a couple of weeks before. Li Ling showed low tolerance for alcohol. It turned his usually thick tongue into cooked linguine, or, at least that was the Governor's impression. Per Li Ling's request, the meeting would be in the privacy of his bank vault office well after hours. He even remembered to screen the space with a whizz-gismo he found online that swept the area for hidden microphones.

Li Ling's chauffer let him off in the alley behind the bank, the same alley Penn used to wait for the end of Trey's burglary. The Chinese Colonel rapped three times, the agreed upon signal. The door must have been eight inches thick of solid live oak with fantastical wrought iron strap hinges shaped like serpents as though the smith was giving all those who entered a warning. The Governor had difficulty with the heavy door but hid the strain it had on him.

"Good evening to you," Li Ling said bowing at the waist. He extended a chubby hand, the same one that pulled the trigger on Lu Zhao. The other carried a tan, leather document case. Both men wore practiced smiles of just the right width.

"Come in, Colonel. It's a real pleasure to have ya'll here," said the Governor heading for the bank vault. Their treads echoed off the marbled rotunda foyer and the obsolete teller cages as they made their way into the spacious vault. Re-designed rows of lockboxes became ranks of file casings. Years back, Helen Russell invested in an antebellum walnut desk covered by heavy carvings imported from England. It became the Governor's bulwark from which Helen's Lord held court.

"Please," the Governor said. "Do make yourself comfortable. If I remember correctly, ya'll have your whiskey neat with a glass of ice water and cubes."

"Your memory, sir, is matched only by your wit," said Li Ling without the least inflection, flat, erased of feeling. The Governor's back to him, he placed the document case on his lap, unzipped it, and extracted a sheaf of papers that he put on the desk for the Governor. The case was closed carefully and shoved into the kneehole of the big desk.

Ice cubes contacted 18th Century Regency, Anglo-Irish cut glass tumblers, a set of twelve bought by phone from the Sotheby-London auction rooms by the Russell family's antiquarian broker in Charleston. Ice animated the silvery glass. It came alive giving off elegant bell tones that angels might have made for the fated Governor.

Drinks were delivered. The Governor joined his guest in a pair of comfortable tufted leather wingchairs. Shiny brass round-headed studs sealed its seams.

"How are the wife and children?" the Governor said.

"Exceedingly well. I thank you for asking. Mao is finishing at university in my footsteps at Cambridge."

"And his College?"

"Christ's College actually. He's reading for a Doctorate in nuclear medicine."

"Congratulations, Dad," the Governor said. They clinked glasses.

"And your daughter?"

"Mia is engaged to be married to a rising leader in Beijing politics."

"Oh," the Governor said, "very good. Isn't it pleasant to have the reins of power in one's family?"

"Oh, yes, indeed it is."

Like a Punch and Judy show, the men boxed familiarities between them in typical and obligatory diplomatic vapidities, meaningless, devoid of genuine sentiment, yet conducive to sneaking up on an understood agenda.

"More whiskey?" the Governor asked.

"Of course, Gaylord." He held up his empty tumbler. "A Western habit to which you have introduced me," Li Ling said, chortling.

His back to Li Ling, the Governor made a stiff one. Li Ling watched every move to make sure they both drank from the same bottle.

The fresh drink delivered, Li Ling shoved the stack of papers removed from the case toward the Governor while taking a long sip. "Our latest quarterly numbers. Go over them at your leisure but I'll cut to the highlights. Shipped water volume is up 23.6%. We have decided to push as hard as we can to make that number pop. Your President is playing trade war games in which both nations lose."

"I happen to strongly disagree with your statement," the Governor said, the whiskey emboldening him. "Your country has had its way with us for decades. The Chinese economy grows faster than ours due partly to the differences in tariffs. We can't do business in China without your government demanding proprietary information about our semi-conductors, or patented drug formulas, and that's just the beginning. This is not right and your blatant and unrepentant theft of our technology is obscene. You take our classified or patented or copyrighted material and use them without either permission or remuneration. Beijing has hacked Pentagon files repeatedly and yet we stand idly by waiting to get skinned. That must stop. Take the BMW assembly plant in the Midlands of our great state. You slap a 25% tariff on those cars if imported into China. What do you suppose is the tariff on Chinese vehicles entering this country to include such products as golf carts, and fork-lifts, and ATVs?" Li Ling shrugged indifference. "Well," I'll tell you. It's a big fat zero. Over the years, we gave you thousands and thousands of billions of dollars for fear of raising your anger. And another strategy you Chinese do is to build your military on the back of American labor, innovation, and hacked technology."

All through the rant, Colonel Li Ling watched his host with a sly smile. Now, it was his turn. "Governor, I am concerned about your health," he said. "A man your age shouldn't have such a red face." He glared at the Governor like his rattler's fixing on a sacrificial mouse. "I will not apologize for anything we have done. Our policy is correct for our people. Whether it is so for the United States, we do not care." He poked a stubby finger at his host. "Be thankful we are a Chinese company able by statute to avoid a 30% tariff that we are now to impose on water imported from the United States." Li Ling held up his empty glass. The Governor didn't stir immediately but did rise to his feet taking the tumbler back to the bar.

"Let's change the subject to matters closer," Li Ling said. "We talked about the break-in to this office."

"No, we did not. What break-in?"

"You had an intruder."

"No sir. I have the best security system money can buy."

"Are you calling me a liar?" asked Li Ling his eyes wide.

"What's your proof, Colonel?"

"It was Trey Lawson and he likely got away with hundreds of copies of your most confidential documents and, even more likely, those documents have everything to do with our, shall we say, arrangements."

"He needs to die," the Governor said.

"Yes, Governor, he does. Let me tell you an intriguing tale," Li Ling began. "You see, I admit to an addiction."

"Oh, and what is that?" the Governor asked in the hope some of the icy exterior of the man would melt from the sharing of a confidence.

The Colonel took on a dreamy look the Governor guessed was not just the whiskey. "You see, dear fellow, I have a fondness for snakes, have ever since I was little. Did you know that my country and our region in the world has thirty-five different types of venomous snakes? Fascinating, don't you think? The creatures live for two reasons; to reproduce and to eat, and you know what, Governor, like me they do not like surprises. Theirs is a simple life. I envy them." Li Ling steepled his pudgy fingers resting them on his nose pleased with himself. "Like your western myth of the Garden of Eden," he went on, "Eve was tempted by the serpent … well, you know the rest."

The Colonel pulled out his Samsung cellphone, swiped it awake, and spoke three Mandarin words into the device.

Li Ling's face turned to stone. "But, alas, this is all for naught, Governor," the Colonel said. "My superiors have issued orders. I am to have no further interaction with you."

"Now, sit down, Colonel, and tell me what that means!" the Governor raged

"Orders, Governor, non-negotiable."

"By who?"

"I believe that's whom. Oh, and by the way, the equity you had in Gu Shui –"

The Governor bolted from his chair like it was a military aircraft ejection system. "What the bloody hell do you mean,' had?' Ya'll can't do that. We have the rule of law in this country."

"No dividend either," the Colonel said enjoying himself immensely.

"I'll close you down!" the Governor bellowed.

"You will do nothing of the sort. First of all, we have diplomatic immunity, and second, you haven't paid a dime in taxes on any money we sent you. Right? Why, Governor, you could go to Federal prison for just that let alone collusion, theft of property, fraud, I could go on with the hit parade but it's late and I have to send a report to our China Ministry of Defense as soon as I reach my plant." His phone chirped. "That would be my driver," he said. The Colonel opened the heavy door himself and left a flabbergasted former two-term Governor and former centillionaire standing slack-jawed in the hall. The Governor shook his head to clear it then went back to his office for another glass of regrets seated at his sumptuous walnut desk, his head once more in his hands.

Three minutes passed. Li Ling called a number on the limousine's secure telecom line. The fireball could be seen from the black car. A thunderous explosion utterly destroyed the Second National Bank of South Carolina incinerating an already destroyed man, his files, and life, all of which were quite literally up in smoke. Only ashes were left of the Governor cremated at over 2,000 degrees Fahrenheit. Arson investigators could say that because gold melts at 1948 degrees Fahrenheit. The wedding ring on his finger for 49 years was a solidified puddle right where his desk would have been. Fire fighters found no trace of the document case Colonel Ling brought with him.

"Trey, wake up, Trey," Penn said gently shaking him. He had fallen asleep on the couch watching an old movie with ear buds so Penn could catch-up on work matters. "There was this big boom," she said, "maybe ten minutes ago. I let you sleep."

"I hear the sirens," Trey said yawning.

"Trey, you gotta see this." She pulled the ear bud lead from the side of the wall-mounted TV. She pointed. "Look, they killed the Governor, firebombed his office." Live shots showed firetrucks, yellow crime scene tape, and a hyper-ventilating young reporter, Lela, who interviewed a distraught widow. Nothing was left of the building but three columns out front and the granite blocks that made up the exterior walls.

Penn turned up the sound.

"Mrs. Russell, we are sorry for your great loss," the reporter said.

"They aren't sure Lord is in there," Helen Russell said looking away. "I can only hope and pray he's somewhere else."

"Was he working late?"

"I don't know."

"Did he have a meeting?" the reporter probed.

"I never nose into his business. Never."

"So, you didn't have any awareness of his whereabouts?"

She examined the ground at her feet. "That's why I have hope."

An older, hard-looking man came to her side and held her elbow. "Helen, you need to come with me," said Roscoe Tanner loud enough the mics could pick it up.

She blinked a couple of times, and with Tanner's help, walked away from the camera.

"Oh, that poor woman," Penn said.

"The ChiComs did it," commented Trey. "Listen, lady, it's time you moved to your family's compound."

"Only if you come too," she said. Trey promised he would.

"You staying up longer," he asked, yawning.

"Yeah, think so. I'm so far behind."

"Well, I think the sofa is where I belong." He yawned again, fluffed the pillow, and rolled away from the light.

An hour and a half later, Penn stretched luxuriantly, closed the computer, and sat by Trey's sleeping body studying the man she had grown to love who, at the moment, looked more the peaceful 10-year-old. She trundled off to bed changing into a long tee shirt for what was left of the night. Penn threw back the coverlet and sat on the bed to take her digital watch off and saw it. She froze in terror. Next to her pillow, a gigantic copperhead was coiled and ready to strike. Penn screamed and jumped to her feet but the poisonous adder was quick. With a strike range as long as its body, the snake bit her on the flesh of her left arm above the wrist. Trey came blazing into the room brandishing his Glock. The copperhead re-coiled ready to strike again. He shot five quick rounds into the snake.

"Ah, jeez," he said holding her arm up. Two puncture wounds oozed blood. He whipped his belt off and used it as a tourniquet cutting off blood flow to slow the distribution of the poison. "Gotta find antivenom and quick," he said.

"No," Penn said coolly. "That's a big one. If it had been small, they're far more trouble because the little ones send all their venom in the first bite. The big ones keep a lot in reserve. Besides, copperhead bites aren't all that serious. I'll just draw water to boil."

He followed her into the kitchen. "Don't tell me you're going to make tea," he said.

"As a matter of fact, I am. It tastes awful but Momma Emiline's Rattlesnake Master will do the job." She rummaged the medicine cabinet and came away with a zip-lock bag filled with dried leaves and stems, went to the steaming saucepan on the stove, and dumped about half of the Rattlesnake Master in the water. She put the back of a hand on her forehead. "Dizzy, a little," she said. Trey took an arm to steady her and guided Penn to the table in the alcove in the corner of the kitchen where green plants grew in a window.

"In the lazy-susan over there in the corner you'll find a sieve," she said, "and above the coffeepot are mugs. Strain the tea into the mug." Penn put her head down on the table. Her left arm was swelling noticeably.

Trey busied himself. "Look, Penn, sweetheart, I understand you're all bought into the old ways but we have instant relief a few minutes away in the ER."

"Oh, thou of little faith," she said weakly. "This herb has saved thousands of my people struck in the fields by the Devil's pet." Trey set the mug in front of her. She drank it off, gasping from the taste and the effort.

"You have exactly five minutes to get better," Trey said.

"Bring me the Rattlesnake Master waste and a sharp knife in the drawer to the right of the range." Trey delivered the stuff. Grimacing, she cut a cross where the puncture marks were, picked up a dab of the wet leaves, and put it on the wound. "Could you loosen the belt?" Penn said, "and make more tea?"

"Yeah, but not before I find a towel to wrap your arm." He left for the bathroom, came back with a purple hand-towel, and tied it tightly around her wrist. Penn's color was better, but she was sweated profusely. Trey brewed another mug-full. She dispatched it like the other one, "Now, water," she said, and told him where the tall glasses were. He found them, added ice to it, and tapped the water feature on the fridge.

"You, okay?" he said needing to be reassured.

"Never better."

"No games," Trey said gently.

"Under the sink, there's a garbage bag. Carry that Devil pet out my house."

Trey did as she asked then supported her down the hall to the guestroom where Penn climbed on the bed. He drew the comforter at the foot to tuck it tenderly under her chin.

"Rest, sweetie," Trey said. "I'm gonna turn this place upside down to make sure there are no other surprises."

Pistol drawn, the guestroom was carefully checked then her bedroom where he looked under the dresser, and in the closet, under the bed then went over every inch of the bathroom. Next was the living room where Trey removed cushions, pulled out drawers, and opened a dark wood cabinet of shelves. Every kitchen cabinet and drawer were explored as was the broom closet. Finished, Trey went to the utility room off the kitchen. The door was partially open, the inside dark. He stretched to turn the light on.

He heard the rattle and knew instantly it was a rattlesnake. Calmly, Trey shut the door to give himself time to think how he was going to kill the snake. He recalled seeing a stubby plastic broom with a sturdy metal top posted on the wall of the broom closet where the kitchen trashcan lived. He retraced steps, found it, and went back to the utility room picturing in his head what he was about to do, rehearsing his assault, a mental exercise that came naturally.

Trey thumped the hollow core door with his knuckles. The rattler responded but he was unable to ascertain its position. His memory said the washer and dryer were on the left and the water heater in the corner next to a series of white metal shelves. The door was inched open. He reached to find the light switch and lit the small room. The snake was nowhere. The rattles became more insistent. He took a small step inside with the thought the snake would instinctively seek a place to hide. He meant to look behind the appliances. Something hit the back of his leg. Trey wheeled. The biggest rattler he had ever seen was hung-up on his pantleg with its long fangs caught in the denim near the back of his knee. Trey wielded the broom to push it off his pants then pin it to the tile floor where it thrashed wildly, rattling at its highest pitch. Using his left foot, the titanium one, Trey stomped it to death.

The snake had hidden behind the door and struck his prosthesis, the lead leg as he stepped into the utility room. Trey got another trash bag from under the sink and disposed of the rattler in the dumpster tossing the heavy body atop its devilish brother.

He watched over her the rest of the night, checking her vitals until first light, day clean, brightened the sky. Her respiration made a return to normal, the sweating was reduced, and the swelling had gone down some. He also checked her pulse. It was strong and 72 beats per minute. Still dark outside, as he mopped her forehead with a cool washcloth, Trey turned the events of the night over in his mind to make some sense of the hash.

And then the stark reality of it hit. Li Ling killed the Governor and tried to kill Penn on the same night. He needed to get his act in gear and take out the Chinese sooner rather than later.

Soon, lemony morning sun cheered the small guest bedroom where Trey dozed in a soft chair at her bedside. He stirred and got up.

"Hey, beautiful, rise and shine," he said cradling her hot face in his big hands. She stretched. "How do you feel, darlin'? You okay?"

"I'll live," she said, "but I gotta see Momma Emiline. She's done Rattlesnake Master many times. Can I have some water?" Penn took a look at her arm.

"Why the frown?"

"Too swollen. Momma Emiline will know what to do. Whoa," she whispered as she swung her legs from under the comforter. "Stop this world spinin'."

Trey had to help Penn to her feet. She took three unsteady steps, and collapsed into Trey's arms. He swooped her up.

Beaufort Memorial Hospital was just four minutes away, ironically, on Ribault Avenue, named for Gauche's old running mate. He screeched to a stop outside the guillotine doors of the

Emergency Room and carried Penn inside to follow the arrows on the gray walls to the waiting room. An orderly in scrubs stopped him in the hall. "Whoa. Whoa, sir. What's up?" he said, eying Penn's inert body.

"Snakebite. She needs antivenom like right now."

"This way," the orderly said leading them to a private exam room. Trey lay her on the hospital bed. He felt helpless and cursed himself for not listening to his instincts. The orderly talked into a shoulder mic. "Ex Room 12. Snakebite victim. She's unconscious, breathing is shallow, pulse fluttery, and now, she's convulsing. STAT."

The room instantly filled with people, some cut her tee shirt away, some hooked up monitors of every sort, and some drew blood.

"Look sir, if you persist in getting in the way," the orderly said, "I will have you removed by security." He indicated an unoccupied corner. "Become wallpaper!"

"Anyone know what kind of snake?" a man asked loudly

"Copperhead," Trey replied.

"Administer 10 CC antivenom," the same voice of the head Doc said. A nurse went scrambling. Machines sputtered and beeped and gave off alarming alarms. The nurse returned with a syringe. She handed it to the ER Doc.

One of the machines shrilled a piercing alarm. "She's flatlined," the Doc said. "Paddles. Please everyone, stand back." A male nurse wheeled yet another machine to bedside, fiddled with it then gave the paddles to the Doc. "Clear," the Doc called out. He placed the paddles on Penn's chest and shocked her. Her torso jerked off the bed. The alarm continued. "Again," commanded the Doc.

Stand clear." He repeated the procedure but Penn didn't respond. "Nurse, I need 1 mg adrenaline.

Begin CPR." A nurse started rhythmically compressing Penn's chest as her associate ripped a long syringe off the wall taped there above the crash cart's station. The Doc counted up four ribs on the left side of Penn's chest then inserted the adrenalin directly into Penn's heart muscle.

She sat up inhaling deeply then fell back but her eyes were open and wild with something Trey could not identify; fear, terror, he knew not.

Later that day, nurses wheeled Penn to a ward room where four hospital beds were segregated by a ring of privacy curtains.

"Please, don't call my parents," Penn said, "not yet but let Joselyn know what's going on."

"I don't think we should share this with anyone."

"I agree, but Joselyn's got to be in on it. She's not just anyone. She's my soul's sister."

"Trey," Penn said, tears leaking from the corners of her pretty eyes making damp circles on the pillow, "I died, didn't I?"

He took her hand. "You flatlined in the exam room."

"It was unspeakably beautiful."

"What was beautiful."

"The edge of Heaven," whispered Penn in awe of what happened. "I floated above the room in like a bubble and watched them work on me. Off in the distance, an angel in a white gown flew down a cylinder filled with bright light. I never felt so content. He landed in front of me. 'Our Father sends His best wishes. Are you ready to meet Him?' the angel asked. Trey, I said, 'no.' I told him I was at peace but unfinished." Penn ran a finger under her nose. Trey pulled a tissue from the box on her tray table and handed it to her. "There on the cusp of the forever, this angel, he spoke clearly mind-to-mind. He said, 'Yes, it is not your time. You have our Father's work yet to do on earth.' He had the most beautiful smile. It overflowed with God's grace. He made the sign of the cross and off he flew without me. My soul reabsorbed into my earthly body. I knew it was so because I felt pain. I am no longer afraid of dying. I truly look forward to it."

That afternoon good news came from the resident cardiologist who told them Penn suffered no damage to her heart, that the reason her heart stopped had to do with the chemicals found in the venom that compromised muscle function. That, and perhaps she had hyper-sensitivities to the venom. Had she not been in a hospital, Penn would have died. The Docs kept her that night for observation.

(27)

Momma Collette relinquished the root doctor mantle when Penn was 15, an unusual decision but one she felt good about. Penn had the eye. Penn had powers, Momma Emiline had kindness and strength and knowledge but Penn, she had the gift. This was why Momma Emiline was surprised to hear from Gauche.

He cackled in her sleep awakening her spirit as a hungry baby's cry does its mother in the middle of a dark night. Gauche bid her to come out onto the porch. Clouds of lacy black crepe clouds imprisoned the moon. A deceptive peace lay over St. Helena Island.

"*Ma cher*, it is good to see you," Gauche said. He swept a deep bow as their wispy spirits floated outside the kitchen.

"What is it, *Arupe*?" Momma Emiline asked, concerned by his unorthodox visit and fearing whatever information he was about to give her.

His bells tinkled in the light wind off the river. Gauche cocked his big head to one side. "Penn is in danger," he said. "Do nothing. She will live but you must allow to happen what will happen. The ancestors and your God promised to guide events effecting your willful daughter who now rests on the arm of a strong and good man whom you will soon meet."

"Is this why you come?"

Gauche paid no heed. "Penn is too weak for now," he went on, tugging at his beard. A tear leaked into it and then another. "Sorry, Momma Emiline. Your daughter cries, I cry. I seem to do it at the drop of a hat these days. Never could stand it when she is weakened. I was a basket case when she had the whooping cough. Remember?"

"And measles, and chicken pox," Momma Emiline added with a smile. "You dance round the drum, old friend. Tell me. What is it?"

Gauche hugged Momma Emiline, his gnarled hands quaking. "Sweet Momma Emiline, I tell you millions of lives are in danger."

With that, he flew off toward the creek to merge with the foggy mist that lay above it.

The Docs cautioned Penn to stay another night. Instead, they drove off to St. Helena Island seeking family.

"You, Mr. Writer, will like our home. It's peaceful out there, but take me by my office first. I won't be long."

"Your parents, they know about me, don't they?" asked Trey, his apprehension thick.

"Yes."

"And what do they think?"

"I cannot presume to steal their thunder," Penn replied.

Trey fed the parking meter and waited in the truck, the windows rolled down, watching Penn's office. He made a pledge to himself to never allow her to be alone. A sports call-in show on satellite radio played. Trey wished for Cerberus whose head would have been out those same windows sampling the air for a Scoobie Snack.

A beater Chevy pick-up slowed some and burbled by. Trey put his Glock on the passenger seat. The truck's throaty V-8 under the hood sounded well-tended. An older black man sat behind the wheel. Not five minutes later, it came by again. This time the driver slowed measurably to make sure Trey understood he was being watched. Trey flipped him off. The driver smiled big and waved.

It was the better part of noon before Penn came out with her laptop under her good arm, the left one still wrapped and in a sling.

Trey told her about the black man scoping him out. "Oh, that's just Juno, my uncle," she said laughing. "He's taken it upon himself to be my guardian. You can bet there's a loaded pistol under the seat. You ever want to hear what Gullah's sounded like way back, Juno, he got it, that's right. He the family mechanic, keeps our farm machinery running and road vehicles, too."

"Do I need a passport to get into your country?" he asked.

"Son," Penn replied, having fun, "I am that passport. Just don't be gettin' all anthropologist on me. Take it for what it is."

As they drove deeper and deeper into St. Helena Island, the more remote their trip became, the more remote Penn became, locking herself in quiet reflection, looking out the window yet seeing little but her internal landscape. Few cars shared the two-lane road out of Frogmore where live oaks made cathedrals of the track.

They whooshed past a ruin. "Wow, what was that?" Trey said rubber-necking.

"Oh, sorry," Penn said. "Turn around and go back. I've seen it my whole life so I don't take much notice anymore." Trey did a three-pointer and turned into the St. Helena Chapel of Ease, a haunting, gutted wreck with only the tabby walls standing. Gusts from off the nearby Coosaw River put leaves in perpetual motion to sound like falling water. The place cast a sad spell on them.

"What does my tour guide have to say?" Trey asked taking it all in.

"St. Helena Episcopal Church in Beaufort built this for their white parishioners," Penn told him, "because it was too far for them to travel to attend church in town. I believe it was put up in the 1740s. My ancestors built this God house here but, of course, never could they worship inside. The Buckra's mostly allowed us to worship our Lord God in the woods like animals. Baptists from up north, they grab the heart of the Gullah 'cause they worship like we worship in Africa with joy and the singing although they weren't real big on the dancing in the aisles part. This Chapel of Ease, it burned in 1886. At first, they talk 'bout Gullah rebuild. It was a lie."

Unsteadied by emotion, Penn stumbled on her words. "Um-m, the Coffins, and Frogmore Plantation, and the Fripp's, and Smith's, they comfortable over there." She indicated a small cemetery surrounded by an ornate iron fence. A fleur-de-lis ornament capped each post. "Come, look," Penn said, sniffling. They stood outside the gate. That was the way Penn felt, an outsider looking back into a white creation. "Gullahs, it was we who built St. Helena Island. Up go the big house, the barn, the stable, the pig house. We grow food to fill they bellies. Gullah dig they graves. Gullah mommas wet-nurse white babies, teach them, love them, and tender the babies back to health when they sick, sing the lullaby, rock them in they cradle made which Gullah hands, and good minds, kind folk, my people. Trey, dear Lord!" Overcome, Penn sought his strong arms where she wept bitterly. "Make this unfairness, my hurt go away. Because I am given the eye, I see things you cannot, horrible things" she said into his chest. "I love you, Mr. Writer, but I shouldn't. Never leave me."

Not a soul in sight, they walked the grounds holding hands and tried to picture what the church looked like in 1750, the white women in long gowns, the men in cutaway coats, embroidered vests, and stockings, house boys tending to the horses, and a house slave taking care of the children. In good weather a picnic would have been packed to be eaten down by the river.

They got back in the truck and headed deeper into the island until Penn murmured, "Right here. This is home." Trey could hardly make out the turn. They drove east down a dirt track. Grass grew in the middle. The margins as well as the center were mowed nicely. After a quarter mile or so the line of trees and palmetto scrub gave way to flat fields in between tree rows to the horizon. The fields were planted in corn with extra wide rows and ready for harvest. They drove past a huge field of shiny-leaved bushes beautifully manicured on raised beds covered in a black material Trey could not identify.

"Blueberries," Penn said seeing his consternation, "and off to the other side, those are strawberries and the tall plants with the big leaves, okra."

Latino men swarmed the okra area picking the tender pods. They tossed them into blue plastic tubs to be dumped into a steel wagon hitched to an idling dill pickle-colored tractor.

"What's that tall plant?" Trey asked.

"Sorghum grass. We press our own syrup. The tradition, the process, and the cane itself came with my ancestors from West Africa. It's close to harvest time. We press the cane using a mule mill that's been on the property for more than a century, then cook the sweet juice down till it's a rich honey-brown."

Talk of the seasonal calendar on the farm seemed to have revived her spirits and for this Trey was thankful.

"We sell the sorghum in groceries in the Low Country and online on our website," she said, "but our biggest market for all our products is the Northeast. The corn we have custom stone-ground for grits and sell that too in hemp bags closed with a red drawstring as well as bulk commercial users under the Smith Family Organic Farms name, copyrighted, of course. And the okra right over there we contract to a Jewish packer in Charleston who pickles it. Over there beyond the corn is another field of pink-eye and black-eye peas, and some crowder peas too. We harvest them for fresh as well as dried. Nothing like it cooked slow with a smoked ham hock and Vidalia onions. All this talk of produce is making me hungry. I wonder what Momma Emiline has planned for supper?"

A mobile home appeared back in the trees. Two men sat on folding chairs out front. They waved.

"Quincy and Virgil, bachelor brothers," Penn said. They passed a double-wide and another modular home. Three more dwellings were visible from the road until they came to the banks of the Coosaw River.

"This is it. Home," Penn said.

It was a neat white clapboard house with cedar shake roofing that rested on a bluff overlooking the Coosaw River. A sea of spartina grass carpeted the way to a cobalt line on the horizon delineating the Atlantic Ocean. A long porch fronted the water that wrapped around the south side of the house to connect with the entryway. And in the back, a wooden walkway led out into the river where a baby-blue shrimp boat was docked. Trey parked in the shade of a live oak grove next to a late model Volvo SUV and a colossal Chrysler Hemi pick-up sporting signage that read 'Smith Family Organic Farm.'

"Out here," came a female voice. "On the back porch."

Momma Emiline and Denmark Smith stood in unison. Neither was smiling. Penn's mother spied the sling. Gauche had been right. "Well, hon, what you done to yourself?" They hugged briefly kissing one another on the cheek.

"The arm is one of the reasons I called and asked if we could stay for a while. I'll not lie to you and Poppa. Someone put a copperhead in my bed."

"Well, forever more," exclaimed Momma Emiline. "Who would do such a thing?"

"We talk later, okay?" Penn said. "Could you take a look? I remember Uncle Sunday got bit and you nursed him well."

"You drink the Rattlesnake Master, did you?"

"Yes'm, I did as I recalled."

"Ma'am, I took her to the hospital," Trey chimed in. He held his hand out to Momma Emiline. "Trey Dawson, nice to meet you, and, sir," he said turning to Denmark, "It's a pleasure to meet you also." Denmark shook his hand unenthusiastically and nodded.

"Come, Penn," Momma Emiline said, her arm around her daughter's waist steering her inside.

Penn's father was rooted to a large wooden rocker. "Sit, Mr. Dawson," he said, "Help yourself to lemonade."

"If it's as good as Lucius makes, it will hit the spot. Only he calls it lemons made."

"Old words," Denmark said.

Trey poured, filled a glass yet struggled to fill the awkward silence.

"Mighty beautiful this place," he said after a bit. "I lived in the Low Country for lots of years and never explored St. Helena. Your family sure knew what they were doing after the war. Penn's clewed me in."

"Em-huh," Denmark said. He rocked through another stubborn minute.

Trey kept on trying to draw him out. "I'm impressed by your operation," he tried again.

"Why?"

"The scale surprised me."

"Em-huh," Denmark said and continued to rock looking out over the marsh. He sipped his glass, set it down. "Who's trying to kill my daughter?" he asked, scowling.

"The most direct answer, sir, is people who abused the heir's property statutes to steal acreage from the Gullah family Grant. Penn is near to filing suit."

"Wouldn't be no problem if she just stuck to her lawyering, mister. You told the police, right?"

"No, sir."

"You better have a reason," Denmark said, his eyes on fire.

"Gaylord Russell."

"Big fish, but he dead and good riddance."

"Yes, sir. The way we figure, if we get police in on this problem, it becomes a political goat rodeo. They'll be slow to act since the conservative kingpin of the Low Country is gone. However, we're close to a solution, but we're missing one critical piece to the puzzle. When we have that, it's time to call the cavalry."

Denmark sipped. The pace of his rocking quickened.

"I have a personal score to settle with the other side, truth be known," Trey said. "Penn and I believe a nearby industrial plant owned and operated by Chinese Communists produces something far more treacherous than the bottled water that is officially disclosed. We captured nearly 10 pounds of gold dust from one of their drones used to transport production to Chinese flagged container ships in the port of Savannah under the cover of darkness. They actually have armed guards to keep employees inside. Yet, what we are interested in is the likelihood Gu Shui Industries filters the water for minerals that could be used by their military perhaps in the production of nuclear weapons, or, super conductors available to make the world's smallest and most powerful computers, or specialized elements specifically designed for war in space, or maybe it's just a vast deposit of precious metals. We don't know. Penn tells me you were in the military."

For the first time, Denmark showed a spark. "Yes."

"Nam?"

"Em-huh," Denmark said, rocking quietly, looking out over the marsh. Trey was determined to wait him out. It was silent until Denmark finally said, "I got drafted as most of the young men of this family. None went to college. They plucked us from St. Helena to right down the road to Parris Island for training and within two months most of us were out front in a war that was going better than the press and politicians portrayed it back home. I was 2nd Battalion, 26 Marines, a rifleman. My unit was ordered to hold the hills around Khe Sanh way up north by the DMZ and Laos. I was wounded three times. Got the Purple Heart and a ticket back stateside to help train incoming grunts to shoot straight."

Trey slipped forward in his seat. "I'll mince no words. Penn and I have shaken the hornet's nest. The only question is; will they come after us this far from their base."

"Chinese Communists invading St. Helena Island?" Denmark scoffed. "You can't be serious."

"Yes, sir," he said. "Would it be possible to arrange for a Smith Family home guard for Penn? You know, like the old-time militia from the Revolutionary War?"

Denmark thought for a few moments. "I sure would like to even the score with those devils myself," he said, "and yes, it's personal for me too to not only protect Penn but to avenge the deaths of two family in a war Washington never intended to win, a cousin and a brother, one to a Chinese-made mortar, the other Chinese cannon fire." He stood. "It is time to call the family together," Penn's father said moving away along the side porch toward the dooryard.

"I'll come with you," offered Trey.

Denmark halted. "Best I go 'til they comfortable with you," he said. "Another ting. You hear of Gauche, the *Arupe*?"

"Yes, sir."

"He come to Momma Emiline last night. *Arupe,* he say millions of lives are at risk. That so?"

"Yes, sir," Trey replied. "The imp may be right."

In a few moments a loud bell pealed out front. Trey found it difficult to comprehend the contrast between this beautiful, isolated place far removed from international politics and the reality that a foreign government wanted to kill them as well as the possibility of millions of others. What were the ChiComs defending so fiercely that two of their men could be killed, three war drones destroyed, and a $200,000 gold payload stolen yet one heard not a squawk on the news nor did the State Police come to arrest them? Maybe the diplomatic channels were burning but that eventually would leak from the information sieve that is Washington.

Hearing her father leave in the Hemi, Penn joined Trey. "Momma say I'm fine. She made a special tea and I feel some better already,"

Trey kissed her. "The bell?" he asked.

"Lets the family know of a death but in this case, Papa rang the three short, three long for our men to gather in the old barn. It means big trouble."

Momma Emiline came out. "You mens and the guns," she said disgustedly, wagging her head.

They ate at the kitchen table that evening. Emiline cooked corn pudding, shrimp day-caught by Pedro on his blue trawler, *Evangeline.* Trey was to learn the name came from a story of a long-lost love who dumped poor Pedro for another man. Everyone knew Pedro still loved this woman but no one ever raised the painful subject. Emiline's signature dish, dirty Carolina Gold rice, was a specialty made with chicken liver and Andouille sausage. Talk centered on rebooting Penn about the comings and goings of her family; who was ill, who was going off to college in the fall, or who was to have a baby. After supper, the women did dishes.

"This way," Denmark said," leading Trey out to the porch where Penn's people seemed to do their business. "I got news," he told Trey. Settled in his rocker, Denmark began, "We got six Smith men who want to hear what you got to say. A morning meeting is set."

Penn and Momma Emiline emerged from the kitchen.

"Look at the moon, so pretty," Momma Emiline said, the gold road to it traced on the Coosaw. "You young folk, go on now to enjoy the shinin'. Papa and me, we got tings to talk to." She patted Denmark's hand rocking next to him.

They strolled with Penn's good arm linked with his, following the path to the long walkway and the dock.

"We need to shush. Pedro, he lives on the *Evangeline,* rises before the rooster to drive to work. Sometime he goes for days down to Key West and Cuba when the white shrimp they not good here. The shrimper, he named it *Evangeline* for a woman who left Pedro for another man."

They rested on a bench at the end of the dock. The soft lapping of the river played a duet with the *Evangeline's* hull.

"Momma, she worried. First time in years, the *Arupe*, he come on her dream and he knows what the Chinese do. He knows what the Chinese think, but Gauche is forbidden to tell us directly. He hints, he suggests. Knowing him as I do, I think the Imp warns us to get on with it." Penn pulled Trey closer. "You go nowhere without me. Do you hear?"

(27)

Trey slept in Penn's old bedroom. She was upstairs in her brothers' room. The family was three boys and two girls in a three-bedroom house so things must have been cozy back then. Penn and her sister, Mary, shared the space growing up. Penn told him Mary was a single parent with two school-age girls working as a third-grade teacher raising her own family on Hilton Head, the biggest of the Sea Islands. Pictures on the wall of former heart-throbs and what were important events then were now very dated. Each girl had her own desk. Trey read that as a none so subtle message about her parent's educational expectations. For the first time in he couldn't remember, Trey felt safe. He slept on sheets dried by the sun and sweet Low Country air with the promise made by Momma Emiline his clothes would be washed and folded by the time he awakened in the morning.

A knock came to Trey's door. The deep bass voice of Denmark Smith said, "0620, Colonel."

A neat pile of his clothing was stacked just inside the door. Denmark was in the kitchen drinking coffee and Emiline was busy over an iron skillet at the stove. She wished Trey a 'good morning,' and said, "Bacon, Smith Family grits, and eggs from Cousin Richard's hens. Good?"

"Yes, ma'am. Thank you," Trey said. "And thanks for the clean clothes."

"Welcome. Help yourself to coffee."

"Have we heard from Penn?" asked Trey.

Momma Emiline looked over her shoulder. "Checked," she said with a smile. "The tea, it help her sleep. She rundown, Mr. Writer."

A radio tucked in the corner of the cluttered counters was tuned to an all-news station out of Charleston.

"Chinese messin' with the grain markets with that tariff nonsense," Denmark said. "Corn prices down the limit. We avoid that."

"How?" Trey asked taking a sip of coffee. "We sell milled corn as, how they say, as artisan, un-huh, organic, there's the word so we get a premium price, all them folk from Ohio or Atlanta invading our islands, many take a food memory with them or order from our website. We win," he said. "But not payback enough for how much of our land they develop."

Breakfast was memorable right down to the Smith Family warmed sorghum on homemade biscuits.

The men gone, Penn and Momma Emiline got the kitchen straight.

"Momma, for sure, we root the yellow man this morning while they gone," Penn said.

Her mother gave Penn an understanding look and put down the frypan she dried with a paper towel. "You right, hon. After we through here, we do it. Em-m, girl, how many time our ancestors in Mother Africa we have did same ting; the men off to war council, de women prayin', and de root doctors a'spinnin' they hexes?"

Penn sighed. "I feel helpless, Momma. Men hunt me like I was some kind of animal like in the slave days and I was a runaway. It's not that I'm afraid, because I'm not, but I am about to jumps ahead of a fit. We fight which what we got."

"Yes, girl, yes."

The kitchen shipshape, Momma Emiline wrapped her head in a purple scarf and gave Penn a scarlet one. She went to the cupboard where the roots were kept. Inside was row after row of glass canning jars neatly labelled. She withdrew four of them and a glassine packet filled with gooler dust from Cerberus' grave Penn brought from her condo. The jars contained desiccated plant material.

From a small stack of Smith Farm's Organic Grits bags, she took one out along with a section of cat gut. Next, a brass mortar and pestle was placed on the counter. Penn and Momma Emiline hummed spirituals while the root doctors shaved bits of each of the four roots, placed them in the mortar and pestle then added a teaspoon of potent gooler dust. Momma Emiline ground the assemblage, smelled of it, adding a little of this, a little of that until it was ready.

"Fetch a kitchen match from off the stovetop, chile," Momma Emiline said.

The house quiet, palm fronds out the window clacking in the onshore winds, they stood at the kitchen table where the heavy iron frypan rested on a brass trivet.

"Momma, I've been thinking de plateye might be the right haint. You know, it the hag with the one eye that pops out when he agitated. The Grant's, they angry with Gaylord Russell and the Chinese for stealing they land. I walked they ground and found a big cemetery full of cement headstones with dinner plates embedded in them, and coffee cups, and glass marbles and an alarm clock, all stuff for the journey over the water. De plateye, it the best messenger in our situation, this Li Ling, this bloody man and, Momma, I'm here to tell ya, he see the horrible plateye till he unable to breathe no more. Take my hand, sweet Momma Emiline."

"We pray Jesus he help us with this enemy," Penn said, her head bowed, eyes closed, "as the Israelites asked our Lord for the manna to sustain them while fleeing the great and powerful Pharaoh of Egypt to find freedom in their Promised Land. God be praised we are set free from the Chinese and their godless mission. Jesus, dear Jesus, we beseech you to hear our prayer. Grant us peace and the freedom for which we have sought for so long. Amen."

Penn induced a shallow trance. She hummed ancient Senegambia war songs while Momma Emiline poured the powdered contents of the mortar into the Smith Family Farm bag, placed it in the center of the frypan, and set fire to it. The smell of sulphur from the striking of the old-fashioned matchstick seemed appropriate to the moment. With cupped hands, they drew smoke to them chanting the same African words in a loop that finished each trope with their enemy's name, Li Ling. It ended when the fire no longer gave mystical smoke to implore de plateye to deal severely with Li Ling. Penn emerged from the trance to sing, *O Death,* to the clacking palms.

Trey and Denmark rode in the huge silver diesel truck over bumpy farm lanes to what must have been a tobacco drying barn weathered now to the color of old blood. Half a dozen trucks of various vintages were parked outside. One in particular was Lucius Aurelius Smith's antique Matilda. Lucius leaned on the truck watching their advance and came to the Hemi when they stopped. He wore army fatigues way to small in the belly.

"Wondered where you be," Lucius said. "Sorry about the dog." He snapped a pretty respectable salute. "Sergeant Smith reporting for duty," he said. Trey returned the courtesy.

Denmark introduced Trey all around as men filed into the barn. A few weathered bootjack-end benches were inside. All but a couple of the men were older. Most looked to be in their 70s, but none showed overt signs of debility. Years of working in their fields and on the ocean seemed to have kept them relatively fit. One of the younger Smith's was Quincy who looked to be 19 or 20, and then there was Penn's brother, Pedro the fisherman, a mountain on two feet standing a head taller than the rest of them. Trey saw him once before. He was the guy in an Atlanta Falcon uniform in a pic on Penn's office wall. Pedro never seemed to smile. Maybe it was Evangeline.

Just as his namesake nearly two centuries before, Denmark stepped forward with violence on his mind, violence not on the native soil of Mother Africa, but the bloody soil of the Low Country. In characteristic Gullah style, Denmark crossed his arms over his chest as he talked, his head cocked at an angle. "We here to protect our own as well as our country," he said. "Our Penn in trouble plenty. We a family. We together. Her enemies are our enemies and this one nearly kill her once't. We are here today to say they have no more chances. This good man, the Colonel, Trey Dawson, he as bloodied as we. What was it in service we hear all the time, we got us a clear and present danger. Well, we got one now, uh-huh. Colonel, your floor."

Trey stepped into the middle. "Your cousin, your niece, your sister is in mortal danger. Our nation is also in grave danger. As Denmark put so well, it is our calling to protect her and the family from attack. This attack is likely to come from the sky from advanced military drones."

"Who is they?" asked Juno.

"The Chinese," replied Trey. The men grumbled. Trey handed out satellite images of the compound he and Penn printed before turning in. "These copies are self-evident, gentlemen. I do not have knowledge that the ChiComs are aware Penn and I are here."

"Excuse me, sir," Pedro said, "you said drones?"

"Yes, armed with lasers and anti-personnel ordinance controlled remotely. Although they do have troops some twenty miles away as the crow flies, we are not sure how big a contingent it is or if they have the appetite to commit armed Chinese combat troops to an act of war with Parris Island just down the road."

The Smith's murmured agreement.

"The entrance to your compound must be manned 24/7," Trey said, "by a sentry equipped with closed circuit walkie-talkies that I will buy today. You are to report to Denmark. He's in charge if I'm not around." Trey smiled. "How long has it been since any of you pulled guard duty?"

The Smith's laughed at that one.

"Further, I noticed as we drove in late yesterday you built what, I suppose is a shelter for your children as they wait for the school bus. The guard on duty should at all times stay inside that shed. Remember, those drones are the ChiCom's eyes in the sky. Their satellite assets will be looking too. You are also tasked with the responsibility to have an ear for the machines. You hear one, you call it in whispering because they're outfitted with sensitive listening devices as well as infrared and night vision light enhancement technologies."

"The devil, he in the sky now," Juno the talented mechanic said.

"That's spot on. A whole new dimensional warfare has emerged since most of you guys were in. It's now earth, sea, sky, and space. Although the ChiComs have state-of-the-art recon satellites, they cannot operate at night, so, if ya'll have to move around, nightfall's the time to do it and that pertains especially to Penn. Next, and you're going to think I'm nuts, but does anyone bow hunt deer or turkey?" Pedro and Lucius raised their hands. "I need to borrow a bow. I assume you have reserves?"

Both men claimed they did. "Good. Hey, don't be looking at me that way. There's method in the madness. And another thing. Does anyone know a pilot, a Gullah pilot?"

Denmark spoke up. "Yes, I do," he said.

"We'll talk," Trey told him.

He handed out another aerial view, this one of Gu Shui Industries to which he added a copy of the interior layout. "Memorize these images," he said. "It might be the difference between whether you live or whether you die."

For the next hour and a half, the men were given missions to fulfill should it become necessary to enter the plant by force. Trey was also careful to fully explain the Pontius Pilate acts governmental authorities had performed washing their hands of an investigation of the Chinese.

"One last detail," Trey said. "Penn must not sleep under the same roof on consecutive nights. Am I clear?"

"What about you, Colonel?" the tender-hearted Pedro asked.

"This is all going to come down fast," said Trey. "I'm afraid I won't be enjoying your hospitality for much longer. And, Pedro, the shrimp were fabulous last night. Thank you. Maybe someday you can teach me how to fish. Questions?" A few hands went up. Trey fielded them then left with Denmark to go back to the house. On the way, Denmark told Trey about his friend, Pompeii, the pilot.

(28)

Li Ling had a tough time staying awake. He looked used but he couldn't remember why he had little energy. You see, de plateye appeared out of the early evening air two days ago as Li Ling walked his garden and tended his pets. At first, he laughed at the apparition with one red eye, a big one too, right in the center of its ugly forehead. It began as a dog, a large species of questionable heritage then it became a glue factory plugger, then half a dozen other animals. To de plateye's amusement, the shapeshifting continued until de plateye morphed into a monkey. Li Ling was petrified of monkeys. De plateye sensed his fear. It opened its mouth to expose dagger fangs then sprung into the night to land on Li Ling's shoulder spewing his head with bloody vomit that smelled like putrefying flesh.

Li Ling shrieked and tried to rid himself of the monkey de plateye but when he grabbed for it his hand went clear through the apparition for de plateye is kin to Gauche, the *Arupe*, images not substance. De plateye howled at the night having fun with the plump, very frightened Asian man. Li Ling didn't know it, but de plateye just adored Chinese takeout.

On the path in front of the pets' pen, Li Ling performed Tai Chi in an attempt to wall-off the clever demon monkey from his consciousness. He assumed basic meditative poses. De plateye did fade yet still clung to the top of his head. A guard approached, Sergeant Zhang. He stood at attention. One did not address the Commandant unless ordered to do so. Li Ling moaned and brushed his right shoulder in agitation. Sergeant Zhang took a chance.

"Colonel, sir, may I help?"

"How long have you been here?"

"A couple of minutes is all, sir."

"Well, don't just stand there like an idiot. Help get this, this; this thing off me."

"Sir, what thing?"

"The monkey. The monkey with one red eye. Are you blind as well as stupid?"

"Sir, there is no monkey."

"Get out of here!" Li Ling shouted and pointed the direction Sergeant Zhang was supposed to leave.

"Sir, I come to tell you supper is ready."

"Serve it in my chambers, Sergeant," said Li Ling.

De plateye jumped to the ground to ooze inside the snake pen. Three rattlers slithered from
hiding, coiled themselves in a neat row, and took turns striking de plateye. The demon howled with
laughter jumping around trying to get them angrier than they were born, reveling in the frustration it
caused them until de plateye vaporized into a red mist that seeped into the open mouth of the largest
of the three snakes to disappear inside the big rattler.

"You two belong together," Li Ling said and hurried away.

"And where do you think you are going, nianqing di shibing - young soldier?" the plateye said
in Li Ling's mother's voice that broadcast from the biggest rattler. The Colonel whipped around.

"No one calls me that except *qin muqin* – dear mother!"

"Come closer," the rattler hissed. Li Ling hesitated but did shuffle to the cage. The big
triangular head with its forked tongue that probed the air wavered as if it meant to mesmerize the
Colonel. "Look at me," the big rattler hissed. "That's it, good boy. You must understand I will not go
away until this land is returned to the Gullah. You are on sacred ground where ancestors sleep.
Leave!"

"I've had enough," Li Ling said. "You are not real."

"Oh, but, yes I am."

Li Ling stormed off in a huff grateful to be rid of the demon.

His back turned, he didn't see the red mist discharged from the big snake's dangerous mouth to form a pool of putrid sludge that silently ambled on two forming legs at his side in the process of transforming into a witchy blob of a woman with thick hairs growing on the tip of her wicked nose from a massive wart the size of a Hershey Kiss.

"Ps-s-s-t, big boy. Look at this month's Playmate."

One sight and Li ling dug for the door, his black leather shoes scorching the pea gravel. No matter, de plateye miniaturized itself in an instant and leapt atop his head to lick him with a foot-long tongue. The dripping saliva smelled of sunbaked road kills so disgusting even turkey buzzards left them alone.

Inside the plant he had to get his act together but even when Li Ling attempted to control his emotions through deep breathing and meditative techniques all officers of the People's Republic of China must learn as military cadets in case of capture, but, de plateye blocked it.

Inside, the guard saluted. In front of the Colonel was a high ceiling room where hundreds of machines whirred and spun covered buckets at high speed. Uncharacteristically, for he was very much a hands-on leader, Li Ling walked right past the guard without interaction. Three more soldiers were disregarded on the way to his chambers where another sentry said, "Good evening, Colonel."

"No, it is not a good evening. Do not under penalty of death disturb me tonight. You are to immediately deliver a bottle of my whisky from the commissary to my chambers then go away. Leave it outside my suite."

The soldier looked puzzled. "As you wish, sir," he said.

"Fetch, Corporal. GO!" shouted Li Ling.

De plateye chortled in glee as it continued to lick and kiss Li Ling's face, enjoying itself sucking his eye sockets, and sticking its tongue up his nostrils exploring the recesses of the Colonel's nasal cavities.

Li Ling felt dirty. He stripped his suit and left a trail of expensive clothing on the carpet. He fled to the shower, turned on the water, and got in without waiting for it to warm. De plateye evidently didn't like water. The hag was nowhere to be seen or smelled. He meditated under the stream until no more discharged from the shower head. Toweling himself, proud of himself, Li Ling heard someone sing, or better said, trying to sing. He went to his sitting room. There, under the wet bar lolled de plateye, its spidery hands conducting its offensive singing, the fatty tissue under each bicep jiggling like so much foul gelatin. An empty crystal decanter that once held good Tennessee corn whiskey lay next to de plateye.

"Oh, Li, I can call you that now that we are such friends and neighbors, right, I mean can't I, Li, sweetums. That was mighty fine whiskey and I thank you." De plateye belched a cloud of noxiousness. "Uh-h, old friend, old buddy, got any more good stuff?"

Li Ling slumped in a chair, his hand covering his forehead. De plateye crawled to him, its great long fleshy breasts swinging from side to side, it's mouth in a hideous smile. "I'm gonna rock your world, l'il honey buns."

The Colonel jerked his head up and bellowed, "Don't ever call me that. It is what my dear wife calls me in private."

"Is that so, young soldier? You loved your Momma, didn't you?" de plateye crooned. "You had dreams in which you soiled yourself."

"Enough!" Li Ling hollered, his face red. The wet towel slipped to the floor. "I will draw and quarter you myself."

"Good luck with that. I'm already dead," de plateye said, laughing at him. It was within a couple of feet now. Li Ling ran to the bedroom, slammed the door shut, and locked it. A red mist seeped into the bedroom. It grew hotter and hotter as de plateye re-evolved into semi-human shape. It opened its mouth to speak but out of it snakes lunged for the young soldier. He cowered in a corner.

"Get off our land," de plateye said pleasantly. The naked Li Ling shook his head. "Well then you're about to have every perverted thought you ever had made real. It's showtime." And with that, de plateye pinned him to the floor and ransacked the young soldier's body inside, outside, out and in for hours until Li Ling blacked out. De plateye lifted him as though he was weightless onto the bed and retreated to the top of one of the four bedposts to guard its prey, it's unblinking red eye fixed on his captive until he sensed the young soldier was in deep sleep. He would then swoop off the bedpost to ravage every orifice until the young soldier could take no more.

Coach Love gave Trey a look that only a former player could translate. It wasn't exactly the evil eye or the 'are you kidding me, kid" look, although he was accomplished at both. No, it was more, 'I care about what happens to you distilled down to don't do it.'

"Now, let me get this straight. You want I should make a shield out of stainless steel like King Arthur used equipped with a padded handle on the underside."

"Yup," Trey said.

Coach cocked his head to one side. "Why?"

"Yours is not to reason why, yours is but to do."

"Twenty-four by forty-eight inches?"

"You got it."

"You'll have it tomorrow afternoon by three. Listen, Roscoe Tanner stopped by here a couple of days ago looking for you."

"Who?"

"Gaylord Russell's bodyguard."

"He's not real good at his job," snarked Trey.

"Everybody knows the Governor kept retired State Troopers on the payroll as, shall we say, well hell, as goons."

"Is that so?"

"He says for you to call him. I got his card somewhere." Coach Love dug through a counter that gave clutter a whole new meaning.

Back on the road, Trey asked the communications console to call the number Coach gave him.

The voice that answered was gruff, no nonsense.

"Who?"

"The one, the only, Trey Dawson. What can I do for you, Mr. Tanner."

"You have information on why Gaylord Russell was killed. Simple, I need that information. There is a public bench in the northwest corner of the public courtyard of the CSA Armory in Beaufort. Meet me there in an hour and a half. I mean you no harm."

The man who sat in the courtyard of the walled and crenellated Armory was sixty-ish, balding with a full beard trimmed to perfection wearing jeans and a Carolina blue fishing shirt. His expressionless face said 'no bullshit.'

"Colonel Dawson," Tanner said.

"The same. What can I do for you?"

"Have a seat."

"I prefer to stand."

"As you like. Here's the deal. Ya'll in divorce proceedings, you're a decorated Special Ops veteran, you consort with a community activist of a different race, and you worked with our late Governor before he was blown to pieces. How am I doin' so far?"

"Not bad," replied Trey.

"Look, I'm a retired career Trooper with plenty of experience on SWAT, plus I got four to five guys itching for a fight with the bastards who killed a man I admired and respected. I tried to do an end-around with the US Attorney for our district but John Porter, why, he allowed as how the Feds refused to snoop those guys, claimed we already had shaky relations with China and that they have no desire to make it worse."

"Yeah, that's about the size of it," Trey said.

"What the hell you up to? And if it's what I think it is, I want in."

"I'm fixin' to take Gu Shui Industries down."

Tanner brightened immediately. "Then, I want in."

After almost an hour of discussion to establish where the sidelines of this new game were, going to be set, they sealed the deal with a handshake.

Trey wasn't five minutes back in the F-150 that the communications center lit up. An 'unknown caller' wanted to talk. Normally he'd disregard the prompt and let it go to voicemail but these were hardly normal times.

"Accept," he said to the dash.

"How are you Lawson, my neighbor and good friend?"

"Having the time of my life," wisecracked Trey.

"I have a proposition for you, a very good proposition, I might add. Come to the park in Beaufort, you know, the one you and the lawyer like so much. Public, right? No games. No weapons. We talk, maybe settle differences."

Running through Trey's head were imaginations of the imminent battle and the unnecessary bloodshed of Gullah, Chinese, and Posse alike. "Okay," he said to Li Ling. "0200 hours at the gazebo." He disconnected then ordered the phone to call Roscoe Tanner.

"Listen, Tanner, we need your help like, right now." Trey outlined what was going down and how the trooper could help.

"Afternoon, Quincy," Trey said to the sentry at Smith Farms. "All quiet on the eastern front?"

"Yes, sir," Quincy said.

The Four Tops leaked from Quincy's ear buds. He warned the Smith's against their use in the barn meeting but said nothing to rebuke the man. He made his way to the house on the Coosaw River where Momma Emiline told him Penn was over to Thomas and Fanny's for the night and that Denmark could be found in the okra fields.

Trey located the doublewide where Penn was to spend the day and night and was pleased they had an attached carport. She wouldn't have to expose herself in daylight to be caught on Chinese satellite imagery. An ancient coonhound greeted him. It reminded Trey of Cerberus. They drove out looking for Denmark and found him supervising the okra harvest beyond the corn fields to the north.

"It would be best if you stayed in the truck," Trey said shutting it down. He pointed to the sky.

Penn gave him a poisonous look. "Why do you expose yourself, then?"

"I'm not nearly as valuable as you, that's why."

Denmark was deep in discussion with a Smith he had not met. Trey assumed the man acted as the overseer of the Latino harvesting crew, an organization not much different than the family's years chopping cotton. The third person in the group was a heavyset Hasidic Jew replete with the tallit, a black brimmed hat, black pants, and now, dusty shoes. His luxuriant black beard was so thick a bird could nest inside. One of Trey's best friends in his first tour in Iraq was a Mossad agent, Joel Rabinowitz, who taught Trey about Jewish religious customs. Joel begged Trey to marry his sister.

He waited for the pow-wow to run its course.

"Got a minute?" Trey asked.

The taciturn Denmark nodded. Penn's father watched him closely as they sauntered down a dirt road by the side of the okra field kicking up puffs of dust.

"You goin' in tonight, ain't ya?" Denmark said.

"Yes, sir."

"Kin tell by the game face. Haven't seen that on a man in long years."

They stopped. "Listen, if I don't contact you or Penn by 0600 hours tomorrow," Trey said, "call a man by the name of Roscoe Tanner. Here." Trey handed him a piece of paper with Tanner's contact information. "Call Tanner if I don't make it. He's prepared to bring as many as six men all of whom are highly trained. My high school baseball coach, Dexter Love from up at Sea Branch volunteered too. Tanner's bunch, they call themselves the Posse. Our objectives are firm. Find the mystery room, discover what they produce besides water and gold, and capture Li Ling."

"This the same Roscoe Tanner who was the enforcer for the Governor?"

"Yes, sir. These men believe the Chinese killed their boss and I think they're right. Tanner also talked with the Feds. They want no part of blaming a ChiCom for anything. The troopers got a dog in this hunt, too."

"Aw-right," Denmark said. "But, you see, Quincy and Virgil done time up to Allendale when they young."

"Whites and blacks, cops and robbers, none of it matters. You bleed red, I bleed red. We owe this to our nation. We owe this to avenge our fallen comrades and I owe it to Caleb."

"I'm with you," Denmark said.

"Thank you for that, sir," said Trey. "You and I, we have another issue to resolve as to whether we involve Penn with my former squad-mate, Cal Hubbard. I mentioned him before. He's our link to local military assets should it come to that. I'm unable to tell you more for fear that when this is over, if we fail our objective, the government will come down around your heads. Penn needs to continue to do good works for the Gullah community whether I'm around or not. We must distance her."

Denmark took a Smith Family baseball cap off and reached to lay a hand on Trey's shoulder. He held it there as he stared into Trey's intensity. "I'm sorry for your boy, Colonel. I wish you good huntin' tonight. The Smith Militia and the Posse, we stand by. You see, we got a tradition go way back to Africa," he went on, "when trouble come as it always do, it communicated by the drum. At the house, the bell we can hear everywhere used to call us to the field before the big war. It tell the family one of us gone 'over the water' to meet our savior. It mean; drop everyting, come to the meetin' barn. This the ancient signal by Senegambia men. Today, I tell them each, the death bell, this time it ring to call us as one people, white and black together."

A shiny black S-Class Mercedes circled the park on the Beaufort waterfront, it's deeply tinted bullet-proof windows gave no hint who the passengers might be. The big car parallel parked after three passes. A blank-faced, liveried Asian got out from the driver's side. He left the door open and popped the trunk lid to show it too was empty. He let Li Ling out leaving that door open too. No one hid inside.

Trey concentrated on Li Ling looking for deceit like an automatic weapon under the driver's seat, or a hand in a pocket but he seemed to be unarmed. The ChiCom Colonel plodded toward the gazebo with his hands behind his back. As he drew near, Trey could see that his spikey black hair was uncombed, and as he climbed the steps, that he failed to shave in a while and the suit was rumpled as though he'd camped out in it the night before. There was a crazed look about him, too, that if the times were better, Trey would have found funny. Li Ling vigorously brushed his shoulders several times, grimacing.

"You look like shit," Trey said. "Are you on a bender?"

Li Ling shook his head, "No," he responded in a subdued voice, the weight of his world on his occupied shoulders.

"One of your Devil's pets bite your sorry ass?"

Li Ling drew himself up. "Unlike you, Lawson, my pets are smart enough not to bite the hand that could feed them."

"Look, lard-ass, I hate being around you so get to the point then get the hell out of my sight."

Li Ling looked like he was in pain. He scrunched his eyes shut then opened them too wide, brushing his shoulders and the top of his head.

"What the hell, you have cooties or something?" Then it dawned on Trey. The curse Penn slapped on him, of course. He couldn't help himself, he chuckled at the Colonel's distress. "De plateye gonna git you," he mocked holding his hands in front of him shaking the fingers as though a fresh curse was being made.

"How about $10 million," Li Ling said through clenched teeth, "deposited in a Swiss un-numbered bank account untraceable by tax authorities."

"Let me get this straight. You just offered me $10 million to leave you alone," Trey said his voice raised in quick anger.

"Yes."

"You know, I might just climb off your back without the money if you told me the truth about what you mine and ship back to the Motherland."

Drool leaked from a corner of Li Ling's twisted mouth where a twisted smile foretold the tenor of his answer. "My nation's business is none of yours," he said then walked slowly away.

Trey could see that the Chinese Commandant talked to himself the entire way to the limo. Once alone, Trey dialed his cellphone. "Hey, did you get it?" he asked.

"Of course," Roscoe Tanner replied putting the video system with an attached, augmented surveillance cone on the passenger seat of his club-cab. The cutting-edge listening device had a State of South Carolina sticker on its pistol-grip handle.

"Now, please don't be gettin' all pouty," Trey drawled.

"What's with this sudden secrecy?" Penn said and then she jumped to an unfortunate conclusion. "It's because I'm a woman, isn't it?"

"Ah Jeez. I already told you; you're more valuable than any of us. You're the leader of your community and your family, the Gullah of the Sea Islands, and a direct contact into another world I will never experience and, frankly, don't understand. There's safer, more essential work for you to do."

She put a hand on his thigh as they drove. "I'm sorry," she said. "You didn't deserve that, but it's just that I can feel you gone and it makes me hurt inside. You're hell-bent on this vendetta, aren't you?" His silence gave truth to what she said. "I thought that when two people fall in love they want to be together no matter what?"

"I have to do what I have to do. Plato, or Sophocles or someone smarter than me came up with that," he said trying to lighten the mood.

Penn punched his arm. "Did not."

"Did too," Trey said. He slammed on the breaks, folded her in his arms, and kissed her long and soulful. Breathless, they pulled apart. "You, Penn, the nation, and getting even with the Chinese is all I care about right now. It's my responsibility to do the right thing. Going in is that right thing."

"Tomorrow is Sunday. We're going to church."

"No," he said.

"What?" Penn sputtered.

"I go tonight. You know what to do if I don't call."

She nodded. "Pappa isn't going, is he?"

"He's the leader in my absence. Please don't tell Momma Emiline."

"Of course, I'll tell her." She wagged a finger at him. "Don't ever lie to a root doctor."

Trey pulled under the carport. They embraced. "Come back to me," she said, and kissed him hard. "We will pray for you, Momma Emiline and me."

"I'll call, promise," he said. "I love you."

On the way to Jonah's Place, Trey bought supper at McDonalds ordering three extra bottles of water. The water from the well at Jonah's Place tasted and smelled of rotten eggs. He'd been back to the rental only once three days before to check on Lucius' repair of the blue front door. Of course, the work had been done beautifully.

He repositioned the mattress on the bed, found a pillow in the corner by a drawer, and lay down on the disheveled bed that Penn once made so neatly. Trey napped for a couple of hours. He awoke feeling refreshed and ready to go. His body thrummed with anticipation, danger a fresh dose of an addictive drug.

He set to the disciplined ritual of suiting up for battle.

The first step was to black his face. Next, Trey stuffed ammunition and equipment into a roomy camo backpack, and buckled on a utility belt that held more ammo clips, more shotgun shells arrayed in special loops, and a long knife he'd owned since basic training. A holster for the Glock finished the belt. He went out into the night to check the F-150 to make sure the Kevlar vest was stowed in the covered bed of the truck as well as Pedro's compound reflex bow designed with a wheel on both ends and mounted with a scope and a quiver of broad arrows. Among the weaponry was the 12-gauge, and the shield. He went back inside where he pulled on a lightweight camo tunic outfitted with a ton of closable pockets, waterproof boots, and an Atlanta Falcons hat.

All the while he was geared up, he went over and over his strategy in the understanding that no battle plan ever went off as initially designed. Whether he lived or died depended on his ability to think on his feet. He checked the charge of his disposable cellphone. The device had a decisive role in the evening's festivities. He almost forgot to silence it, but remembered at the last instant averting potential disaster. The phone was stuffed into a Ziploc bag and put in the top left Velcro closable shirt pocket.

His mind strayed from business to Penn, her face, her smell. An image of his mother shaking an accusatory finger at him flashed in his head. He could hear Thelma say, "Your father prayed every day. You should too, young man." For the first time in preparation for battle, Trey dropped to his knees, reflexively crossed himself, and prayed for Penn, and Caleb, and Thelma, and for, Robert' the father he never met, and Cerberus, and the Smith's. "Lord, please keep my family safe. I beseech you to hold Penn's hand, and Caleb, too, if you can hear me little guy, your father loves you, and Mom, that goes for you too." Trey choked on the words. "Thanks be to God, and, I guess, amen," he finished in a voice roughed by love.

(30)

Wei Luezing, MD, loathed his current posting in what he considered the unwashed anus of the world, South Carolina. He detested the climate, the tedious routine of office visits to examine patients afflicted with nothing more interesting than a cold, and, especially, he loathed leaving a lucrative practice in Hong Kong because he received unappealable orders from the State Food and Drug Administration. Dr. Luezing held two degrees from the prestigious Peking University Health Science Center, one in internal medicine, the other in oncology and now, of all things, he had to take seriously the psychosomatic wailings of a neurotic Commandant.

"I think I've gone mad," Li Ling complained to the doctor. The chunky man sat on the end of the examining table stripped to his underwear. "I can't sleep and when I do this thing, this old hag, abuses me then sits atop the bedpost with one red eye staring, all the time staring ... staring."

"I am aware of your erratic behavior, sir. That is why I asked you to come see me." He listened to his patient's heart and lung function, palpated his back, and probed the fleshy belly. "Any aches, pains, headache?" he asked finding nothing.

"No, just this thing. I haven't slept in four days. Since it is always dark in the confines of our dormitories, this plateye, this monster never sleeps and when I do it wakes me doing the vilest things." Li Ling slid off the table. He paced around the exam room thoroughly distracted.

"Colonel," the doctor said and when he didn't answer, Dr. Luezing said it louder nearly shouting. "Colonel!"

"Yes, what is it?" Li Ling finally said both dazed and annoyed.

"Please, sit, sir, you're making me nervous."

"Alright."

"Commandant, I believe you suffer from stress, overwork, and sleep deprivation. I will order the pharmacy to deliver medicine to your quarters to help you rest. In the meantime, I shall file a report with the Executive Commander –"

Li Ling cut him off. "You do and I will have your head, no, a brilliant idea arrived. Better yet, I shall put my pet alligator to work, a glorious ten-footer, like me, a killing machine who lives just up the road in one of those foul freshwater lagoons. It will be great fun watching you try to outswim it."

The Colonel went back to his digs dreading de plateye. As soon as he opened the door, it let out a scream of joy as de clever monkey plateye tilted its big head and howled. It flew off the bedpost. On the way, de plateye morphed from the clever monkey to the hag. It plastered the Colonel with its fleshy body knocking him over.

"I am thrilled you're home, young soldier," it said as de plateye drained more of Li Ling's soul.

A knock came to the door. De plateye flew back to the bedpost to become the clever monkey leaving a misty contrail. It was the courier from the pharmacy. Snatching the plastic bottles out of the courier's hands, Li Ling went directly to the bathroom, opened the bottles, didn't bother to read the directions, and chewed three of each washing them down with 10,000-year-old water. Within seconds, the chemicals began to fuzz the edges of de plateye. The clever monkey first lost its tail, then its feet, then the body, but the head remained even after five or six minutes.

"See, you aren't real," Li Ling said triumphantly.

"Oh, but Colonel," de plateye said, "this is only the beginning of wonderful, not the end. I'll tell you one thing I will do for you. I'll give you a treasured piece of advice. My sweet sticky buns, you ride your staff like they are step-children. I will leave you be if you ease up on the people. Stop ruling by fear. Rule from respect."

"I agree," Li Ling said hoarsely. He was fuzzy but liberated and fell getting up from the couch only to regain his equilibrium with difficulty. The Colonel bumped from wall to wall down the hall. Ecstatic, relieved, joyous to be free, off he wobbled on the way to the command center.

On wooden legs, Li Ling went unsteadily to the middle of the room and entered the control post. He spoke into the mic in a soothing, drowsy monotone, "There is no God," he announced in a gentle voice. "There is no Heaven, no Nirvana, or Paradise. We have glorious China instead. Our President, our most beloved, our revered, our sacred Hua Jungxing fulfills all our needs; healthcare, nourishment, housing, transportation, education; all the elements of a good and serving life. Most of you have no idea what we really do in our happy plant. I tell you in broad terms; we help make China the greatest military and economic power the world has ever known. I fail to tell you often enough how much your service means to China and to me, this your benevolent Commandant. We are all a very long way from our families. My trusted friends, you work too hard," he said, chortling.

"Therefore, I declare that all personnel are ordered to stand down by half. We are winning; therefore, we have no reason to overwork ourselves. In our never-ending quest to provide something uniquely powerful for our China, something no one else will ever have, minerals come up from the earth to put China in the front of all nations. Because of what we do every day, I can tell you with extreme and unwavering certainty the United States of America is finished because of the honorable work you do daily. Enjoy the respite, my people, as I enjoy a respite of my own."

(31)

Trey drove to Monk's Corner where he wheeled into the Beaufort County Municipal Airport looking for Hanger 4. It was the only one lit that late night. A single prop aircraft idled on the apron waiting for him. A dark figure got out of the cabin and came toward the F-150.

"Pompeii Thornton," the Gullah man said holding out a big hand.

"Trey Dawson."

"I seen you in church that time," Pompeii said. "Can I help with your gear?"

They took the equipment to the crimson plane whose fuselage advertised Low Country Jump School and stowed the gear in the area behind the seats, climbed in, and started to taxi.

"Thanks for doing this. We appreciate it," Trey yelled above the noise.

"We all in this together, Colonel Dawson. That's right," Pompeii said.

"Nice old plane you got here."

"Yeah, this here, she my baby. A '44 Stinson. What with the high over-wing, it's nigh unto perfect to jump from."

"Denmark told me you had an MC-1 chute," said Trey as the Stinson arrived at the end of the only runway.

"Yes, sir. My personal favorite. Aw-right, we're about to takeoff, so, if you would, I need to concentrate 'til we reach altitude."

Pompeii throttled up. Glued to the mid-line, the Stinson used only a third of the runway and was lifted skyward as light as a leaf on an autumn wind. In the light crosswinds, the Stinson bobbed and weaved as she rose into the night. Trey felt a twinge of familiar fear. The mission had begun, yet the pang was particularly acute now that Penn was in his life. He had a lot more to lose than his tours of duty carried. Back then, he had only Ned maybe somewhere in Arizona. Aunt Mimi was long gone having passed from ovarian cancer a year before he enlisted, an ironically cruel way to go for a woman who never conceived.

At five thousand feet, Pompeii pushed the yoke in and leveled her out.

"Aw-right, then," he said to the windscreen. "No worries, Colonel. Denmark likely told you, but I served with the 101st Airborne Division out of Ft. Campbell for two tours. Did lots of jumps, combat or otherwise, plus they taught me how to drive a plane. I own this jump school now, give instructions to the tourists, you know. Strange how folks will pay good money to fall out of planes."

"The night selector on the chute's altimeter in working condition?" asked Trey.

"Of course."

Few lights were on at this hour in the Low Country other than the reddish hue of the horizon evidencing Savannah to the south and Charleston to the north.

"What altitude are you thinking about for the jump?" Trey yelled.

"1,200."

"Yeah, I agree. This outfit I'm after has a fleet of drones capable of laser fire as well as air-to-ground missiles. I sure as hell don't relish the idea of becoming target practice during a long descent."

"Yes, sir. Denmark, he say so. I planned on coming in at 5,000 then dead stick it to 1,200, get you gone, then gun it for all the old gal is worth to higher altitudes on the way home. Drones don't operate so good above 1,000 feet."

"Even with the danger, you still volunteered to help us. I can't tell you how much that means to me."

"Right is right, Colonel. She a Gullah treasure, yes, sir, that Penn Smith. I hear they tried to kill her like the Romans did to Cleopatra with an asp in her bed."

"I appreciate what you're doing," Trey said betraying nothing about the Copperhead.

"What's our ETA?"

Pompeii looked at the array of modernized navigational instruments. "Twelve minutes."

"Whew. Better get my tail in gear."

Trey climbed into the parachute with difficulty. The inflexible Kevlar vest under his shirt plus a cartridge belt made him feel exactly like a stuffed sausage.

"If you don't mind my asking," Pompeii said, his face illumined by the red and green instrument lights, "why a bow and arrow?"

Trey laughed. "What's old is new. Call it stealth technology."

"Aw-right, now, you got eight minutes."

Trey did a mental check of his equipment then opened his cellphone to glance at the weather. Winds were out of the SSW at five to fifteen knots with clear skies.

"Position yourself, Colonel, I'm fixin' to dive," Pompeii called out. "When the time it come, and we smooth, I will give you a verbal countdown starting at three and ending at one." The engine sputtered, spooled to idle, and the Stinson tipped over.

His belly churning, Trey gave Pompeii a thumbs-up.

The lights that surrounded the plant could be seen out the windscreen.

"The jump light is lit," Pompeii yelled above the wind. "Aw-right, here we go. I give you three … two … one, jump!"

Trey fell into the blackness. Stars were his companions as he quickly released the chute before he picked up too much speed. The nylon filled above him with a resounding pop that jolted him. He reached for the hand grips on the left and right that would allow him to steer to his objective; the roof of the building that was such a mystery to him and Penn.

Quickly, it became clear Pompeii misjudged the drop time, that, or the winds picked up. Trey was way short. He had to go firm right but fast. In his anxiety, he pulled too hard on the cord. It came loose in his hand. Trey did the only thing he could. He yanked on the right harness strap. It helped, but another gust pushed him even further toward the razor wire chain-linked fence. He was going to miss and miss big. The only question was by how much.

He hit the ground a good fifty feet away from the plant's north façade, tried to roll as he had been taught, but was pulled backward sharply. The parachute was ensnared in the razor wire. He listened to his body to assess any damage. His right shoulder hurt and the stump for the prosthesis ached, but then, when didn't it? Vulnerable out in the open, he instantly decided to leave the chute where it was and not waste time cutting it free, yet the harness was another matter. The main release coupling didn't work so he pulled his combat knife from its sheath on the web mesh belt and cut the nylon reinforced webbing. Free, he ran for the north wall. There was no way for him to know it but the destaffing ordered by the Colonel meant fewer eyes on electronic surveillance of the perimeter. No one had fired at him yet. That was a good sign.

Panting from the exertion, nervousness, and an over-abundance of adrenalin, Trey scrounged in his backpack and came out with a coil of twisted steel rope tipped by a featherweight titanium grappling hook designed for rock climbing.

He understood that if the technicians who serviced the drones reemerged too early, the noise of the hook landing on the roof would kill the raid as well as him. He wound up like King David standing before Goliath revving his slingshot to toss the rope over the top of a low wall surrounding the rooftop at whose base were a series of pipes he noticed on satellite imagery. The first toss came away with only air. He reeled it back.

"Come on, baby," he whispered and tossed it again.

This time it stuck.

Trey walked up the windowless wall. He was cautious. He peered over the edge. No one was outside! He finished climbing and took cover behind a series of commercial air conditioning condensers. The bow was readied. Five arrows tipped by wickedly sharp broadheads were locked into a specially designed, notched carrier along the median length of the bow to facilitate quick firing.

Trey found an opening between the condenser units that gave an unencumbered line of sight to the landing zone. The metal shield ready, he hunkered down waiting for his chance. If the shield didn't work, he was about to be fried.

Half an hour passed, precious minutes lost as the clock raced to the fail-safe 0600. He questioned whether he had given himself enough time to complete the mission, but then, a mule drone whirred overhead, floated momentarily, and landed. Saddlebags were clearly evident in the wash of light. When the fans shut down, three technicians popped out of their station thirty feet away.

Trey nocked an arrow, stepped from behind the unit to sight the scope, and let fly. The first arrow pierced the man's throat, the broadhead passing clean through the neck. He looked surprised before he died. The carotid must have been severed. Blood spurted in rhythm with the last beatings of the dead man's heart. The second soldier died instantly of a chest shot, but the third arrow hit the wall next to the frantic technician fleeing for his life. Trey nocked another. This time the arrow found the last soldier's skull at the back. The broadhead protruded from his forehead.

Because of the stealth of the ancient weapon, Gu Shui Industries' drones and proximate security heard nothing that would betray his presence.

Wary in case the drone awoke, Trey advanced on the sleeping machine leading with the Glock in case more than three soldiers were on this detail. Unfastening one of the two saddlebags the size and shape of a brick, Trey found brown powder inside then zippered it closed to stash it in his backpack. The drone was turned into scrap metal.

As Trey stood over the wreckage, above the noise of the air conditioner units, he heard another drone. It zipped over his head then reversed, lasers lit. He dove behind an air conditioning unit. A wide shot caught the unit next to him on fire. Flames and smoke rolled from the unit. Trey grasped Coach Love's shield to hold it between him and the attacking drone then inched on his butt toward the door. He could feel both the heat and the power of the laser pulses that silently slammed the steel. Errant shots meant for him sizzled the prostrate technicians burning holes through their uniforms and frying their skin. The smell of roasted human flesh nauseated Trey. And then the drone flew off. Hhe guessed it ran low on juice and had intended to land to take on new batteries.

In the calm, Trey struggled to drag the largest of the dead men to the entrance still warm from a quick death. He caught a break. The Chinese built a short roof over the doors.

Another drone flew in. Its laser cannons caught the roof on fire. Expecting more drone strikes, he unslung the 12-gauge just in time. The remote Chinese pilot of one of the machines took a chance and drove it down to three feet off the rooftop and opened up on him. Using the dead ChiCom as an additional shield, Trey blew the drone away with two shotgun blasts. Unmolested, he stripped the largest man's uniform except for the boots. Trey wore 13E. This guy might have been a 9. He climbed into the jumpsuit to complete the ruse.

The shotgun at his hip, ready for anything, he entered the plant.

The room was small, maybe 20 X 20, and uninhabited. A battery charger station occupied a far corner. Trey spotted cameras in opposing corners. He blasted them. Claxons blared outside the door. Excited orders hailed from the PA.

Trey smelled war, his to win or lose, the kinds of terms he understood.

Second in command, Lt. Colonel, Liu Shen, was livid at the helm of the command center. Its walls were covered with video screens, all but two of which gave live feeds of the plant. The air zinged with tension.

Nothing was going right.

"What do you mean he's asleep?" Liu Shen bellowed. Veins popped out of his thin neck.

"The doctor gave him medicine to help our Commandant sleep," a junior grade officer replied.

"You donkey! Beat down the door! Now! We are under attack."

Liu Shen picked up the microphone, depressed the red button, and said, "Sector seven, sector seven, red alert, intruder, repeat, intruder, an American law breaker. Capture if possible. Otherwise kill him."

Liu Shen turned over in his mind if he should call his superior at the Department of Military Defense in Beijing but thought better of it. One point everyone in the plant agreed on; if you wanted to live and not die a disgusting death, you never went over the Commandant's head.

Liu Shen settled to the fact that a return to full force could not happen until Colonel Ling gave the order. How long would that take? He was stymied by both military protocol as well as personal risk. Until the Commandant was deemed incapacitated by a competent medical professional, he had no choice but to deal with Trey as best he could with what he had. A thought came to him. He opened a file of internal telephone numbers. On the third ring a sleepy Dr. Luezing picked up. "Doctor, this is Liu Shen, acting Commandant. You met with Colonel Ling yesterday. Is that right?"

"I did."

"What was his condition?"

There was a pause before the doctor answered in careful words. "I recall you have a wife and children as do I. Our Colonel is well enough to do his job," the doctor said and hung-up.

(32)

Trey picked his way toward the mystery room moving along a catwalk high above the floor of the area. The disposable phone was held to his ear. It was 0532.

"I'm in," he whispered. "I have a sample. Penn, Penn; no time for that. The room you said contained water purification systems is filled with the type of centrifuges used in uranium enrichment. There must be a hundred of them. I'm gone, sweetheart. Yes, yes, I know the brown stuff could be radioactive. Penn, stop now, please don't be upset. Think about what we're going to name our first baby? I love you," he said and dropped the call.

Penn ran downstairs. Her father sat at the kitchen table gazing off into space. The radio this morning was mute.

"Time to go?" he asked when he saw the wreck that was her face.

"Yes, and Pappa, I'm just as qualified as anyone," she said, "plus, I've had more training than most of our men."

"Get the Kevlar on," her father said. He rose and went to the wall phone to alert Roscoe Tanner. It turned out the Posse were in three trucks parked at the entrance to the farm chewing the fat with Virgil, a man Roscoe Tanner arrested and convicted of grand larceny auto theft twenty-one years ago.

"I'm goin' to ring the bell now," he said to Penn.

Momma Emiline came in covering her ears with her hands to block out the peels. She went to Penn and embraced her. "Oh, dear Lord," she said, her hand raised to cover her mouth. "While you play man, I pray to our Lord and the ancestors to bring you home safe."

The same bell that once called them to the fields before Emancipation continued to peel in the dark; three long, three short, three long, three short.

They met in the tobacco barn. Denmark's headlights shone on the group. "We go," he said. "Everyone know they jobs? Right? Lucius, you and Pedro are the spearpoint. The rest of us, we follow."

Roscoe Tanner stepped into the light. He and the rest of the six-man Posse wore Kevlar and each carried an AR-15 semi-automatic assault rifle. "Time is important so I keep this tight. Yo, Billie," he said to one of his men. A high-rise string bean who came forward passed out Kevlar vests to the Smith's. "You men are gonna need these," predicted Tanner. "Plus, plus I got three dynamite bundles, you know, for party favors. I'm counting on all ya'll. Got it? Denmark, the Posse, we gone."

Denmark scanned the Smith's, got unanimous thumbs-up, and said, "Three trucks, you, Pedro and Lucius in the lead, the rest of us in the others. God's speed, men."

Penn rode shotgun with her father. A 12-gauge and two deer rifles hung on a gunrack behind her head. She called Cal Hubbard. No one picked up.

Four Chinese soldiers over in the corner below Trey loaded onto an elevator. All of them held long guns. He figured they were on the way to meet him for a little chat. Trey pulled down a weighted ladder that led to yet another level above him probably there to facilitate changing light bulbs on the ceiling fixtures. He climbed it then ran in the opposite direction as the team coming at him. He could feel the prosthetic go wonky but he pushed on ignoring the shooting pains each step as Trey headed for he knew not what.

Suddenly the walkway's iron mesh vibrated with men's boots. They were coming at him. He hid behind a structural abutment. They came closer and closer trotting past his position. Trey unloaded a magazine of steel shot. Two dead soldiers were blown off the walkway to tumble to the cement floor falling on a couple of the centrifuges that clattered to a stop, brown dust everywhere. More claxons wailed.

Trey stepped over the bodies and kept moving until he came to another weighted, maintenance ladder that led to the centrifuge floor. The space that appeared to be unoccupied, no doubt a tribute to the Chinese proclivity to use robots instead of humans. The climb down was hairy. He was target practice should they spot him, but he made it.

Penn's phone buzzed. She had never bothered synching it with her father's new truck. She swiped it in the hope it was Trey. It wasn't. "Morning, Major Hubbard. I have you on speaker phone with ---"

Hub cut her off. "Where's Trey?" he demanded, an edge to his voice.

"What?" Penn stammered, taken off guard but she forged on concentrating on giving the military information Trey needed to convey. "I talked with Trey. He said to tell you we have breeched a company called Gu Shui Industries near Franklin, South Carolina. Trey asked that you furnish the GPS coordinates and send two Marine helo attack squads to assist in operations to take the building over. In addition, he asked that an Apache guard the perimeter. This company is a threat to the sovereignty of the United States."

"He's inside, isn't he?"

"Yes. You know him as well as anyone. I called fifteen minutes ago. You were supposed to be on alert."

"Yeah, yeah," Hub said. "Listen, do you remember that glove he found aboard the *Edge of Heaven*?"

"Of course."

"I sent it to a specialty chemist in Oak Ridge, Tennessee and forgot about it," he said hiding the fact he had the alarming results for quite a while. "I didn't put a rush on it," he added for good measure extending the lie.

"Why not?"

"Because, frankly, I was pissed off with Trey for getting me involved in something I have no business doing. I've had it with him. It's always about his needs, not mine."

"So, you have no results?" said Penn.

"Bingo."

"You don't know if they are or aren't legal."

"Yup, you broke the code."

"Hubbard?" Denmark said.

"Who are you?"

"This is Penn's father. We got us a dozen men and my daughter within five minutes of the place."

"Oh, for the love of God! Do not, I repeat, do not breach Chinese property. You imbeciles will buy us a Third World War."

"You'd be surprised what a woman and a bunch of old men can do," Denmark said.

"Amazing, truly amazing. Do not confront the Chinese!"

"Too late," Denmark told him.

"As usual, Trey will get all the accolades and I'll be court-martialed. No doubt the perfect bastard left instructions for his lackey boy."

"His plan was to enter the north side of the building," Penn told the Major, "on the rooftop where drones are serviced. Trey has all the physical evidence we need. This place is dirty. Send in the Marines, Major."

The circle at the bottom of the cellphone screen went red.

(34)

Trey walked through the centrifuge room as though he belonged in it doing the classic bootleg football move to hide the shotgun from cameras he felt sure followed his every move. A double door exit was at the back of the room but his memory told him not to go there. It led into the main offices. You could bet Li Ling would not be doing paperwork. If he could find the way out to the garden that would put him reasonably close to the north wall where he could recover the grappling hook to get him the hell out of there. His objectives were met except for the capture of Li Ling. He envisioned scaling the fence and hunkering down in a protected place to wait for the militia. The chances he would take against a diminished drone squadron were better than staying inside to be cornered by their cameras.

He felt the Chinese bear down on him, a sixth sense that saved his peaches many times. He spotted an exit with a red light above it in the far corner. Next to it was a bank of electrical boxes. He tried the door. It was locked. Chinese characters covered the surface that he guessed read – Use Only in Emergency. Surely his militia was close. He shoved more shotgun shells in the box magazine of the 12-gauge, used two to demolish the latching system and the rest were pumped into the electrical box's cabling. Sparks arced from them. The centrifuges stopped spinning and the irritating claxons ended. Because the mystery room was designed with no windows, it went coal mine dark.

Trey slammed his good foot at what had been the lock of the emergency exit.

As they had agreed in the barn, the militia convoy parked off the road on the grassy shoulder just short of the Gu Shui campus. Pedro and Lucius got out of Matilda. They picked up reflex bows and two quivers of arrows and off they went in a crouch seeking the heavy vegetation on the sides of the dirt road for cover. Thirty feet away from the guard posts, undetected, Lucius put a hand up. Both guards were riveted to their computer screens by what little they could now see of the interior. Pedro dug into a flapped pocket to take out a handful of rocks just the right size to throw. The first one sailed through the night air then a second and a third. The sentries jumped out of the guard post, weapons drawn. Seeing nothing, they looked into the sky for clues to what had just happened. Pedro and Lucius slipped away from their cover, drew bows, and sent silent death to the Chinese. They fell pulling at the shafts, writhing in agony, their wounds mortal.

Pedro unholstered his pistol to shoot two rounds in the air.

They advanced on the downed men. Neither moved.

The two pick-ups hurtled toward them. Lucius nocked another arrow. He stole a glance at the trucks. It was then that one of the Chinese got off two shots at Lucius, one hit his left arm, the other ripped through the upper thigh close to the groin where the femoral artery was slashed.

Pedro put three rounds in the shooter's body.

Lucius sat groaning in the dust where a growing black circle of blood soaked into the earth. "Cain't rise up none," he said to his nephew. "When you done, pick me up. You a good boy, Pedro. Go on. They here."

Pedro put a meaty hand on his uncle's shoulder. "I see you on the other side, uncle. The Lord and I love you."

Pedro vaulted the fender of Roscoe Tanner's pick-up. Tanner gunned the big V-8, bumped over the bodies of the fallen guards, busted through the gate, and steered for the front entrance.

The Hemi skidded to a stop. Denmark got out. He kneeled next to his brother. "Come on which us, now. You be fine."

"No, that ain't so. I want you should go. Pick these –" Lucius groaned. "Pick these ole bones up on the way home maybe. Go on, now. I love you, my brother."

Denmark stood and hurried to the truck. "He'll be fine," Denmark said to Penn although he knew it was not the truth. They hurried after Tanner's speeding truck.

"Willie, get that satchel ready," Tanner yelled above the roar and came to a skidding stop at the front entrance encountering no resistance.

Long, tall Willie jumped off the bed and ran to the glass front doors then raced along a wall to the left to avoid being hit by glass blowback, the shaped charges specifically prepared to blast in a focused direction rather than a big boom that covered 360 degrees. Tanner and Denmark drove trucks to the end of the east wall.

Nothing happened. A minute clicked by then another, then another.

"Well, I'll be go to hell," Tanner said.

Penn got out of the truck. Standing on the running board, she sighted-in a 30-06 hunting rifle and scope. Side mirror supports became a muzzle rest. "Fire in the hole," Penn yelled pulling off a shot. The satchel atomized. Four sticks of dynamite erupted in yellow, orange, and red flames. Debris rained all over the compound. The entire vestibule and office suites were gone all the way to the entrance to the bottling line.

On the other side of the exit from the centrifuge room, six soldiers leveled AK-47s at Trey, three knelt, three stood firing squad style.

"Drop your weapons, Lawson," demanded Liu Shen.

Trey glared at him. "It's Dawson, lame brain. You've herded me out here to Ling Ling's Garden of Eden, haven't you?"

"I said, drop your weapons," the officer shrilled a pleased smirk on his face that confirmed Trey's suspicion.

No choice left, Trey did as he was ordered.

"Knife and pistol, too," the officer said. "Up, the hands up, now, turn around. Face the building where video cameras can record this." Trey hesitated, "I said turn around, don't you understand English?"

Trey did what he was told.

An arm held aloft, Liu Shen yelled "Fire!" in synch with the explosion of Billie's first satchel charge.

Denmark and four men, some Smith's, some Posse to include Dexter Love, jumped out of the truck. "Tanner, you and the rest take the left. We take the right. Now, we huntin' for the head of the snake."

Working cautiously, each office that was yet intact on the corridor was swept. They encountered no resistance but the double door entrance to the darkened bottling line where all the lights were out was a different story.

"They set a trap," Denmark said. "Lure us in to the killin' field. Hold behind the wall. Say, Virgil, chuck that chair by you into the big room. Go on now."

Virgil took hold of a twisted desk chair to toss it into the cavernous room. Semi-automatic fire and what sounded like a heavy machine gun ripped it apart. The ChiComs were decidedly jumpy.

"Which way did the chair hop?" Tanner asked.

"Left to right," Clem Dexter said. "Means the bastards are to the left as we go in."

"Aw-right, great call Denmark," Tanner said with a big smile. "Willie, me boy. Plunk your magic twanger, son. Chuck one up under the bottling machine to the left and, now, listen up, all ya'll, we use the blast for cover. Once inside, hide behind the equipment, stacks of water bottles, anything, AR-15s on full automatic, shotguns pumping like billy hell. Colonel Dawson said there might be stacks of filled water bottles toward the walls. If so, find them. It'll be all the better for us. The lights are out save exit signs. That gives us an advantage. You men on this side of the door go with me, other side, go with Denmark. Figure out where the fire comes from. Run away from it and take defensive positions. They have automatic weapons too but we gotta spray them hard as soon as we get in. In the chaos, Posse members are to toss grenades as you take your position. That should give us enough light to set up a firing line as well as to encourage them to duck their pinheads."

"Don't bunch. Keep spacing," Denmark added his training from long ago resurfacing. "We got to take out the muzzle flashes. Fire and move, fire and move."

"Poppa," Penn said in his ear. "I'm headed back outside to look for Trey." Before her father could object, Penn sprinted for the entrance.

Acting like he did this every day of the world, a stoic Willie armed the satchel charge then gave the squad a verbal countdown,

Willie's khaki satchel frisbeed into the big room. The explosion shook the building. It rained dust and debris. Somewhere a loud sound of water escaping a pipe under high pressure came to the men, but the more dominant sound became the moans of Chinese casualties.

Of the six rifles pointed at Trey, two fired rounds that impacted Trey's prosthesis, tore it clean off the stump rendering the appliance scrap metal. What flesh was left of his leg blazed with pain. He thought the shock very likely shattered it. Trey thrashed on the ground in agony, righted himself, and in a fury chucked the bent piece of junk that had been his artificial leg at his tormentors.

"You got company, assholes," snarled Trey. "Did you hear that? Out front, my family is here to welcome ya'll to hell."

"Get up," Liu Shen said.

Trey struggled, managed to get to a crouch, and tried to raise himself, but fell back with a grunt. Liu Shen kicked him in the side with a steel-toed boot. Breaking ribs could plainly be heard. Trey cried out in pain.

"Get up," Liu Shen said gritting his teeth.

Trey kneeled on the good leg then gave a mighty heave with all he had groaning as he righted himself, hopping to maintain his balance using the burnt and scarred shield to steady himself.

"You, American, you come in the front with me."

The pea gravel on the path was deep. His whole body ached screaming at him to stop, but he endured. Dancing on the rim of shock, he hallucinated. The green of the grass and the halo of yellow light that streamed from tall metal poles reminded Trey of night baseball games on flawless summer evenings with not a care, the illuminated green space the limits of the immediate world delimited by the wattage of the nightlights. Maybe he was losing it, but he swore he was about to relieve the pitcher. Coach Love, a chewed White Owl blunt in the corner of his mouth, held the ball out to him.

Trey stumbled and fell curling up in the fetal position in preparation for the next brutality. Liu Shen kicked Trey repeatedly.

"American dog!" he yelled each time.

"Bite me," Trey grunted. "I get the message. Alright, I'll get up."

They rounded a bend where Li Ling circled the snake cage antagonizing the Devil's pets. He pulled at his hair, skipped around it like a child, all the while looping in Gullah, "De plateye he dead, dat right, he dead. Naw what we got here?" he said turning from the snakes to Trey. "I knew you would seek beauty out to my wilderness with other wild animals, Lawson. Your name, Lawson, right?" Li Ling said, chuckling then his round face became stone. "You fine with a fight with my friends, your neighbor the Diamondback Rattler?"

The Chinese Colonel came to Trey and stood nose-to-nose, impassive, his fists balled at his side. He hit Trey in the face. .

Trey went down.

There was nothing but whiteness all around.

(35)

Penn prayed as she ran along the east wall, the shotgun and the 30-06 Springfield clacking together slung over her shoulder. The sounds of a fierce firefight reached her from inside the plant.

"Dearest Lord, I beseech you that we militia do not die this morning as your day clean arises just as your Son did to give light to your world. Praise you and please dear Lord, preserve my Trey and Poppa. Amen."

She turned the corner. The shiny braided rope was a silvered line down the middle of the north façade. Penn put one gloved hand above another and climbed with skill. As Trey had done, she stopped at the top to peer cautiously over the rim. Once over the wall, her senses on overdrive, Penn armed her Glock. She took in the arrow-shot dead soldiers, the smoldering air conditioning unit, and the roof.

Voices came from the ground below, Chinese voices, and they were none too happy.

Dawn brought a wan natural light into the bottling area as the old men ran like they were 18 again, their primordial battle cries echoed in the hall, sounds unheard in the Low Country since the Civil War. A machine gun opened up on them spraying heavy rounds, a big one, maybe a .50 caliber. Shots pinged off the metal equipment making the concrete floor come alive with deadly fireflies. A Gullah went down. Two Posse members dragged him to refuge. Another Posse member wailed, "Hit!" Confusion. Chaos. Still too dark to make out faces. They fought as one.

The Posse and the Smith Militia absorbed bullet strikes to torsos or sides, bruising ribs and bellies, the Kevlar designed for just this kind of tactical situation. Another fighter cried out in pain yet the rag-tag coalition returned fire as best they could, angry hornets whizzing by their heads, some impacting metal with a zing much like a sword withdrawn from a scabbard.

"Cover fire," Tanner shouted. The militia lit the place up with as much firepower as they had. "Now, Willie!" Tanner yelled.

Willie stood and did his David and Goliath wind-up building centrifugal force and let fly the last satchel at the machine gun nest. Illuminated in the dim light by the flash, the men could see parts of three bodies rise in the air in slow motion. Cordite smoke was thick laced with the coppery smell of blood and earthy feces of partly digested rice. Willie's toss, reduced in half hostile fire. The Posse and the Smith Militia now outnumbered the Chinese. Juno and Clem and Pedro calmly sighted in their deer rifles picking muzzle flashes until no more resistance returned fire except for one, a stubborn shooter hidden behind the bottling line control panel who spit sporadic fire.

"Hey, sports fans," Coach Clem yelled, "I got one grenade left. Watch this high hard one." And with that, he pulled the pin, stood, and tossed the pill. "Strike three, sucker, you're out of here!" Coach Clem gloated until three bullet strikes to his upper chest sent him flying backwards. The grenade exploded against the south wall.

Quincy crawled on his knees and elbows to where Coach Clem lay moaning.

"Hit?" he asked in his normal economy of words.

"Yeah, slapped the crap out of me."

"Kin you move?"

"Maybe tomorrow."

"Here, my hand."

Quincy pulled Coach to cover, raised him to a sitting position, and put an arm around his shoulders.

"Man, nice throw," Quincy said.

Chinese opposition ended in the next few minutes. Excluding the groans of wounded or dying men, the place was graveyard quiet. Three unarmed Chinese walked out of the smoke with their hands in the air. "No shoot, no shoot," one of them said. Two of the three had been hit. Blood soaked one's left arm, the other had a head wound.

They'd live as long as they stayed in America.

Li Ling stood over Trey, his stubby arms crossed and a foot on Trey's heaving chest. "Your foolish scheme will not end well. Americans are jesters. Americans cannot match Chinese. You are a thoroughly degraded and impure race damaged by inbreeding. Isn't it ironic America dies as the sun rises on the Chinese Empire. Poetic, don't you think?"

"You need a slow death," Trey said getting to his feet with great difficulty. Blood streamed from his broken nose to flow over his lips. He blew air out of his mouth to speckle the Commandant's face.

Li Ling responded by smashing a fist just above Trey's left eye. The skin instantly split as did the eye socket underneath. Blood dripped into Trey's left eye. He wobbled, lost his balance then fell heavily on the pea gravel again, but this time he rose to his feet laughing at the ChiCom.

The Commandant put his fists on his hips glaring at Trey. "I'll not hit you again, American. I need your senses intact for the fun ahead. Lawson, you simply must come closer to see my pretties. You pay now."

"That's Dawson, butt lick."

"Ah-h, so it is, Lawson. You," Li Ling meant one of his soldiers. "You, useless soldier, help the prisoner." He indicated the walk-in entrance to the cage.

It was then that Penn fired on Li Ling. She went for a head shot but he moved. The bullet took off his right ear. He stumbled, lost balance, and crashed into the cage. Four thick, triangle-headed snakes slithered to him eagerly striking over and over. Li Ling screamed then went silent with the biggest rattler, at least a seven-footer and as big around as a baseball bat, still attached to his chubby cheek pumping venom from inch-long scimitar fangs. It may have been shock, it may have been that he was already dead, but Li Ling moved no more. His face froze, the eyes forever startled.

Penn squeezed off another round meant for Liu Shen then another. A soft tip load pierced the officer's throat blowing half of it away. Rather than return fire, the soldiers beat feet back into the safety of the plant. Penn let them go. The militia will handle it. She was intent on destroying the snakes before they too scattered or messed with Trey. She hurriedly switched to the shotgun and pumped round after round into the cage. Steel shot contacting the chain link fence sent sparks into the dawning light.

"Trey, up here," Penn cried out.

He waved, grew dizzy then the world went white again. He fell to the ground.

The heavy thunk-thunk-thunk of helos grew closer.

Penn hurried down the metal rope and ran to Trey's side to cover him with kisses.

He was alive!

An Apache attack helicopter loitered over Gu Shui Industries as thirty Marines from two landed Chinooks discharged inside the fence of the compound. Regular Marines out of Parris Island made quick work of mop-up.

Late to the fray, a Marine two-seater scout chopper also landed, but on the west side of the plant. The pilot with helmet still on and pistol in one hand climbed out and trotted to the building to eyeball the perimeter. As the figure turned the corner gaining visual access to the north façade, it saw the dead Chinese officers, the bloodied remains of the Devil's pets, and Penn, her back to the figure, cradling Trey in her lap waiting for medics to come. With pistol armed, the figure set off for the pieta.

Penn wheeled around on a man's voice.

"Where is it?" Mother Hubbard grumbled leveling a .45 at Penn's head. "Come on! Wake the sonofabitch."

"Where is what? Penn said.

"The gold," Hub replied. "Get him awake!"

Penn pinched Trey's pale cheeks. He came around a little.

"Hub, that you? How'd we do?" Trey asked, groggy with pain.

"Where's the gold and don't play me. You of the big bucks, writer, war hero, and what did my service get me? Huh? A shit job patrolling swamps. The idiot Chinese that night we were on the *Edge of Heaven*, they weren't supposed to send drones. They screwed up. That gold shipment was meant for me, not you. Where is it?"

Trey slipped back into unconsciousness.

"In a lockbox at the bank," Penn replied. "Free us and it's yours. You can't possibly escape."

"On your knees," he said arming the pistol.

"Trey, if you can hear me, know that I love you," Penn said. She kissed his cheek and gently lay him on the ground. She kneeled beside him a hand on his heart. "Our Father who art in heaven hallowed be thy name," she prayed, "Thy kingdom ---"

Mother Hubbard put the cold muzzle to the back of Penn's head but before he could pull the trigger, a large caliber rifle bullet tore through his body. Hub was dead before he hit the ground.

Denmark lowered the .308 Winchester.

EPILOGUE

Seven men nursed bruises from hits to their vests to include Virgil whose collarbone was broken by impact through the Kevlar. Higby must have stopped a .50 caliber round because he had what likely were three broken ribs, painful but not serious. Denmark was hit, too. He took a bullet that passed through his bicep breaking the humerus. Two of Tanner's men weren't as fortunate. One was hit in the shin. The joint would need total reconstruction and three operations as did another Posse member who took hits to his knee and thigh. Roscoe Tanner had a finger shot off, as it turned out, the middle one on his right hand. "I cain't be nearly as eloquent as I was," Tanner said as he was tended by a Marine medic. His shadow, String Bean Willie said, "Why, Roscoe, that's enough to make you want to slap your Granny."

On the way back to Smith's Bluff, Coach Love and Pedro lifted Lucius into the back of his brother's Hemi and set him down tenderly. Medics pronounced Lucius dead at the scene. Penn was unaware of her favorite uncle's passing until a day went by. She was busy giving support to Trey who was swarmed by Marine medical personnel. He came away from the fray with serious physical issues. His remainder femur suffered a compound fracture from the impact of the AK-47 rounds. The Chinese boot in the side broke four ribs, two of which punctured his left lung. The face pounding cracked the eye socket, and bruised the left eye. His docs said everything would heal just fine but would require months to mend and many more months in rehab to relearn how to walk again. Penn kept him upbeat.

Chinese casualties were high. Eleven died and twelve were wounded. Six of the survivors petitioned for political asylum in the strong and probably accurate belief their country would put them to sleep. Wei Luezing, MD, was among the asylum seekers. He never saw his family again.

(35)

Diplomatic relations between the two superpowers collapsed. Within twenty-four hours, Washington closed our embassy in Beijing. International stress pushed the temperature of the world to Defcon 3, a tension level not seen since the 1973 Yom Kippur War when the Soviet Union sent a ship steaming to Egypt laden with nuclear weapons intended to turn Israel into glass. Meeting after meeting and myriad news conferences tirelessly dominated the media publicly chewing on the cud of public fear.

Thirty-six hours after the report of the Gu Shui Industries incident, Mary Thomason, American Ambassador to the United Nations, asked for and received permission to address the General Assembly. The former Pennsylvania US Senator stood on the raised dais in front of the familiar wall of verde antique marble, her eyes keen, her resolve annealed like the Pittsburgh steel made in her hometown.

"I stand before you today to inform the world of a threat to the balance of nations," she said. "You have heard by now of a team of local militiamen and a brave American black woman who stormed a Chinese factory in South Carolina that produces not just the water they shipped back to China, but something far, far more dangerous to the world's balance of power. A brown powder was found onsite. Chemical analysis of the powder showed it to be a blend of three naturally occurring but exceedingly rare earth minerals. Our chemists reported that the minerals were in an unrefined state but highly concentrated. They cautioned President James Lowry's staff that if mixed in the correct proportions, the black powder would produce laboratory-grown crystals that were capable of becoming the genesis of the most powerful lasers the world has ever known, lasers able to shoot down ICBM's, airplanes, helicopters, burn through the spent uranium armor of our most advanced tanks, and sink aircraft carriers from over the horizon. The unlawful production of such provocative technologies would allow China to use conventional airpower to fire lasers from within the stratosphere to destroy our ability to communicate with one another, in short, the destruction of the western world's satellite fleets. This, ladies and gentleman, places too much capacity in the hands of any one super power.

You must know the United States has limited quantities of the minerals in government stockpile, but not nearly enough to accomplish much more than laboratory experiments. God bless the bravery of our homegrown heroes for preventing an international crisis we have not borne since WWII. I believe the world can agree that no one nation should possess these minerals in abundance. I repeat, no one. The James Lowry administration offers the following solution: Close the site to anything but the production of water and gold. Staff the production center with United Nations personnel to monitor every phase of any ongoing or future production. Not an ounce, not a microgram of minerals should ever be produced again. Today, let us join hands to find a diplomatic solution to this ominous threat to world peace. Thank you, ladies and gentlemen."

Later that day, United Nations staff released estimates of the amount of material Gu Shui Industries produced that ranged from 8.5 kilos to as much as14 kilos. Either extreme was enough to change world order. Through the United Nations, the United States and a long list of allies demanded the Gu Shui inventory be dumped in the Pacific Ocean where repossession would be impossible. In an announcement that surprised the world, Vladimir Putin's Russia locked arms with the United States in a quick accord pledging solidarity. With that, China was effectively rebuffed by all of the world's nuclear powers except North Korea and Iran.

For all intents and purposes, China stood alone.

In the clean-up that followed the raid, sixty-two Chinese nationals were arrested to include the doctor, Wei Luezing, and his staff, Li Ling's gardener, Miss Chen the China doll, and dozens of lower echelon Red Army members. The survivors were bussed to the brig on Parris Island where they were subjected to intensive interrogation by the CIA and the FBI. Of course, Beijing hammered the table for their immediate release. When the plant was running normally, the operating census approved by the State Department was supposed to be twenty-six people such as; engineers, chemists, mechanics, drivers, and the like. No one had any idea how so many foreign nationals could sneak so easily onto American soil as well as the positioning within our borders of sophisticated military drones, cutting-edge radar technology, GPS systems, ammunition, and weapons. Backroom chatter reacted to leaked information that the interrogations exposed a trail of illegal, undisclosed materiel and personnel transported from Chinese container ships.

The first outrageous Chinese provocation was predictable. They disabled one of our military communication satellites then had the gall to say it was an accident. Talking heads on the Sunday news shows suggested the stunt was ordered so that potential antagonists could witness China's superior capabilities and be suitably intimidated, but the Pentagon was less than impressed. Sure, the Generals at the news conference that announced the incident were steely-faced but several couldn't help grin a little at the Chinese for tipping their hand, as well as the crudity of their delivery system. Although the Pentagon never publicly admitted it, they have an ace in the hole. The United States operates a fleet of aircraft that can penetrate outer space and return at will. The SR-72 Aurora scramjet, known in some circles as 'The Son of Blackbird,' is a hypersonic drone capable of air speeds in excess of Mach 5, or said another way, five times the speed of sound. The world's fastest aircraft theoretically could take down all of China's communication satellites in a morning's work and return to base for refueling.

The next outrageous stunt was to increase confrontational naval engagements in the international waters of the South China Sea coupled to the test firing of a new intercontinental ballistic missile cloaked in stealth technology they claimed was developed in close coordination with North Korea and Iran. Public and private discussions of the possibility of a nuclear holocaust were deliberated in every nation. The populations of New York, Washington, Northern Virginia. the North East metroplex, Los Angeles, Dallas/Ft. Worth, Chicago, and anywhere proximate to key military bases shrunk overnight as people fled areas with no-brainer red X's on them. Overnight, it became difficult to find hotel rooms in flyover country and it was impossible to book flights to Canada, Mexico, and the islands of the Caribbean. Hotels and motels were booked solid in Omaha, as was Sheboygan, and Mobile, and Billings, and Abilene.

Nervous diplomats met at the UN to turn the temperature of the planet down in the hope the lids on underground silos could be encouraged to close. As time clicked off the clock, little by little the world took a collective deep breath.

Two months after the incident, intimidated by the forces aligned against them, China signed an agreement brokered by Vladimir Putin and President Lowry that secured 14.2 kilos of the minerals to be securitized by the United Nations. Pundits remarked that Putin helped broker the deal to save his rickety nation from falling further behind in the technology cold war. The same day the United Nations took receipt, the minerals were given to the wind over a one hundred square mile swath of the Pacific Ocean. Nuclear Armageddon was narrowly averted.

One mystery took a while to solve; the puzzle Trey found when he walked atop the mystery room, the same one they were told housed dual water purification systems. At the time, Li Ling led them to a viewing platform. Their eyes and ears told Penn and Shell they saw the towering systems tended by bots, but the reality was what Trey saw; hundreds of clacking centrifuges. How? Quite simply, the Chinese hid their treachery behind a sophisticated hologram. The Pentagon was thrilled by the revelation. The captured projector was rushed to the fabled FBI Laboratory in Quantico, Virginia for dissection.

(36)

The Smith Family and the Posse came to be known throughout the world as The Low Country Thirteen, a group excoriated on some news channels and metropolitan newspapers for being too individualistic to the point of placing the United States on the doorstep of a Third World War. Globalists fumed at the loss of face their devotees believed they had suffered. No, the talking heads reasoned in unison, this should have been accomplished through diplomatic channels in Washington or New York. The Carolina Cowboys, yet another moniker manufactured on-air, were derided daily, ironic because South Carolina was the state where the term 'cowboy' was coined. Globalists were especially unenthusiastic, though, what they would have thought if their children had to fight a war without satellite communication is hard to tell.

However, the vast majority of Americans lifted The Low Country Thirteen to the pedestal on which heroes belong.

The yard bell tolled for Lucius the transitive day of the raid. At the visitation as well as his memorial service, family and friends gathered to send him away to enjoy the perpetual love of his Lord and Savior.

Media swarmed the First Free Baptist Church parking lot the day of the funeral blocking entrances with their satellite trucks. News crews gave live broadcasts for networks across the globe in such quantity that it was impossible for the hearse carrying Lucius to find a parking spot by the side door used for such occasions. The Reverend Owen Potter of the big voice was not pleased that one of his flock was denied the normal, the natural service he would have enjoyed viewed from a front row seat in Heaven compromised by his emergent international fame.

The old church threatened to burst at the seams. Ushers politely refused admittance to non-members and a blanket prohibition on cameras was directed to everyone at the doors. Rather than sing in the choir, Penn stayed at Trey's side. She worried about him, his emotional breakdowns, his periods of blinding hurt, and the amount of pain killers he sometimes had to consume to dial back its intensity. Her doting nature, her abundant love, and the affection of the family Smith healed Trey, albeit slowly. He even had a call from Ned, his older brother now living in Las Vegas. They promised to get together once the dust settled.

Lucius' service was SRO filled by a congregation brimming with hope, convinced by a belief in the rightness of the path to the Lord, and the celebration of a martyr's purposeful life, an American hero, Lucius Aurelius Smith. Roscoe Tanner attended the service, too, as did his wife and the other Posse members and their wives, two of the men, like Trey, in wheelchairs. Trey sat in the aisle next to Penn, and Denmark, and Momma Emiline. Trey fell asleep during Owen Potter's thunderous and patriotic sermon.

The Department of Defense sent their most highly decorated Marine Honor Guard stationed at Camp Pendleton, California to assist the ceremony that included a special jar of sand from Omaha Beach in Normandy. At the Smith Family Cemetery on St. Helena's Island, they accorded Lucius the distinction of a thirteen-gun salute, one volley for each Carolina Cowboy. Trey loved the man with a whole heart, his self-professed caretaker, his re-introducer to the Lord, and the man who delivered him up to Penn. When it came time for the Marine Corporal on the Honor Guard to blow Taps, Trey broke apart in tears. So many good men had died under his command. A stoic Denmark was presented with the flag that draped his brother's coffin.

That afternoon, one hundred and sixty-two mourners attended a feed in Denmark and Momma Emiline's back yard that Smith's would talk about for decades to come. The family agreed that media was to be barred at the entrance to the compound but that did not prevent networks from flying drones over the feed, an ironic development not lost on Penn and Trey.

Two pigs roasted all night over good hickory wood were chopped into barbecue. On a special grate over a post oak fire, twenty chickens grilled. The ladies brought coleslaw, tons of skillet cornbread, baked beans in barbecue sauce, hushpuppies, shrimp and okra, red rice, dirty rice, anything you wanted plus gallons of sweet tea but the bounty of the sea was everyone's favorite. An old-fashioned steel panel over a wood fire helped shovel full after shovel full of sweet Coosaw River oysters steam under a wet burlap sack. Atlantic blue crab by the bushel and extra-large Carolina shrimp and whiting, all came from the bounty of the sea by Pedro's hands. The tender-hearted giant had a lady on his arm. The Gullah say she Evangeline.

"Yes, sir," Momma Emiline said, "the Lord he take, and the Lord he restore, em-huh."

Trey took Mother Hubbard's duplicity hard. The blow softened some when he spoke to Linda, Hub's wife, to express his condolences. It seemed Hub was diagnosed with PTSD two years ago and received therapy a couple of times a week at the VA Hospital in Savannah. According to his counselors, the disease exacerbated a chronic inferiority complex that bedeviled Hub since childhood. It spawned a compulsive gambling addiction that sapped family savings and forced them into debt. The Hubbard's were three months behind on their mortgage, had run through all they put back for their two girls for college, and hawked Linda's grandmother's jewelry to keep the lights on. Plus, Katherine, their special needs daughter, maxed-out her annual medical spending limit with three months to go in the calendar year. Linda exhausted her ability to stop Hub. It was always the next bet, then the next, then this next one would take care of all their financial problems and make him feel better about himself. Of course, it never did. Like other losers, he looked for his money where he lost it. Not even her threat to leave him and take the girls to her parents in Hinsdale, a tony Chicago suburb, worked on Hub.

Trey wrote a check to the bank to bring their mortgage current.

Falling in with the ChiComs was Hub's final big bet. His job necessitated knowledge of those Low Country companies that did business with the Savannah Port Authority to include where their enterprise was located and who ran it. Gu Shui Industries was the only Chinese national business on that roster. The call Hub made after first contact with Trey was to threaten the company with any number of violations; unlicensed drone usage the starter of trouble. He met with an angry Li Ling several times settling on a shakedown for an initial $500,000 in gold coins, bars, or dust, the most fungible asset anywhere in the world with one very distinct advantage, cash sales could be closed at any time and any size to licensed dealers or collectors or hoarders. The cash would first be used to pay off gambling debts. That was transparent. Everyday expenses like gasoline, or groceries, or deposits to replenish raided college savings accounts for the girl could be done in cash, too. Deposits to their checking account were safe as long as they stayed beneath the $10,000 threshold in accordance with Federal anti-money laundering rules. The fact that the ChiComs never made good on a payment was the only reason Hub called in the Marines.

The DOD kept Mother Hubbard's story out of the news by officially stating that a Coast Guard officer was injured in the firefight and that he later died of his wounds. Only then did they release his name but it took months to get that far. Linda said that at first the DOD informed her they planned to erase her retirement benefit, GI life insurance, and military medical insurance. It was then that Trey got to work tirelessly making phone call after phone call advocating for his fallen teammate's family. He maintained that Hub had no idea what he was doing, that his mental condition caused him to develop the gambling addiction, and that it was grossly unfair to withhold a benefit for which he risked his life simply because he was mentally impaired. The arguments took time but they were successful. Linda and the girls received Hub's pension as well as his life insurance proceeds. The house went up for sale. They did indeed move in with her parents in Hinsdale.

As for the whereabouts of the off-campus droneport, GPS data from the wreckage of the broken machine on Gaylord Russell's workbench led to a site a couple of miles outside Hardeeville, South Carolina in a dilapidated but private farmhouse long gone to seed. The worn-out farm had a creaky barn that technicians used for a hangar. Inside, the place was incredibly high tech overloaded with instruments the CIA confiscated even though the ChiComs took pains to bust them with a discarded axe handle. The farmhouse revealed little but they did find four different sets of DNA and fingerprints for which no match could be made in the Federal or Interpol database. Five sabotaged drones were captured.

Investigators were certain the four Chinese drove a stolen vehicle. An oil spot next to the barn was found where the grass was matted and shorter because it received less sunlight underneath the vehicle. No driver's license issuances or vehicles purchased by a green-card Chinese alien had been recorded in the last several years other than the occasional college student. The odds favored an edgy drive to either Charleston or Savannah the morning of the raid, the men eventually were absorbed in the bowels of a Chinese container ship.

The FBI visited every food establishment in the Hardeeville area to ask proprietors if they did business with an Asian man or men who spoke broken English and paid in cash. The single positive response came from Jose Rodriguez at Tienda Maria, a small grocery in a strip center serving the Latino community. Security cameras showed a nervous Asian man perhaps 25, smiling, smiling, smiling, bowing, bowing, bowing, and buying canned food and bags of rice plus household and personal hygiene items.

The damaged drone at the Governor's house gave up yet another secret. Officials determined there was zero evidence they were piloted in the farmhouse. No joystick stations were found. Two-way communication did exist through a satellite dish fastened to the farmhouse's roof, however, in the end, it was settled; the droneport was used solely as a remote parking and maintenance depot. Trey had been correct. The drones were piloted in Beijing, specifically, from the basement of the Ministry of National Defense of the People's Republic of China.

Either the ChiComs held superior military intelligence or just got lucky evading radar imaging in Savannah and Parris Island. No one could see tiny blips flying at less than 200 feet. But, some of the more hopeful investigators thought it might be the coating on the titanium machine that transformed them into ghosts, a feature that investigators pledged to research.

What did go boom in the night after all? A team of hydrologists and oilfield service specialists were tasked to figure out the mystery. Production logs found in the plant exposed a change in operational strategy when Gu Shui engineers attempted to address a decline in recoverable minerals. The Chinese borrowed an American technique from the oil patch and used a process called fracking that entails the deep injection of water or other liquids under high pressure into the layers of rock through which the underground river flowed. This wasn't traditional vertical drilling. This was horizontal, in fact, an extensive spiderweb of drilling tracks was discovered by a special machine made in Dallas, Texas that used deep soil sonograms to find oil. Every time steam was injected, the underlying strata of granite bedrock cracked open with a boom.

Months after the raid, the Congress of the United States authorized President James Lowry to issue thirteen Medals of Freedom, one posthumous for Lucius Aurelius. The medals were awarded in the White House Rose Garden one glorious bluebird morning in late May.

"I'll be damned if I attend that ceremony trapped in a wheelchair," Trey blustered with Penn.

"Well, hon, you do whatever you like," she said patting Trey on the top of his head like one would a fussy toddler.

"Standing. That's how I'm going to receive that decoration."

A crutch was needed but he managed just fine.

It was late at night. Penn couldn't sleep in the recliner at the Naval Hospital on Beaufort's Pinckney Street. They assigned Trey to a private room fitted with a wide window overlooking the city. A necklace of lights delineated the harbor that night as Penn mused over their future.

"Ps-s-st," came from behind her then a giggle. Penn turned to see her old friend Gauche and what was apparently his lover, de plateye, who draped over Gauche like a mink stole. Penn couldn't help but be cheered to see the Imp.

"Time to celebrate," Gauche said, his big head absorbing de plateye's attention. "So, *ma cher*, this is Trey Dawson?" De plateye left Gauche to perch next to Trey providing a red glow over his battered features. She looked him over.

"Pretty cute," de plateye said stroking his bruised face. "Can I do anything for him?"

"That's nice of you, but he's going to be fine," Penn told de plateye who flew to Penn to hug her around her knees then hovered at eyelevel.

"Anything. Just think it and Gauche and I, we'll make it happen."

"You guys an item are you?" asked Penn.

Gauche laughed heartily. "She loves French food," he quipped.

De plateye whisked away to plaster herself to Gauche, the little man kissed all over his face. De plateye turned to Penn. "This man is tasty," she said smacking her lips.

"I'm so happy," Gauche said, the waterworks flowing. Requisite tears soaked his beard. "Dear sweet Penn, de plateye is genius." Gauche whispered in de plateye's ear.

Instantly, a striking African woman dressed in a long skirt of vivid colors stood before her. Fahima looked exactly like Penn save her darker skin.

"We finally meet," the apparition said. "I come to give you warm greetings from your ancestors and their encouragement to keep doing what you have been doing to lift our people up, to crack open the bounty that awaits the Gullah under your guidance directed by your bountiful imagination. Penn, we know you can do it. I bid you farewell until we work side-by-side for an eternity in the spirit world."

The image faded to de plateye.

"I mean, isn't she the most beautiful woman?" asked Gauche. That turned the tears back on. Gauche sniffled. "We leave you in peace," he said and swept a courtly bow to Penn, took de plateye's hand, and together they walked through the hospital door.

America fell in love with the Gullah. The nation thirsted for their story. As one would imagine, Penn became the face and voice of her people. Tirelessly and with great passion, she made the media rounds in New York and Washington telling the story of heir's property and how slavery has been perpetuated because of flawed land titling practices used during the Reconstruction years of 1865-1877. The Gullah message resonated. Donations to a new 501(c) 3 called Gullah Magic that Penn pitched every time she could flowed like the River Jordan.

They lay awake in the new queen-sized bed in Penn's old room, night sounds coming through the open window. The blue light of a full moon on a cloudless night added to their contentment.

"I've been thinking," Trey said. "Why don't we petition the powers that be to deed the Gu Shui property over to Gullah Magic? My guess is there would be little if any objection, kind of like reparations. I mean, ya'll should take over the plant, rehab it, and run it as a business. It was confiscated by the Feds, right?"

"Yes, as far as I know," Penn said, "and shuttered, plus, I believe a UN guard unit is deployed too."

"If I'm not mistaken; isn't property seized as the result of a felony able to be held on permanent forfeiture."

"That's right. It usually happens in drug cases," agreed Penn, "but, the process would be incredibly easy. A simple quit claim deed could suffice."

"I thought as much. People who buy Gullah Magic water will feel good about drinking the product," Trey speculated, thinking out loud. "They could ... they could tour the plant, hear stories about the raid, and learn about your Gullah culture. You could hold festivals honoring your traditions.

Sweetie, you studied the balance sheet. If one can believe the ChiCom's accounting, how much do you think the plant could make?"

"Wow, you missed your calling," Penn said propping herself on an elbow. She spun an idle finger through his chest hair. "You should have gone to Wall Street. I like the idea, no, I love it. Li Ling said they bottled 20,000 units a day. Let's say the line ran six days a week. That's 120,000 units, then let's say we can, I'm being conservative, now, we can ask $1.00 a bottle wholesale less expenses of, oh, let's say 25%. That makes $90,000 a week tax-free in profits times four is $360,000 a month. That means net annual sales could reach over $4 million. Man, I'm thinking schools, daycare centers, a fund for repairs on Gullah homes, scholarships for smart kids, nutrition programs, oh, Trey, this is beautiful." In her excitement, Penn raise up to sit Indian fashion. "We have enough cash from donations to at least begin reconstruction, repair, and redesign the front, and restore the bottling line. What were once Chinese offices could be repurposed as a Gullah showcase for commercial foods, crafts like sweetgrass baskets, art, woodworking, a theatre streaming videos of our history, you name it."

"I'm here to tell you," Trey piped in getting excited too, "the talk shows and news outlets would love it. Maybe we could sell the water super-premium, or develop a whole new line of naturally flavored sparkling waters that seem to be all the rage. I believe the UN agreement prohibited all mining of those rare earth minerals but it didn't say anything about halting the production of water or gold. The drone I captured on the *Edge of Heaven* carried about 10 pounds of it. That quantity of gold dust is, like, almost $200,000 melt value. How long did it take them to separate it? Was that shipment a week's worth of work, a day, a month, what? And, could the centrifuges already in place be retooled to spin heavy gold flecks out of the water but not the dangerous minerals? I'd bet they could."

"Good Lord a'mighty," Penn said. "We have us a Gullah gold mine."

"You know, your buddy in Columbia, Shell, could be a big help. She's got the guilt bad for siding with the ChiComs. Offer her a strong position, a board seat maybe. That would instantly develop a link to Columbia that could be useful plus give us creds with the save the planet folks."

"Think of it," Penn said dreamily, "for the first time Gullah will have more clout than the developers who have stolen our people blind."

"You're so beautiful," Trey said shifting to sit next to her. "You want to play house with me?" he asked, low and tender.

Penn took his hand. "Any time, big fella. Speaking of a house, I love the lot on the Coosaw by the okra fields."

"Me too," Trey said. "By the way, we've been so busy I forgot to tell you. Morty wired another fat royalty. He pushed me for a memoir on the raid talking some smack about a big bonus and movie package. Morty from Flatbush wants to be a part of the healing of a nation."

"So do I," Penn said, "as long as I'm with you." She kissed Trey. "You know, I've been thinking about the question you asked me when you called from inside the plant. Do you remember … about a name?"

"Sure, sure. And?"

The answer is; Lucius or Thelma. We could call them, Luke and Thellie. So, Mr. Warrior, I'm two months late. Just when are you going to make an honest woman of me?"